W9-CXZ-392

"I am Daunton," he announced, watching her closely. "Lawrence Daunton."

Immediately the humor left her face and she retreated a step.

"*Rake* Daunton?"

He grinned, saying with some satisfaction, "So you *do* know me."

"I know of your *reputation*," she retorted. "When I said we keep to ourselves I did not mean we do not know what is going on in the world. I have an aunt in town who writes regularly and the society pages of the London newspapers provide a rich source of entertainment. Your name is never out of them!"

"All gossip and innuendo, I assure you."

"Oh, heavens!" She put her hands to her cheeks. "This is so dreadful!"

He folded his arms. "More dreadful than it was five minutes ago? I thought we were getting along famously."

Her eyes flashed.

"Not only am I stranded miles from my home, but my companion is one of the country's most notorious rakes."

Lawrence spread his hands.

"I pray you will acquit me of planning this!" Some spirit of mischief made him add, "I have never yet had to employ such base tactics with any woman."

* * *

Snowbound with the Notorious Rake
Harlequin® Historical #321—December 2011

Author Note

When writing a book, it is not unusual to be describing one sort of weather while living through something quite different. However, when I was writing *Snowbound with the Notorious Rake* I was experiencing just the same winter weather as my characters! Living high up on the Pennines, we can have quite harsh weather, and this winter we had a prolonged spell of ice and snow, which turned the moors into a winter wonderland but made the roads impassable. Luckily I love this kind of weather, and wrote most of this book curled up with my laptop before a roaring fire, with the snow flinging itself against the window—sheer heaven!

Being snowed in can be wonderful—as long as everyone is safe and there are sufficient supplies of food and fuel. There is a great sense of isolation; the rest of the world seems so distant that it no longer matters. This is what happens to my heroine, Rose, when she finds herself stranded at a lonely house on the moors. It is an escape from the tedium of her real life. Is it any wonder that Rose soon finds herself succumbing to the fairy-tale setting and the charms of the house's owner? It does help, of course, that Sir Lawrence is just the sort of man to melt a maiden's heart!

I was born in the West Country, and it was such a pleasure to set this story on Exmoor. However, I decided not to use real places for the major settings of my story, preferring to let my imagination run wild—something that is very easy to do in such a wild and beautiful part of England. I do hope you enjoy *Snowbound with the Notorious Rake* and I wish you all the happiness of the season.

Snowbound with the Notorious Rake

Sarah Mallory

TORONTO NEW YORK LONDON
AMSTERDAM PARIS SYDNEY HAMBURG
STOCKHOLM ATHENS TOKYO MILAN MADRID
PRAGUE WARSAW BUDAPEST AUCKLAND

If you purchased this book without a cover you should be aware that this book is stolen property. It was reported as "unsold and destroyed" to the publisher, and neither the author nor the publisher has received any payment for this "stripped book."

Recycling programs
for this product may
not exist in your area.

ISBN-13: 978-0-373-30630-5

SNOWBOUND WITH THE NOTORIOUS RAKE

Copyright © 2011 by Sarah Mallory

All rights reserved. Except for use in any review, the reproduction or utilization of this work in whole or in part in any form by any electronic, mechanical or other means, now known or hereafter invented, including xerography, photocopying and recording, or in any information storage or retrieval system, is forbidden without the written permission of the publisher, Harlequin Enterprises Limited, 225 Duncan Mill Road, Don Mills, Ontario, Canada M3B 3K9.

This is a work of fiction. Names, characters, places and incidents are either the product of the author's imagination or are used fictitiously, and any resemblance to actual persons, living or dead, business establishments, events or locales is entirely coincidental.

This edition published by arrangement with Harlequin Books S.A.

For questions and comments about the quality of this book please contact us at Customer_eCare@Harlequin.ca.

® and TM are trademarks of the publisher. Trademarks indicated with ® are registered in the United States Patent and Trademark Office, the Canadian Trade Marks Office and in other countries.

www.Harlequin.com

Printed in U.S.A.

SARAH MALLORY

was born in Bristol, England, and now lives in an old farmhouse on the edge of the Pennines with her husband and family. She left grammar school at sixteen to work in companies as varied as stockbrokers, marine engineers, insurance brokers, biscuit manufacturers and even a quarrying company. Her first book was published shortly after the birth of her daughter. She has published more than a dozen books under the pen name of Melinda Hammond, winning the Reviewers' Choice Award in 2005 from Singletitles.com for *Dance for a Diamond* and the Historical Novel Society's Editors' Choice in November 2006 for *Gentlemen in Question*.

To Marianne, Paul and Steven,
who lived with a distracted mother and had to
fend for themselves while I wrote this book.

Chapter One

The drawing room of Knightscote Lodge was considered by many to be the ideal room for a cold winter's night, the beamed ceiling and polished oak panelling being declared perfect by the romantically minded. Certainly with a cheerful blaze in the huge fireplace and the golden glow of the candles, the room looked warm and welcoming. However, its present occupant was sunk low in his armchair, his booted feet resting on the hearth as he stared moodily into the fire, a half-filled wineglass held casually between the long, lean fingers of one hand.

It had started to snow earlier in the day and now it was swirling against the tiny diamond panes of the windows, driven by the howling wind. Sir Lawrence Daunton raised his head as a particularly fierce gust rattled the casements. It occurred to him that if the blizzard continued no one would be able to get along the lane for days.

'Good,' he muttered the word aloud as he drained his glass.

It was Christmas Eve. When he had ridden down to his hunting lodge on the edge of Exmoor a few days earlier he'd had two objects in mind. The first was to avoid all company during the festive season; the other was to get very, very drunk. With the second of these worthy aims in mind, he reached for the bottle standing on the table at his elbow. It was empty and he was making his way to the servants' quarters in search of another when he heard a loud hammering at the door. Lawrence stopped.

'Who the hell can that be?'

With great deliberation he put down the empty bottle and picked up a lantern. His footsteps rang on the flagstones as he walked to the door. It took him a moment to wrestle with the locks and the catch, but at last he flung the door open.

A blast of icy air took his breath away.

As did the vision standing in the shelter of the porch.

Before him was a young woman enveloped in a powder-blue-velvet travelling cloak. The hood was edged in white fur that framed a pale, delicate face with a straight nose, generous mouth and a pair of blue-grey eyes fringed with dark lashes.

All this Lawrence took in immediately, but even as he blinked to see if the vision would disappear, she stepped quickly into the hall, saying, 'Do not keep me standing in the snow! Pray tell your mistress that Mrs

Westerhill would like to see her. Immediately.' This last word she added a little sharply, for Lawrence was still staring at her. She continued, 'And my groom is outside with the horses. Perhaps before you shut the door you could direct him to the stables.'

Lawrence blinked. A gust of wind sent another flurry of snow into the hall where it fell gently onto the dark flags and dissolved.

'Yes. Excuse me.' Quickly he stepped outside, pulling the door closed behind him, and ran across to where the hapless groom was holding the reins of two horses. A few words of instruction and Lawrence hurried back into the house. The hall was empty, but a trail of wet footprints led off towards the drawing room, where he found the lady warming her hands by the fire. She had discarded her cloak to reveal a high-necked gown of deep-blue wool, unrelieved by any ornament save a small edging of white lace at her throat and wrists. The severity of the gown was alleviated by her abundant honey-brown hair, which fell in soft ringlets to her shoulders.

'Well? Have you told Mrs Anstey that I am here?'

'Er…no.'

She straightened, fixing him with a frowning look.

'This *is* Knightshill Hall?'

'Alas, no,' he replied. 'This is Knights*cote* Lodge. Knightshill is on the Stoke Pero road.'

'Oh, heavens. Then this is *not* Mrs Anstey's house.'

'No. You must have missed the turning.'

Lawrence watched as her small white teeth momentarily gripped a bottom lip that was as full and red as a ripe cherry. Her eyes travelled about the room and for the first time she seemed aware of its untidy state.

'*Is* there a mistress in this house?'

Lawrence's eyes danced. 'Not at the moment.'

'Then perhaps you would inform your master...' She trailed off as she looked up and read the merriment in his face. 'Oh, heavens.' Her hands came up to her mouth, and her eyes with those ridiculously long lashes stared at him in horror. 'Oh, pray do not tell me *you* are master here.'

'Very well,' he said promptly, 'I won't.'

Her eyes twinkled, but she said severely, 'Pray do not be absurd. If you are the master, then tell me your name.'

'You do not know?'

She shook her head.

'I must appear dreadfully ignorant, sir, but I do not venture abroad often; we keep very much to ourselves.'

'I am Daunton,' he announced, watching her closely. 'Lawrence Daunton.'

Immediately the humour left her face and she retreated a step.

'*Rake* Daunton?'

He grinned, saying with some satisfaction, 'So you *do* know me.'

'I know of your *reputation*,' she retorted. 'When I said we keep to ourselves I did not mean we do not know what is going on in the world. I have an aunt in town who writes regularly and the society pages of the London newspapers provide a rich source of entertainment. Your name is never out of them!'

'All gossip and innuendo, I assure you.'

'Oh, heavens!' She put her hands to her cheeks. 'This is so dreadful!'

He folded his arms. 'More dreadful than it was five minutes ago? I thought we were getting along famously.'

Her eyes flashed.

'Not only am I stranded miles from my home, but my companion is one of the country's most notorious rakes.'

Lawrence spread his hands.

'I pray you will acquit me of planning this!' Some spirit of mischief made him add, 'I have never yet had to employ such base tactics with any woman.'

She did not appear to believe him and looked about her anxiously.

'Are there any other females here?'

'Not one.'

'Oh, good gracious!' She snatched up her gloves. 'Then I must go immediately.'

'Go where?'

'To Knightshill Hall. Coming here was a dreadful mistake. The snow was covering the sign at the gateway and only the first few letters were visible. I was sure this must be it.' She straightened her shoulders, put up her head and announced formally, 'I will take my leave now; I beg your pardon for disturbing you.'

She walked to the door, but Lawrence made no effort to open it for her.

'Oh, but I cannot let you go.' Her eyes widened with sudden alarm and he added, 'You cannot cut across the moor in this snow, and it is too far to travel by road; it is a good mile back to the crossroads and another few miles from there to Knightshill Hall.'

'Oh. Well, there must be another family close by who will give me shelter.'

She fixed her hopeful gaze upon him and for a moment Lawrence was almost sorry to disappoint her. Almost.

'I'm afraid not. This is a hunting lodge, you see. Designed to be away from all other habitation. We are in the middle of nowhere.'

She took the news very well, her dismay only showing in her eyes, which darkened a shade to slate grey.

'Well,' she said at length, 'then we must try to get home. If you will show me the way to the stables, I will talk to my groom.'

Lawrence shook his head.

'He has probably just finished settling the horses.'

'Then he must unsettle them,' she retorted. 'We must be on our way again, and as quickly as possible.'

Lawrence walked over to the window.

'Of course, but I do not think that will be tonight.' He held out his hand, inviting her to join him. 'Come here and look.'

She approached, but was careful not to stand too close to him as she peered out. It was still snowing heavily, the wind driving the flakes almost horizontally across the window.

'But we might get through it, at least back to Exford…'

'Out of the question.' He drew the curtains together,

belatedly shutting out the night. 'There is no house or shelter within miles of here, and in this blizzard it would be madness to attempt it.'

'Then what am I going to do?'

For the first time Lawrence heard a note of uncertainty creep into her voice. He put his hand under her elbow and guided her back to the fire, gently pushing her down onto a chair.

'I am going to fetch a bottle and you are going to drink a glass of wine with me.'

As soon as she was alone, Rose jumped to her feet again. She walked back to the window and peeped out through the curtains. Perhaps she had been mistaken; perhaps it was not as bad as she had first thought.

If anything it was worse. The snow continued to fall in thick white flakes, tossed about by the wind that gusted and howled around the old house. Restlessly she picked up her cloak and spread it over a chair to dry, then she returned to her seat by the fire to consider her predicament. She was alone in this house with a libertine. No, not quite alone—Evans, her groom, was with her, although she had no idea exactly where he might be. Perhaps Sir Lawrence had overpowered him. Poor Evans might even now be languishing in a cellar! Quickly Rose dismissed such thoughts, scolding herself for being fanciful. So far Sir Lawrence had behaved with perfect decorum. True, he was dressed very informally, but then he had not been expecting visitors. A fierce gust of wind rattled the window and whined down the chimney, reminding her of the tempest raging outside. She had not taken much notice of the house as they rode up, too thankful to see the welcome light shining from the window. It was similar to other old manor houses in the area, a low, rambling building with a gabled roof. Inside, it was furnished for comfort rather than fashion: heavy dark furniture and panelling was alleviated by richly coloured cushions and wall hangings as well as quantities of gleaming brass and copper. She looked about her. The room was clean enough but it had an air of untidiness, cushions disturbed, empty glasses on the mantelpiece, as if there was no one to clear up after the master.

The master.

Rose found her thoughts turning to that disturbing individual. Really, it was no wonder that she had thought him a servant, appearing in topboots and breeches, with his waistcoat undone and his shirt open at the neck to display a very improper view of his chest with its smattering of crisp, black hair. And that dark shadow on his jaw, too, signalling the fact he had not shaved today. When he'd opened the door to her she'd had the impression of a giant, his black hair brushing the lintel and his wide shoulders filling the doorway. Standing together in the narrow hallway, she had found him quite overpowering. That was why she had made her way to this room, preferring to have a little more space between them. Of course, now she knew just who he was, she realised she was right to feel nervous.

She jumped as the door opened and her host came in carrying a bottle. He went to a sideboard and proceeded to fill two glasses. His hand was steady enough, but it occurred to her that he might be drunk—that would account for the glitter she had noticed in his blue eyes. It was more of a glint, really, a twinkle, inviting her to share his amusement. She found it both alarming and attractive, which was extremely worrying. She would need to keep her wits about her and resolved to take no more than one glass of wine with him.

'Where is my groom?' she asked as he handed her the wine.

'In the kitchen. I told him to make himself comfortable there. And if he keeps the fire going it is one less task for me.'

'You have no servants here?'

'No. I sent them away to enjoy Christmas with their families.'

'Why—?'

He shook his head, lowering himself into a chair on the opposite side of the hearth.

'I have answered enough questions. I think you should tell me what you are doing abroad on such a wild night.'

Was there anything she could say that would not add to her vulnerability? Playing for time, Rose took a sip of the wine. It was rich and fruity and surprisingly comforting.

'I have been taking flowers to my husband,' she said at last. 'I am a widow, you see. My husband died on this day four years ago, and since that time I have visited Exford twice a year: on his birthday, and every Christmas Eve, to place flowers on his grave.'

'But that is not where you live now?'

'No. I live at Mersecombe.'

'Mersecombe! It must be all of ten miles from there to Exford.'

'No more than eight, surely. And it was not snowing when I left home.'

'And of course one expects perfectly sunny weather in December.'

'I have made the journey quite safely for the past three years!'

'Only a ninnyhammer would set out on such a journey at this time of the year.'

'Then I am a ninnyhammer,' she said, sitting up very straight.

For a moment he stared at her and she tensed herself, expecting another sharp response. Instead he said quietly, 'I beg your pardon. To make the journey to Exford in the middle of winter—I admire your devotion.'

Almost without realising it Rose fluttered her hand, dismissing his comment. It wasn't devotion that had drawn her away from Mersecombe that morning. A touch of guilt, perhaps, that her husband was so rarely in her thoughts these days, combined with a restlessness that was increasingly hard to bear. Riding to Exford with just her groom for company gave her a temporary freedom from the ties of duty and responsibility. Not that she resented those ties, they were forged out of love, but when she had left home that morning she had been aware of a longing to be free to do just as she wished, even for a short while.

Seeing the gesture, Lawrence smiled.

'At least accept that you have great determination.'

'Thank you, but it does not help my predicament. There is no getting away from the fact that I am in the most horrendous fix, being here, alone, with you.'

'Many women would envy you.'

'And I would gladly exchange places with them!'

Her candour made him laugh.

'Point taken, madam—by the bye, what is your name?'

She shook her head at him.

'I do not think I should tell you. It is not fitting that we should know one another.'

'Dash it all, I cannot call you "ma'am" for ever! Besides, I have only to ask your groom.'

Rose imagined an undignified race to the kitchen, where she would order Evans not to disclose her name. It would be too foolish.

'I...am Rose Westerhill.'

'Very well, Mrs Westerhill, let me assure you that I have no designs upon your virtue. I came here to get away from the world.'

'Why?'

'That, madam, is no concern of yours.'

He sounded irritated, which suited Rose very well— surely there was less chance of him becoming amorous if he disliked her? She replied with great cordiality, 'No, thankfully it is not. Well, there is no hope of going anywhere until the morning.' She slanted a challenging look at him. 'Is there a spare bedroom, or shall I be obliged to sit up here all night?'

'Oh, there are plenty of bedchambers, but none is prepared.'

'If that is all, I am sure I can manage to put sheets on my bed.'

'Yes, but it's where to *find* the sheets.'

A smile tugged at her mouth.

'If you will show me your housekeeper's quarters, I will endeavour to locate them.'

'Very well.' He emptied his glass and jumped up. 'Shall we go and look now?'

She put a hand to her rumbling stomach.

'I would rather find something to eat first.'

He nodded.

'To the kitchen, then!'

Rose followed her host through the dark, chilly passages to the kitchen, where they found Evans sitting in a chair beside the hob-grate. He took off his cap and rose as they came in.

'So you have banked up the fire here—good man.' Lawrence nodded. 'You found all you needed in the stables?'

'Aye, sir. I shall check the 'orses again before bedtime, but they are snug as bugs out there.'

'You will need somewhere to sleep,' said Rose, casting an enquiring glance at Sir Lawrence.

'There's plenty of space above the stables, but the scullery boy has a bed in the small room off the kitchen—behind the fireplace. You might be more comfortable there.' Lawrence paused as another icy blast spattered against the window. 'You would certainly be warmer.'

'Aye, I spotted the bed.' Evans nodded. 'I'll settle down there, if you've no objection.'

'Just make sure you take your boots off before you climb between the sheets,' Rose warned him and earned a pained look.

'I's lived in a gennleman's 'ouse for long enough to know *that*,' the groom retorted.

Lawrence strode across the room and lifted the lid of a small black cooking pot balanced on the hob. An appetising aroma filled the room.

'I guessed this was for your supper, sir,' remarked Evans, 'so I put it in the flames to heat up.'

'Yes, my housekeeper, Mrs Brendon, said she had left something for me. Hmm. Not much for three of us.' He went into the larder and began to investigate the pots and tubs kept there. 'There's a little bread, and a ham—plenty of rice and flour—and a basket of vegetables. Oh, and lemons.'

Rose had found an apron and tied it over her gown. She picked up a wooden spoon and gave the soup a stir.

'Is there a hen house?'

'Why, yes,' said Lawrence, backing out of the larder. 'I believe there is, on the far side of the yard.'

'Then there may be an egg or two, even at this time of the year. Perhaps you would go and fetch them.'

Sir Lawrence's black brows went up.

'Me?'

Rose gave him an innocent smile. 'I would ask Evans, or course, but I need him to fetch in more peat for the kitchen fire.' She held out a small basket. 'You may need this.'

Without a word Sir Lawrence took the basket and slouched out of the room.

'I could've done that *and* fetched in the peat, Miss Rose,' opined Evans, when the door had closed again.

'I am sure you could,' murmured Rose, stirring the soup. 'But it will do Sir Lawrence no harm to cool his— er—head out of doors for a while.'

Lawrence pulled his hat a little lower over his face and tucked his chin into his muffler as he bent into the wind that howled across the yard, throwing icy needles of snow against his cheeks. Damnation, he had been looking forward to a quiet evening, drinking copious amounts of wine and perhaps helping himself to a little soup and bread before he went to bed. Now all that had changed and he was obliged to find enough food for his visitors.

He wished it had been a man at the door; then they might have enjoyed a drink together, perhaps played at cards and made do with the ham and cheese from the larder. Or even a lightskirt—that would have been entertaining! Instead he was saddled with a respectable widow who looked set to take over his kitchen. One, moreover, who expected him to work for his supper! A laugh shook him. This was *not* how he had envisaged spending his Christmas!

Half an hour later Sir Lawrence was back in the kitchen, shrugging himself out of his greatcoat.

Rose counted the eggs in the basket.

'Half a dozen, how clever of you to find so many, and in the dark, too!'

'Thank you, ma'am.'

She glanced up at him, her eyes alight with laughter.

'Oh dear, do I sound as if I am talking to a child? Forgive me, but you remind me very much of my own little boy.'

Lawrence almost winced. A masterly set-down, designed to put him firmly in his place! He looked around the kitchen.

'Where is Evans?'

'I sent him to the drawing room with more logs. I thought we should eat there; I had a quick peep in your dining room, but it is so cold it would take for ever to warm up.'

'You are willing to risk dining alone with me?'

'It cannot be helped. Poor Evans would not eat a thing if we imposed ourselves upon him here in the kitchen. I shall have to trust you to behave yourself.'

Again that minatory tone.

'I believe I can remember how to act as a gentleman.'

'I do hope so. It will be much more comfortable for us all if you do.' She treated him to a smile. 'Perhaps you will be good enough to set the table? It will take me but a moment to cook the eggs.'

'I take it you know *how* to cook?' he challenged her.

'But of course. My mother thought it very important that I should learn something of the art. I am going to make a pancake of the eggs and add a little ham. We will follow it with the soup.'

'Excellent.' Lawrence realised how hungry he was. 'I will fetch out a bottle of good wine to enjoy with our feast!'

* * *

Sir Lawrence said nothing untoward during dinner, but Rose could not forget his fearsome reputation. Since her husband's death she had not dined alone with any man and sitting at the small dining table with Sir Lawrence seemed almost indecently intimate. She was disturbingly aware of her companion. With his tall, athletic form and darkly handsome features she could understand why he was so successful with women; even his informal dress and the dark shadow of a beard on his chin did not detract from his charm—if anything, it was enhanced by the element of danger. She sipped at her wine, determined to have no more than one glass: Sir Lawrence might be a model of propriety now, but there were many long hours to go before morning.

As the evening wore on and his behaviour towards her remained perfectly correct, Rose began to relax and their conversation became more natural. He asked her about her life and she found herself telling him about the home she shared at Mersecombe with her mother and her young son.

'Why did you not stay in Exford, if your husband is buried there?'

She made no comment as he filled her glass again. Should she tell him the truth—that she had wanted to escape from the pitying looks and whispers? That she had found the memories just too painful?

'I was obliged to sell up to pay his debts.' That was also the truth. Suddenly it was a relief to talk to someone. 'Harry was a dreamer. When we moved to Exford he thought the farm would provide a living, but he would not listen to advice.' She sighed. 'He sacked his manager, who was a local man, and brought in another who knew nothing of the land. By the time Harry died there was nothing left but debts and the deeds to Hades Cove, a worthless mine. I sold the house and the farm, but by the time I had paid off the creditors there was precious little left. I took Samuel back to Mersecombe, where my mother has a neat little house. We manage very well and I supplement our income by running the church school.'

'Ah.' His eyes glinted as he smiled at her. 'You are a schoolteacher. That explains your managing ways.'

His smile robbed the words of offence and she found herself smiling back at him, fascinated by the way the candlelight gleamed in his blue eyes. It really was very attractive. A tiny wisp of desire stirred deep inside. She looked away, conscious of the need to maintain her defences.

'You should be thankful for my managing ways,' she replied crisply. 'Heaven knows what would have happened if I had not taken charge of the kitchen this evening.'

'I would not have been sent off like a lowly scullery boy to collect eggs!'

'Oh dear, did you really object to that?' She turned back to him, a laugh gurgling in her throat. 'But you did it so *well*!'

'Do not try to turn me up sweet with your flattery, madam.'

The glinting smile in his eyes reassured her.

'Well, if you had not been such a ninnyhammer as to send all your staff away…'

He laughed at that, a real, full laugh, and Rose thought how much younger he looked. How carefree. Again she felt that little tingle of desire and quickly repressed it. The man was a rake; she must keep her distance.

Their meal over, Evans came in to collect the dishes and carry them away to the kitchen. Rose would have followed, but he shook his head.

'You prepared the meal, madam, 'tis only right that you should rest awhile.'

She sat back, glancing across the table at Sir Lawrence, who said, 'I am in your debt, Mrs Westerhill, I do not know when I have dined so well. Since the rest of the house is so chill, I cannot suggest that you withdraw, so instead I will invite you to join me in a glass of brandy.'

It was tempting—the glowing candlelight, the wine, the roaring fire—but Rose dared not relax her guard.

'That is very kind, sir, but there is more work to do. We have yet to prepare a room for me.' She spoke as if it was the most natural thing in the world for her to be sleeping in his house. Not by a blush or the flicker of an eyelid would she betray her nervousness. 'Perhaps we could seek out the linen cupboard?'

She tensed, half-expecting a knowing look or *risqué* comment, but Sir Lawrence merely nodded and pushed back his chair.

'Come along, then. I am not familiar with Mrs

Brendon's part of the house, but I am sure we shall find something.'

The house was cold, dark and full of echoes. Rose kept close to Sir Lawrence, who was carrying the lamp. Too close. When he stopped suddenly she cannoned into him. His hand shot out to steady her, but his warm touch through the thin sleeve of her gown made her tremble even more.

'I—I beg your pardon.' Her voice was little more than a croak. 'I stumbled. The uneven floor…'

'Ah.' His hand slid down her arm and he caught her fingers. 'Then let me help you.'

She did not pull away. It was only sensible to accept his support. And she felt so much safer with her hand tucked into his large, comforting grasp.

They walked on in the little pool of lamplight until they reached a corridor with a series of cupboards built along one side. Lawrence began pulling open the doors. One was crammed with pewter dishes and an old dinner service, another held neatly folded suits of servants' livery. A heady scent of summer herbs wafted over them as he opened a third door.

'This is it,' murmured Rose.

Sir Lawrence stood to one side, holding up the lamp to display orderly stacks of white linen.

'Very well, madam. Help yourself.'

Rose stepped up. Soon she had a pile of sheets, pillowcases and bolster covers in her arms.

'Let me carry those for you.'

Rose shook her head at him.

'No, no, they are not heavy. If you will just show me the way to the bedroom?'

He placed his hand under her elbow and guided her back along the corridors.

'I think you would be most comfortable in the Blue Room,' he told her. 'It is one of the smaller chambers, but that will make it easier to keep warm.' He threw open a door. 'Here we are.'

Rose did not move from the doorway as he went around the room lighting the candles in the wall sconces. A large tester bed took up most of the floor, the mattress shrouded in a plain white cover.

'It has no hangings, I'm afraid,' remarked Lawrence, twitching off the dust sheet. 'But there are plenty of blankets and an elegant cover, embroidered by some previous lady of the house, no doubt. And the mattress is very comfortable.'

Rose found herself wondering how he knew that— what sort of guests had he entertained here before?

Best not to think of that. She put down the pile of linen.

'Thank you,' she said briskly. 'Now, if you will excuse me, I will get to work.'

'Can you manage on your own?'

'Perfectly well, thank you. I am not such a lady that I cannot make my own bed.'

'Very well. Then I will light the fire for you.'

'Oh, there is no need. Evans can—'

'Evans will have plenty to do checking on the horses before he retires.' He added, 'I am not such a gentleman that I cannot light a fire.'

'No. Of course.' She smiled at him. 'Very well, then, thank you.'

In a remarkably short time the bed was made and a fire was burning steadily in the hearth. Sir Lawrence stood to admire his handiwork for a few moments.

'It is still early,' he said, turning to her. 'Will you join me in the drawing room for a little while and give the fire a chance to warm the room?' When she hesitated he shook his head at her. 'I have nothing more sinister in mind than conversation, madam.'

'I thought you had sent your servants away because you wanted to be alone.'

'I did, but your presence in my house precludes me from carrying out my original plan, which was to drown my sorrows in a bottle.'

He spoke lightly, but Rose heard the underlying bitterness in his voice. She caught the fleeting shadow of pain in his eyes.

'Perhaps you would like me to prepare some coffee?'

'No, we will save that for the morning.' He was smiling again. '*I* shall make us some hot punch!'

Chapter Two

The fragrant aroma of lemons and cloves greeted Rose when she returned to the drawing room a short time later. A small iron pot was suspended over the fire and Sir Lawrence was leaning over it, thoughtfully stirring the contents. He did not look up immediately and she took the opportunity to watch him, noting the way the dark coat strained across his broad shoulders, admiring the long, powerful legs encased in buckskins and top-boots. The firelight glinted on his black hair and heightened the strong lines of his handsome face.

Many women would envy you. His earlier words flitted through her mind.

He looked up and smiled as she approached.

'I thought you might have fallen asleep.'

'I went to speak to Evans.'

'And is he comfortable?'

She chuckled.

'Very. Especially so since you gave him leave to help himself to the cider!'

'I hope he will not regret it in the morning.'

'I trust Evans not to drink too much; he knows we will need to be on our way as soon as may be once it is light.' She sat down in one of the two armchairs he had pulled close to the fire. 'You are shaking your head, sir. Do you think I am too optimistic?'

'If the snow continues, then the roads may well be blocked.'

She shrugged. 'Then we will ride across the fields. I have done that before.'

Lawrence filled a rummer with hot punch and handed it to her.

'What a resourceful woman you are, Mrs Wester-hill.'

'I am a widow, sir, and needs must be resourceful.'

Rose settled back in her chair, savouring the hot, sweet punch. What had happened to her resolution not to drink more than one glass of wine? She pushed the thought aside.

The wind had dropped and the only sounds in the room were the steady tick of the clock and the crack-le of the fire. Lawrence occupied the chair opposite, his booted feet resting on the hearth. His gaze was fixed on the leaping flames, but Rose sensed that his thoughts were far away. The drooping curve of his mouth reminded her of his earlier words.

'What did you mean, sir, when you said you wanted to drown your sorrows?'

She thought for a moment that he would not answer

or would change the subject with a careless word. She was about to offer him an apology for her impertinence when he spoke.

'Some fourteen months ago, my fiancée died of a fever.'

'Fiancée!' She flushed as his scorching glance swept over her. Her incredulous exclamation was insulting. After all, she knew nothing about the man, except gossip. 'I b-beg your pardon,' she stammered. 'I thought— I did not know—'

'How should you? It was never announced. The betrothal was of very long standing. Even her death was accorded no more than a line in the society pages, easily missed. Our betrothal was not a secret, but it was unremarkable.' He held up his glass and stared at the dark liquid. 'It has always amazed me that my indiscretions are emblazoned throughout the society news sheets, but my sweet Annabelle, whose short life was so full of kindness and charitable acts, was not considered worthy of a paragraph.'

'You say it was a private arrangement, sir. Were her parents against the marriage?'

'Oh, no. Why should they be, when it would mean the combining of our two estates? It had been arranged between the families when we were children. We are neighbours, you see, and it was always understood that a marriage between the Cravens and the Dauntons would be most advantageous.' His lip curled. 'But I was not to be constrained. I would go to London, sow my wild oats, then return to Hampshire to the family seat and marry my childhood sweetheart. Only before I could do so, she caught a fever and…died.'

'I am very sorry.'

'So, too, am I. Last Christmas I returned to Daunton House. It had become the custom, you see, for both families to be in Hampshire during the winter season. My parents died some years ago, but there are the aunts, uncles and cousins, as well as the whole Craven family. They descend upon Daunton and the Craven estate to spend Christmas together. But with Annabelle gone—' He broke off, giving his attention to refilling his glass. 'It was the condolences,' he said harshly. 'Everyone was so dam—dashed sympathetic. What had I ever done to deserve their compassion? Instead of commiserating with me on my loss they should have berated me for neglecting poor Annabelle, condemning her to her quiet life with her charities and her good works while I scorched my way through society like a—a comet, bent upon my own destruction. That is why this year I determined I would not go back. I would come here and—'

'Wallow in self-pity.'

His head shot up.

'Why should I not?'

'No reason at all.' Rose held out her rummer, not speaking again until he had refilled it. 'What was she like?'

'Annabelle? An angel. Patient, forgiving—'

'She sounds more like a saint,' observed Rose. 'To sit at home year after year while you spent your time on routs and revels! Good heavens, if *we* could read about your…exploits here, so far from London, surely she must have done the same?'

'Of course.'

'And she never once took you to task over your wild ways?'

'Never.' His black brows snapped together. 'And just what does that look mean?'

'I beg your pardon. It is none of my business.'

He pushed himself upright in his chair.

'You are quite right, of course,' he said, fixing his hard eyes upon her, 'but since we have come this far, pray do not stop now. Explain yourself.'

Rose hesitated.

'I do not understand why her family—or yours—did not express their disapproval at your excesses. I admit they make very entertaining reading—my mother is an avid follower of the crim. con. and the latest *on dit*—as is my aunt and most of her friends!—but I think they would feel very differently if it was anyone connected to us. The lady's family must have been aware of the damage you were doing to yourself.'

'Of course they were. Annabelle's brother George spends his time in town and he knew exactly what I was about. But as long as I did not damage my *fortune*, they were all happy to turn a blind eye.'

Again she heard the bitterness behind his words. Pity stirred, but instinct told her it would not do to show it. Instead she said thoughtfully, 'Well, I think it is a very good thing that you did not marry her.'

The silence that followed Rose's announcement was as brittle as glass. She sipped at her punch, trying to look unconcerned while a pair of piercing blue eyes bored into her.

'Would you care to explain?'

His voice was dangerously quiet. She had the impression of sitting opposite a tiger who was ready to spring and she had to steel herself to continue.

'I cannot see that you would have been happy. Unless, of course, you intended to live apart.'

'That is not at all what I intended.'

'So you planned to settle down with a woman of whom you knew nothing—'

'I beg your pardon! I told you we were neighbours. The families had known each other for years.'

'Truly? Did you grow up together, like brother and sister?'

'Of course not. I was sent off to school before Annabelle came out of the nursery.'

'Perhaps you played together during the holidays?'

'Well, no. George and I were friends, but Annabelle did not enjoy good health…'

'And once you had reached your…*understanding*, she was quite happy to let you go off and…sow your wild oats.'

'By heaven, ma'am, I am no worse than her brother, or most of the men in town!'

'Pardon me, sir, but if only half the reports I have read are true then you are *much* worse than most!'

He gave a savage bark of laughter.

'Only because I do not hide my peccadilloes. In actual fact, they are not so very bad—my worst crime is that I enjoy the company of beautiful women and they seem to enjoy mine. But I will not pay to have my name kept out of the news. I am not such a hypocrite.'

'That, of course, is to your credit, sir.'

Rose returned his furious gaze with one of limpid innocence, but she noted how those long, lean fingers whitened around his glass. She thought it just possible that he might strangle her.

He drew a deep breath, as if containing his anger. 'I never lied to Annabelle. She knew what I was.'

'It seems you made no effort to conceal it.'

'She also knew I would change when we were wed.'

'Hah!'

'The devil, madam! You dare to dispute with me?'

'Well, there has certainly been no shortage of news about you this past year, sir.'

'With Annabelle gone I have had no reason to change my way of living.' When she said nothing he put his rummer down with a snap. 'Do you think a man cannot change?'

She fixed her eyes upon him.

'A snake may shed its skin, Sir Lawrence, but it is still a snake! If you had married this poor woman, then one of two things would have occurred: you would have been heartily bored within a month or you would have continued your wild career and broken her heart. You might even have managed both.'

With a smothered curse he leapt out of his chair.

'Confound it, how dare you say such things to me!'

'Well, it is about time someone said them,' Rose retorted. 'It seems to me the poor girl was to be married without any consideration for her happiness, or yours. Do you honestly believe she was content living her solitary life, waiting for you to decide when it was time to settle down?'

'Yes! Yes, she was. In fact…' She waited, watching him as he strode about the room. After a while he stopped and rubbed a hand across his eyes. 'I admit I was surprised that she was so content with her lot. I sometimes wondered if she really *wanted* to marry me.'

'Perhaps she did not.' She added drily, 'Charming as you may be, a libertine does not make a good husband.'

He came back to his chair and threw himself down again, slanting a quick glance towards her. 'You really do not think very much of me, do you?'

Rose looked away.

'You do not think enough of yourself, sir.' She finished her punch. 'It is getting late, I should retire.'

Immediately he was on his feet.

'I will escort you.'

'Oh, no, that is not necessary—'

He was already at the door, holding the lamp. He tilted his head, listening as the long-case clock chimed the hour.

'I remember how nervous you were earlier. How much more so will you be now it is midnight?'

His kindness surprised her. She had angered him, criticised his way of living, yet still he could consider her comfort. She did not argue, merely took the proffered bedroom candle and allowed him to lead her up the stairs. Their conversation rattled around in her head. Perhaps she had been too outspoken, but he was a rake and she despised rakes. But it was no business of hers how he chose to conduct himself. Still, she was a guest in his house and she did not like to think that she had been impolite. A fleeting glance at his face told her nothing.

'This is your room.' He stopped. 'Goodnight, Mrs Westerhill. Let us hope the snow has eased by the morning and you can continue your journey.'

'Sir Lawrence! What I said earlier—if I offended you, I am most sorry.' The look he bent upon her was unfathomable, but the flickering shadows made his features seem harsh and uncompromising. She hurried on, 'I was taught never to let the sun set upon a quarrel.'

'I thought what you said to me was more in the nature of…home truths.'

She dragged up a smile.

'You are regretting your kindness in giving me shelter.'

The harsh look fled from his eyes. He said with a touch of humour, 'I cannot recall I had any choice in the matter.' He reached for her hand and raised it to his lips. 'Goodnight, Rose Westerhill. Content yourself with the fact that you have given me much to think on.'

Rose stepped into her room and leaned her back against the closed door. She was trembling, but not with cold, or the effects of their harsh words. It was shock at the bolt of wanton lust that had shot through her when he had pressed that final kiss upon her hand.

Lawrence opened his eyes and lay very still, watching the play of light upon the ceiling. Something was amiss.

He was at his hunting lodge, it was Christmas Day, but his head was unusually clear.

Then he remembered.

He slid out of bed and reached for his dressing gown. He had a visitor. A respectable schoolteacher who dared to lecture him—him!—upon how he should grieve for Annabelle. Well, the sooner Rose Westerhill was on her way and out of his life the better.

It took only a glance out of the window for him to know she would not be going anywhere today. The snow had fallen heavily all night, covering the ground with a thick white blanket and piling heavy drifts against the walls. There was a knock at the door.

'Come in!'

Evans entered.

'The mistress's compliments, sir. She sent up hot water. Said as how you would want to wash and shave before you came down to breakfast.'

'Did she, now?'

'Aye, sir.' The groom fixed his eyes somewhere over Lawrence's shoulder. 'She also said you shouldn't dress too fine, even though 'tis Christmas Day. She said there's work to be done!'

The clock was chiming ten when Sir Lawrence strode into the kitchen. Rose heard his impatient tread and turned towards the door. Her heart, which had become very unreliable recently, leapt to her throat and then began to hammer against her ribs.

I knew it. I knew he would be unbearably handsome!
When she had seen him last night with his hair

untidy, clothes dishevelled and a day's growth of beard upon his cheek she had thought him a rogue, albeit one with kind eyes and a blinding smile. Now he appeared before her clean-shaven, his hair brushed until it gleamed glossy as a raven's wing and she was sure the snowy whiteness of his starched neckcloth would not have looked out of place in a London salon. His brown jacket appeared to be moulded to his frame, but no more so than the tight buckskins that clung to his thighs. She had heard that some gentlemen deliberately shrunk their breeches to make them fit so tightly. His certainly left little to the imagination. Her mouth was so dry she could not speak.

'Well—' his deep voice was rich with laughter '—do I pass muster?'

She blushed vividly.

'I asked Evans to tell you not to dress up today.'

He glanced down.

'This is my usual country wear. Nothing special. The coffee smells good. May I have some?'

'What? Oh—oh, yes. Of course.'

With a supreme effort Rose pulled herself together.

'I found some muffins that your housekeeper had left for you. And there's honey and butter...'

'Excellent. Have you eaten yet?'

She shook her head.

'Then we shall break our fast together.'

They sat down at one end of the big table and toasted the muffins before the fire. Rose found herself relaxing, enjoying the companionship—there could be no false airs when one was licking butter from one's fingers. Sir

Lawrence was watching her over the rim of his coffee cup. She smiled.

'Oh dear, have I made a terrible mess? There is no dainty way to eat these things!' She picked up her napkin and wiped her lips.

He put down his cup.

'You have butter on your cheek. Here—let me.' He took the napkin from her fingers and leaned closer.

Rose held her breath. His hand was on her cheek, but his face was just inches from hers, so close she could see the tiny laughter lines around his eyes, follow the curl of each dark lash, study in detail those incredibly blue eyes. When she breathed in she was aware of the clean, fresh scent of him. She had heard that the Prince Regent used a perfume water scented with roses. Whatever fragrance Lawrence favoured it was not roses, but a much more subtle blend of herbs—lavender, perhaps. His hand stilled on her cheek and he looked down, exposing her to the full force of his gaze. Rose knew she must say something, and quickly.

'Wh-what is that fragrance you are wearing, sir?'

The blue eyes never wavered from her face.

'It is from France. Eau de cologne.' The corners of his mouth twitched. 'I am sorry to say Bonaparte's endorsement has made it rather unpopular in England. Do you not approve?'

Oh, yes, she thought, her senses swimming as she breathed in the heady fragrance.

She cleared her throat.

'It is not for me to approve or disapprove, sir.'

He was still hovering over her, tantalisingly close.

'Most ladies seem to like it.'

The words were provocative. She should give him a set-down, but it was impossible. He was still staring at her and she could not tear herself away. But then, she did not wish to. All her virtuous resolutions had deserted her. She was drowning in a pair of blue eyes.

'By gum, 'tis a cold 'un.'

A blast of icy air enveloped them as Evans came in, knocking the snow from his boots before shutting the door. The groom's entrance had freed Rose from her inertia. Heavens, how close she had come to disaster! She rose quickly and began to gather up the dishes, clattering them angrily together.

'Bad, is it?' Sir Lawrence asked him, unperturbed.

'Aye, sir. Nothin's travelling today, that's for sure. Miss Rose asked me to go down as far as where I guessed the main track should be, but the drifts are terrible deep. Once the packhorses have pushed through, then we can follow their trail, but I don't expect to see 'em today. 'Tis Christmas Day, after all.'

'So it is!' Sir Lawrence turned back to Rose. 'Let me be the first to wish you a Merry Christmas, madam.'

'Do you mean to say we will be stranded here for another day?' she demanded.

Sir Lawrence grinned.

'At least.'

It occurred to Rose that her host was not at all upset by the news.

'When do you expect your staff to return?'

He shrugged.

'I had told them to come back tomorrow. However,

if it snows again that may change. If we cannot get out, *they* will not be able to get in.'

'You do not seem very put out by the prospect.'

'Why should I be? Mrs Brendon has left the larder well stocked with ham and cheese, probably biscuits, too.'

'Enough for you alone, perhaps. But…cold meats on Christmas Day?' She rose, brushing down her apron. He had accused her of being a managing female—she would prove him right! She said briskly, 'Very well, then, we must get to work. Evans, have you checked the stables yet?'

'No, ma'am. There's a gert snowdrift across the door.'

'Well, I think you should dig it away and look after the horses.'

Sir Lawrence stood up.

'I'll give you a hand—'

'No, sir, I have another job for you.' Rose gave him her sweetest smile. 'I am afraid, Sir Lawrence, that the occasion calls for a sacrifice.'

Sir Lawrence scowled. 'This is a damned unusual Christmas!'

Rose chuckled.

'I know, Sir Lawrence, but needs must, as they say.'

They were in one of the outhouses, surrounded by feathers.

'I only hope these birds were not the best layers,' he muttered. 'Mrs Brendon will have something to say when she returns.'

'But, my dear sir, we must have something to eat today.'

He cast a fulminating glance in her direction.

'My requirements were quite minimal. A slice of ham, a bottle of wine...'

'But it is so cold I am sure your housekeeper will be pleased to know you are going to eat a proper meal,' replied Rose, trying not to smile. 'I have almost finished plucking my bird, Sir Lawrence. You do not seem to be making much progress with yours. But I acquit you, since you were the one who had to despatch the poor things.' She looked up and laughed. 'Fie, Sir Lawrence! I do believe that, at this moment, you wish it had been my neck that you had wrung!'

His mouth curled in a reluctant grin.

'I admit I was sorely tempted, ma'am, when you told me what you wanted me to do.'

'But you will enjoy your meal, sir, I promise you.' She put aside her own bird and reached for his. 'Let me finish that for you, Sir Lawrence.'

He looked at her, his brows raised.

'Why do I have this suspicion that you will find me something equally onerous to do now?'

'No, no, not at all.' She laughed at him. 'I only want you to go and make sure the fires are banked up! Evans has fetched in more peat, but you might wish to refill the wood basket.' She added, in the way of a treat, 'When you have done that and I have prepared these birds for the spit, perhaps we should step out and see for ourselves just how bad the roads are.'

The blizzards of the previous evening and the overnight snow had given way to a gloriously clear blue sky.

The glistening white world shone just outside the door. Rose was dazzled by its brightness. She longed to go out and explore it, but she had spent years teaching her pupils that leisure time was much more enjoyable when it was earned, so she carried the two hens to the kitchen and set everything in readiness for dinner before she allowed herself even to think about going out of doors.

When she ran upstairs to collect her cloak she stopped for a moment to gaze out of the window. The world was transformed by a blanket of white. She thought of her family back at Mersecombe. They would have realised how impossible it was for her to get home. She hoped they would not be too anxious; little Sam would not worry at all, he would be much too excited by the first real snow of the winter, but Mama—she knew Rose had Evans with her and would surely believe her daughter was sensible enough to take shelter. Rose gave a little laugh. Sensible! If her mother could see her now she would think her anything but sensible, stranded in a large old house with a man whose licentious reputation was known countrywide! But, in truth, what else could she do? The sensible thing had been to remain at Knightscote and it was eminently sensible to make sure they had a good meal. Humour bubbled in her throat again. Perhaps she could have fainted off, or had hysterics when she realised just who her companion was, but Rose could not see that such behaviour would have benefited her at all. No, she would just have to make the most of it. Her family would be at church now, so she uttered up a little prayer for them as she picked up her cloak and set off to join Sir Lawrence downstairs.

The sun was high over head as they left the house.

'I am surprised you are willing to quit your new domain,' remarked Sir Lawrence as they set out across the courtyard.

'It is not my domain,' she told him. 'Evans is only too happy to sit in the kitchen, smoking his pipe and keeping the fire in. My presence is not required.'

They left the grounds by a little wicket gate that led directly to the lane. Rose walked behind Sir Lawrence, placing her boots in his footsteps, but still it was necessary to hold her cloak and skirts high to avoid them dragging in the snow. It was only one hundred yards to the end of the lane, but by the time they reached it she was breathing heavily, her boots and the hem of her skirts caked in snow. Sir Lawrence, she noted, in his country jacket, York tan gloves and stylish beaver hat, looked as fresh as the moment he had stepped out of the house. He had not put on his greatcoat and his only concession to the cold was a muffler wrapped about his neck.

She came to stand beside him and they gazed down upon an alien landscape, only the black outlines of the trees and bushes showing against the dazzling white of the lying snow.

'Evans is right,' said Sir Lawrence, shielding his eyes against the glare of sun on snow. 'It would be hard going for you to push your way through those deep drifts.'

'But how long must we wait for the packhorses to go through?'

He shrugged. 'A couple of days at the most.'

'Oh, no!'

He turned to smile down at her. 'You need not worry; livelihoods depend upon the business. They will be on the move as soon as they can.'

'Well, it cannot be soon enough for me.'

'Ungrateful woman! Is my house so lacking in hospitality?'

'Indeed it is,' she retorted, 'when I have been obliged to cook my food and to make my own bed!'

'Neither of which was necessary. Mrs Brendon left plenty of cold food and my bed was made; I would happily have shared both with you.'

Rose gasped.

'How…how dare you!' she stammered, her cheeks flaming.

'Oh, easily.' He grinned. 'I am quite notorious, you know.'

'Y-you are quite outrageous,' she retorted, trying not to laugh. 'You are trying to put me to the blush.'

'And succeeding!'

'Well, I wish you would not. It will make for a most uncomfortable time if I have to spend the rest of my stay in the kitchen with Evans.'

'It will, indeed, and I would not have you do that for the world. Shall we go back?'

The return journey was easier, for they had a beaten path to follow and Rose now found it possible to walk beside Sir Lawrence. His outrageous remarks had not disturbed her—quite the contrary, for there was understanding in his blue eyes and an invitation for her to share the joke. He was obviously in good spirits and she was a little surprised therefore, at the serious tone of his next remark.

'What you said to me last night,' he said, gazing up at the sun, 'do you think it true? That Annabelle never really wanted to marry me?'

'Sir—'

'No, tell me, if you please. I feel I have been surrounded by sycophants, people who only say what they think I want to hear.'

'Whereas I will tell you the truth as I see it.'

'Yes.'

Rose drew her breath, awed at the responsibility he was placing on her shoulders.

'I did not know your Annabelle. Perhaps she *was* a saint, content to wait, but if she truly loved you, I wonder that she did not remonstrate with you.'

'She never did. Not one word. As I told you, she was an angel.'

'However much you might grieve for her, it will not bring her back. She is gone and the best you can do for her now is to make something of your life.'

He gave a mirthless bark of laughter.

'And just what am I good for? Spending money, charming women...'

She gripped his arm.

'You are young and strong. And rich! At the very least you should work to improve the lot of those you employ. And even if your land is in good heart and supporting you and your people, there are others who need help. For example, those poor wretches who fought at

Waterloo. Soldiers, proud men who are now cast off, unnecessary to the government. One sees them sometimes, even in this out-of-the-way place, starving at the roadsides. They should be honoured, protected. If you have the means to help them, then you should do so.'

He stopped.

'Aha, so you *do* think a man can change?'

'No, sir.' She returned his look. It was easy to be brave when the winter world was so bright and fresh. 'But I do not think that *charming women* is all you need do with your life!'

The house was in sight, long and low, the leaded windows twinkling in the sun beneath the covering of snow on its gabled roof. All around them the drifts were piled against walls and hedges, turning everyday outlines into magical forms. Rose breathed deeply: the clear air was as heady as wine.

'It may interest you to know, madam, that my reputation is somewhat exaggerated. I do not go out of my way to attract females.'

'But you do not *go out of your way* to avoid them.'

'Well, no, but your sex can be quite…resolute.' He grinned. 'Especially when the prize is so worth the catching.'

When his blue eyes smiled in just that way Rose could understand why so many foolish women succumbed to his charms, but she was determined not to be one of their number. She said severely, 'You value yourself very highly, Sir Lawrence.'

Again he flashed that wicked smile.

'Who am I to dispute what the ladies say?'

They were approaching the wicket gate and he strode ahead of her so he did not hear her indignant gasp.

'Why, you…smug…arrogant…*conceited* man!'

She scooped up a handful of snow and squeezed it between her hands, taking aim as he applied himself to opening the gate.

Her snowball caught him only a glancing blow on the shoulder so she quickly formed another and hurled it after the first. Her aim was hurried and the snowball would have sailed harmlessly past his head, if Sir Lawrence had not turned back at that moment and taken the full force of her missile on his hat, which was knocked clean off his head.

'Well, that was most satisfactory.' Rose dusted her hands together, a grin tugging at her mouth, until she realised that Sir Lawrence was about to retaliate.

She turned away, uttering a small scream as his first attempt splashed on her neck, some of the snow finding its way onto her skin. She remembered the adage that the best form of defence was attack and fired off another couple of shots. However, she quickly realised that she was no match for Sir Lawrence's deadly aim.

'Enough!' she cried, laughing. 'Truce, sir, truce!'

'Oh, no, this is a duel to the death!'

Another well-aimed shot hit her shoulder and showered her face with icy flakes. Rose picked up her skirts and fled for the shelter of the hedge. Sir Lawrence followed and Rose set off across the field with its covering quilt of snow.

'Got you!'

The hand on her shoulder sent her tumbling, Sir

Lawrence following as he lost his footing on the icy ground. They sprawled together, laughing and gasping for breath.

'Unfair, sir,' declared Rose, when she could at last speak. 'Do you know how difficult it is to move when one is hampered by skirts?'

'Hah! Who was it struck the first blow, when my back was turned?'

'That blow was well deserved!'

She was about to rise, but Sir Lawrence rolled over, pinning her down.

'Well deserved? What had I done?'

'It was punishment, for your arrogance!'

'My—' His black brows rose. 'Is it my fault if women find me irresistible?'

'You are incorrigible!' She was laughing up at him, finding it quite impossible to disagree and responding unselfconsciously to the humour in his eyes.

They continued thus, smiling at one another, blue eyes locked on blue-grey, for a long, long moment. Time stopped, everything around them was hushed and still, as if the world was holding its breath. Suddenly it occurred to Rose that she had never shared such a moment before, even with her husband.

She realised her situation: stretched out on the snow with Sir Lawrence almost lying on top of her, his lips only inches from her own, his breath feathering her cheek and the faint tang of eau de cologne filling her senses. In her imagination she reached out for him, pulling his face to hers and kissing him passionately. He would respond, of course, but it would not stop at kisses. Suddenly she knew why she had been feeling so restless… Panic filled her and she struggled to sit up. Immediately Lawrence rolled away.

'Very well, Mrs Westerhill, let us now agree to that truce!' He jumped up and held out his hand to her. 'Will you cry friends with me?' Even the touch of their gloved hands was unsettling. As soon as she was on her feet Rose pulled her fingers free and turned away, knowing she was blushing, but the thoughts of making love to him refused to leave her mind. He said quickly, 'I hope I did not hurt you?'

'N-no.' She concentrated on shaking out her skirts, speaking sharply to cover her discomfiture. 'But that was very irresponsible of us. Our clothes will be wet through.'

'Here, let me help you.' She started when he began to brush the snow off her back. 'There.' He turned her to face him. 'Forgive me,' he said gently, 'I did not mean to alarm you.'

Her eyes flew to his face. She was nervous, overset, but he had done nothing, save be there.

'Oh, no—that is, it was as much my fault as yours.' She struggled to smile. 'I fear the snow has made me a little light-headed.'

'It makes everything different,' he agreed, looking around them. 'It is like living in a fairy-tale world.' He held out his arm. 'Friends?'

She nodded.

'Friends.'

When they reached the kitchen garden Sir Lawrence stopped.

'It is Christmas Day and I have no present for you.' He reached across to a snow-covered bush and pulled off a small twig. 'Here. Rosemary, for remembrance.'

Rose took the spiky little branch and held it to her face, breathing in its scent. She never wanted to forget this day, however dull and respectable the rest of her life might be. The smell of rosemary would for ever remind her of Sir Lawrence.

'Thank you.' She tucked the stalk carefully into her pocket. 'But now I am in your debt.'

He put his fingers under her chin. She yielded to the pressure, tilting up her face, and he kissed her.

'Now we are equal.'

His kiss was brief, light as a feather, nothing like the impassioned, ravaging embrace of her imagination. It meant nothing, she kept telling herself. It was a friendly gesture, to reassure her that he had no designs upon her virtue. She was not sure she wanted to believe this argument, but as they walked back to the house she made a great effort to regain her composure. By the time they walked into the kitchen she had recovered sufficiently to smile at Evans's look of surprise.

'We have been very imprudent,' she told him, pulling off her cloak. 'Sir Lawrence will be able to change, but I shall have to rely upon a good blaze in the drawing room to dry my skirts.'

'Aye, well, I did build up the fire there for you and banked up the fires in the bedrooms, too, but you'll never sit around all day like that, Miss Rose,' declared her groom. 'Why, I can see from here that the back of your gown is soaked through!'

Sir Lawrence had been arranging their gloves on the mantelshelf, but now he turned, saying, 'If you would like to follow me, ma'am, perhaps we can find something for you to wear while we dry your clothes.'

Rose shook her head. 'I must put the chickens on the spit to roast—'

'I can do that for you, Miss Rose,' said Evans, waving her towards the door. 'You had best get out of those wet things before you catch your death.'

'That is the problem with servants one has known since a child,' she remarked, frowning at her groom, 'they tend to bully one.'

'But you know he is right,' replied Sir Lawrence. 'Come along, ma'am.'

There was nothing but friendliness to be read in his expression, so with a nod Rose followed him up the stairs, aware that her wet undergarments were becoming increasingly chilly against her skin.

'This is my bedroom,' he announced. 'You may come in or stay outside, but pray do not keep the door open, you are letting all the heat escape.'

Rose knew she should retreat and wait for him in the corridor, but the warmth of the fire was too tempting so she stepped into the room and closed the door. While Sir Lawrence delved into drawers and searched through a large linen press she looked about her. The painted walls glowed ruby red in the brilliant sunshine, matching the red-and-gold bed hangings. The ornately carved chimneypiece depicted hunting scenes that were repeated in the plaster frieze around the ceiling. In the daylight the chamber looked rich and warm; Rose imagined it at night, with the curtains pulled across the windows and the warm candlelight adding to the fire's glow. How much more comfortable to lie beside Sir Lawrence on that huge bed rather than in the cold snow...

Her body grew quite hot at the idea. Heavens, did merely being in the company of a rake make one prey to such dissolute thoughts? Rose quickly reached for the door handle.

'Perhaps I should wait in my own room...'

'No, no, I have found it now.'

Sir Lawrence came towards her, a floating confection of lace and ribbons in one hand. Despite her nerves Rose laughed.

'I cannot wear that,' she declared, gazing at the gossamer-thin nightgown. 'It would be most improper. And besides, it would afford me no warmth at all.'

Sir Lawrence grinned.

'One of my—er—guests left it here. And I cannot recall thinking it improper.'

Rose choked. She must not laugh at his outrageous comments. He continued as if he had not noticed. 'However, I agree it would not be very warm, but you might wear this over it.' He held up a grey woollen wrap. 'It is a banyan and a trifle small for me.' Rose hesitated and he added, 'Surely it would be better than risking your health by keeping on those wet clothes.'

'Very true.' She held out her hand. 'I will go and change.'

'Do you need help?' asked Sir Lawrence. 'I am not unfamiliar with…'

'No—thank you!'

Rose snatched the clothes from him and fled.

Chapter Three

'Well, it may not be stylish, but it is certainly respectable.'

Rose regarded her image in the mirror. Sir Lawrence's dressing gown almost wrapped around her twice, held in place by the belt which was knotted tightly at her waist. It covered her completely from her neck to her toes; if she had not folded back the sleeves, they would have hung down past her fingertips.

Thankfully her serviceable leather boots had been laced tightly at the ankle and not leaked, so she was able to put them on and protect her feet from the cold stone flags of the lower floors. When Rose left her chamber she was conscious of the soft silk and lace of the nightgown against her skin. Enveloped as she was in the dressing gown, no one could consider her dress immodest, but without her stays or chemise she felt decidedly underdressed.

The succulent smell of roasting chicken greeted her as she entered the kitchen, making her realise how hungry she was. She reached for the cook's apron hanging behind the door and was tying it around her when Evans brought in a basket of vegetables from the cold room. If he noticed her unusual garb, he said nothing about it. Neither did Sir Lawrence, who came in shortly after, but she was aware of the way his eyes wandered over her and she had the uncomfortable feeling that he knew exactly what she was—or was not—wearing beneath the enveloping wrap.

'So you are going to cook Christmas dinner for us, ma'am?'

'I am.' She tried to keep her attention firmly fixed upon basting the chickens. 'I am quite adept at the art of cookery.'

'I am very glad to hear it.'

He sat down at the big table. Rose frowned.

'What are you doing?'

'Nothing. That is, I am watching you.'

She turned back to the fire.

'I wish you would not.'

'Why? I like watching you.'

Rose knew it was not just the fire that was heating her cheeks.

'Well, I do not want you to watch me,' she said crossly. 'It is very off-putting.'

He laughed. 'Very well. Is there anything you would like me to do?'

His good-humoured compliance disarmed her. She stood for a moment, wiping her hands on her apron.

'Well,' she said at last, 'the table will need to be prepared...'

'Then I shall do that,' he said promptly. 'If you are to be cook and serving maid, I will be footman—oh, and butler, of course. I will find a bottle of wine for us to drink!'

The drawing room looked very inviting. The heavy velvet curtains were pulled across the windows to shut out the cold night. On the table, candlelight twinkled on the array of glass and silver, and Sir Lawrence had even collected a few evergreens to decorate the table. A dish of steaming vegetables was placed in the centre and a chicken, golden and succulent, rested on a platter waiting for Sir Lawrence to carve.

'A simple meal,' declared Rose, surveying her handiwork as she took her place at the table, 'but I think it preferable to cold meat and cheese!'

'Infinitely so,' agreed Sir Lawrence. 'I congratulate you, madam. It looks, and smells, delicious.' He raised his glass. 'A toast. To the most resourceful woman of my acquaintance.'

Rose was thankful for the dim candlelight to hide her blushes.

'It is nothing. Any good housewife could do as much. And credit goes to you, too, sir, for the excellent smoke-jack in the kitchen; it turned the spit most successfully.'

'Ah. That was one of the conditions Mrs Brendon placed upon me when I purchased the place. She said she would not consent to work here unless I improved the kitchen.'

'When did you buy Knightscote?' she asked him. 'It is strange we heard nothing of it at Mersecombe.'

'I have owned it for a couple of years now, but I have seldom used it, so my coming made little noise.'

'What, was there no gossip?' she dared to tease him. 'Even when you brought your less-than-respectable guests here?'

He frowned at her, but she was not deceived, for she read the laughter in his eyes.

'Be thankful, Mrs Westerhill, that my disreputable guests *did* visit, else you would have nothing to wear.'

Instinctively her hand went up to the neck of the dressing gown.

'I had hoped my own clothes would have been dry by now…'

'I'm afraid we did too good a job of making them damp.'

Rose bit her lip and tried not to recall her wicked thoughts of that afternoon, but they were always there, in her head.

'At least you are most decorously attired,' he continued. 'You have only to cover your hair with that napkin and the result would be positively nun-like!'

She could not resist a retort.

'Some might suggest it is a necessary defence, sir, given your reputation.'

He bared his teeth.

'Put away your claws, vixen. I will not fight with you on Christmas Day. Tell me instead about your life in Mersecombe. Do you have a large establishment?'

'No, a modest house with a couple of servants.'

'Yet you keep a groom.'

'Evans has been with me since I was a child. He came with me when I married, and when I sold the house at Exford he agreed to come with me to Mersecombe, although he is obliged to work in the house as well as look after the horses.' She smiled. 'They are my one luxury. I will buy a pony for little Sam, when the funds allow. Evans will teach him to ride—he put me on my first pony. I should like him to do the same for my son.'

'It must be hard, bringing up a boy on your own.'

'I have my mother to help me. But you are right, he misses his father. Sam was only four when I was widowed, so I am not sure how much he remembers of his papa.'

A good thing, perhaps, recalling the tears and the arguments.

'How did he die?'

Lost in the past, Rose looked at him, uncomprehending, and he said quickly, 'I beg your pardon, if you would rather not—'

'No, no. I have no objection to telling you. A riding accident. His horse slipped on the ice and threw him. He broke his neck.'

She did not add that he was returning from a tryst with his current mistress. Everyone in Exford might know the truth, but there was no reason she should admit it to this stranger.

'I am very sorry.'

She shrugged as if to evade his sympathy.

'It was four years ago. We have managed very well

since then.' She added brightly, 'And now we have Magnus.'

'Magnus?'

'Magnus Emsleigh. He is a shipping merchant and owns a substantial property just outside Mersecombe. He is a pillar of the local society. An excellent example for my son to follow.'

'And does he wish to become Sam's father? Ah. I can see by your look that that is the case. Why have you not mentioned him before?'

Rose had wondered that herself. Surely to tell Sir Lawrence that she was betrothed to a wealthy, respected local gentleman would have added to her consequence. It was not a love match, but a prudent arrangement, designed to provide security for her and for Sam. It now occurred to Rose that she was reluctant to admit, even to herself, that she was soon to marry Magnus Emsleigh.

He spoke again, saying lightly, 'Have you set a date?'

'Lady Day.' She pushed a slice of chicken around on her plate. 'Magnus has no experience of children. Sometimes Sam can be…difficult.'

Lawrence sat back, his fingers playing with the stem of his wineglass. He remembered his own stepfather, a deeply religious man whose repressive regime of sermons and beatings had only made a spirited young boy even more determined to rebel.

'It can be hard for a young boy to accept another man in the house. It will take time and patience.'

'Yes,' she nodded eagerly. 'That is what I have told Magnus.'

Lawrence took a sip of his wine.

'But what is this pillar of society thinking of, to let you ride unattended in such weather?'

She put up her chin at that.

'He is not my keeper. I will not allow him to dictate to me.' Lawrence's brows went up and she added, 'Besides, he is in Bath at present and does not know what I am about.'

Rose turned her attention to her plate and Lawrence took the opportunity to study her. She looked absurdly young in her borrowed dressing gown, but it did nothing to hide her charms. The belt was pulled tight around her tiny waist and accentuated the full, rounded swell of her bosom. The ordered ringlets of yesterday had given way to more natural curls that she had caught back from her face with a wide ribbon, and her cheeks were still delicately flushed from her endeavours in the kitchen.

'I applaud your wish for independence, Mrs Westerhill, but I pity your suitor.'

He thought she might blush at that, but she surprised him by chuckling.

'Poor Magnus. He thinks I am not capable of managing my own affairs and he is eager to relieve me of all my burdens. As if I had any! My meagre savings require little effort and, no matter what I say, I cannot persuade him that Sam is *not* a burden! Magnus is a dear, but he is inclined to lecture me and I get quite cross with him sometimes—' She broke off. 'I beg your pardon. I should not be telling you all this.'

'You may tell me whatever you wish. In fact—' He stopped, slightly alarmed to discover that he wanted to know everything about her. He got up to throw more logs on the fire. He must be careful; this woman was getting under his skin. He enjoyed her company, enjoyed teasing her, watching the delicate colour mantle her cheek, but she was not of his world. The seduction of a respectable schoolteacher was not something he wanted on his conscience.

When he looked up again she had walked to the window and pushed apart the curtains.

'We have had more snow this evening. It has stopped now and the moon is rising. Do come and look, it is almost as bright as day.' She glanced over when he came to stand beside her. 'Is it not beautiful?'

Almost as beautiful as you.

The words were on the tip of his tongue, but he swallowed them, saying instead, 'If we have no more snow, then the packhorses should be able to get through tomorrow. You can be on your way.'

She looked a little startled at his harsh tone, then the lashes dropped, veiling her eyes.

'Yes, of course. And this little idyll will be over.' There was a hint of sadness in her voice that surprised him.

'An idyll? Is that how you have seen this?'

Her smile not only lit up her face, it illuminated the room.

'Stranded here, having to fend for ourselves—it has been so different from my everyday life.' She added shyly, 'Of course, I was a little frightened of you at first, but you have proved yourself to be most—'

'Be careful,' he warned her. 'Do not make a hero out of me!'

'—most *restrained*,' she ended, one corner of her mouth lifting a fraction. She looked back to the window. 'I wonder what might have happened if you had been less honourable.'

'I beg your pardon?' Surely he had misheard her? The faint blush on her cheek told him he had not.

'We have been given this opportunity to escape from our ordinary lives for a few days. Tomorrow, I will go back to Mersecombe and I assume you will soon return to London. It is unlikely that we shall ever meet again. I just wonder what it would have been like…'

For a long moment she held his eyes.

'Forgive me.' She looked away, giving her head a little shake. 'I think I have had too much wine. Please, ignore what I said.' She turned back to the table. 'I had best get these dishes to the kitchen. Evans will have finished his own meal by now and will be waiting to clear up.'

'Let me help you.'

She did not refuse and he followed her through to the kitchen, his mind buzzing with conjecture. Was she really regretting the fact that he had not tried to seduce her? He shook his head. No. She was far too respectable for that. His gaze was drawn to the proud line of her back, the narrow waist and the full hips that swayed so invitingly as she moved. It was unconsciously done and therefore all the more alluring.

Evans had already cleaned the spit and cooking pans and he would allow them to do no more than bring the dishes into the scullery.

'A kitchen's no place for the likes of you, Miss Rose,'

he muttered, 'nor you, sir. If you will forgive me for saying so, I think you'd be more hindrance than help.'

Lawrence laughed at that. 'I fear you may be right. I'll go away.'

'Aye, do, and be so good as to take my mistress with you!'

'Really, Evans is growing quite autocratic,' grumbled Rose. She was kneeling before the drawing room fire, jabbing the poker between the logs. 'He knows I am more than capable of helping him!'

'Yes, but you should not have to.'

Sir Lawrence reached out and took the poker from her. She shook her head at him, smiling.

'I want to do *something*!'

He dropped down beside her and finished stirring the fire into a blaze.

'Then find something a little less harmful to your hands.' He took her fingers in a firm, warm clasp. 'Look how rough they are.'

Rose tried to pull away, embarrassed.

'That is not just from the last couple of days…'

He ignored her and continued to examine her hands. They were trapped in his gentle grasp. His intense scrutiny was unsettling; her heart was pounding, fluttering in her chest like a caged bird.

'You have even burned yourself.'

'A tiny mark!' She tried and failed to keep her voice steady, conscious of how near he was. The tug of attraction was almost palpable. He continued to study the small red weal on the edge of her palm. She swallowed.

'And one expects that in a kitchen…' Her words trailed off as he lifted her hand to his lips.

It was a gentle, intimate gesture and it took her breath away. Without thinking Rose tightened her fingers around his. She leaned closer and kissed him full on the mouth. His hands slid up her arms and rested lightly on her shoulders, holding her to him. Rose had closed her eyes, but the next instant they flew open and she drew back.

'Oh, my! I beg your pardon!'

'There is no need; I am not offended.' He was smiling at her in a way that made it difficult to think.

She knew she should get up off her knees, but his hands remained on her shoulders, the thumbs tracing the line of her collarbones through the wool of her wrap. She did not want him to stop.

'I—I do not know what came over me.'

'Curiosity, perhaps?' His smile grew and she felt her bones begin to melt.

'It…it is the snow,' she stammered. 'And the wine. I am not normally so…wanton. What must you think of me?'

He skimmed one hand down her arm and even through the soft woollen sleeve her skin tingled beneath his touch.

'I think you are adorable.' He lifted her hand and began to kiss each of her fingers.

'Wh-what are you doing?'

'Trying to decide,' he murmured, between slow, deliberate kisses, 'if I most want to make love to you here on the rug in front of the fire, or in my bed, between silken sheets.'

The images conjured by his soft words made her tremble. If she had not already been kneeling, she thought she must have collapsed on the rug in a damp heap of desire and anticipation.

'Im-impossible,' she stammered. 'You will do neither of those things.'

'No?' He raised his eyes from the contemplation of her fingers, and what was left of her insides liquefied. 'It was *you* who kissed *me*. And you yourself questioned whether we were wasting this opportunity.'

She swallowed and ran her tongue nervously over her lips.

'Are…are you joking me, Sir Lawrence?' The look in his eyes told her he was in deadly earnest.

'One night,' he whispered. 'After that we will go back to our separate worlds and need never meet again. What do you say?'

It was the edge of a precipice. He was still holding her hand, his thumb rubbing gently across the soft inner side of her wrist and sending arrows of heat through her body. They were still kneeling, and so close that she would only have to lean forwards a little to be in his arms.

Rose searched his eyes. Behind the intense blue was a shadow of sadness.

I could dispel that, she thought. *I could make him happy, at least for a while.*

'No.' Gently she disengaged her hands. 'I am very sorry if I led you to think—'

'You did, but I shall get over it.' He held out his hand to her. '"Since there's no help for it, come, let us kiss and part,"' he quoted, smiling.

Her throat swelled. Tears burned her eyes as he pulled her to her feet.

'Oh, *please* do not say such things to me!'

'Do you not like Drayton?'

'Too much!' She blinked. 'It—it has been a long day. I should retire now.'

He released her, and with another mumbled apology she ran out of the room.

Damnation!

Lawrence stared at the closed door. She had rejected him.

And quite right, too, argued the voice in his head. *She is too respectable for you, despite that unsolicited kiss.* But he had thought, for a while, that she might just count the world well lost. She had certainly considered it. He sighed. Such a heady mix of innocence and honesty. She had begged him to ignore her. How much better if he could have done so! Indeed, he had intended to keep his distance, until the moment he had taken her hands. The mere touch of her skin and all his honourable resolutions had fled. All he knew was that he wanted her in his arms. In his bed.

He had not felt such desire for months, possibly years. He was happy enough to attend the constant round of parties and balls that filled the London social calendar and was willing to indulge any of the ladies who threw themselves in his way in a little flirtation. Mostly it was no more than that, but he had only to escort a lady to her home for the gossips to claim she was his mistress. He had stopped trying to correct them, but the lies and intrigue of town life had begun to pall—society would be aghast if they knew how many nights he spent alone. He collected a glass of wine and threw himself down in a chair. Another lonely night would be nothing new. The rattling of the window reminded him of the weather. Pray heaven it did not snow again—he needed Rose out of the house. He was only flesh and blood, after all, and she was too damned desirable.

Rose shut and locked the door of the guest chamber. The room was warm and she sank down in front of the peat fire. What had she done? To kiss a rake, and so wantonly; she might as well have begged him to take her! It was to Sir Lawrence's credit that he had let her go so easily.

But you didn't want him to let you go.

The thought shocked her, but honesty compelled her to acknowledge it. Ever since she had arrived at Knightscote she had felt the tug of attraction. It was not just that he was wickedly handsome, it was the smile in his blue eyes, the way he made her laugh. She had not felt so alive since those early years with Harry, when he had courted her so assiduously. Her thoughts moved on from there to the marriage bed. Since Harry's death she had never craved another man's touch, until now. It was loneliness. She wrapped her arms about herself and inched even closer to the fire. That was the true reason for her restless state. She was lonely.

And she had read loneliness in Sir Lawrence's eyes, too. He had forsaken the world this Christmas to mourn his lost love. Rose's heart went out to him. He might be a rake, but he was sincerely grieving.

So why not comfort each other?

Rose shook off the insidious thought. It would not do, she was betrothed and she was a mother, although that life seemed a world away. She took off the wrap and slipped between the sheets. The bed was cold. She toyed with the idea of going downstairs in search of a warming pan, but abandoned it. She might see Sir Lawrence and then her noble resolve would crumble. It had been hard enough to walk out of the drawing room.

She shifted restlessly in the bed. Her body was on fire, aching for a man's touch, but not just any man. With a tiny cry of frustration she turned over.

'A rake makes the devil of a husband. You should know that by now.'

But her agitated mind would not be appeased. She was not looking for a husband, only a little comfort. An escape from her loneliness. A sweet memory to keep in her heart when she returned to her real world. Rose pummelled her pillow and lay down again, pulling the covers up to her cheek. She pictured Sir Lawrence in the drawing room, her stomach clenching as she imagined him smiling at her, felt again his gentle touch.

One night, then we need never meet again…

Lawrence remained in the drawing room, staring into the fire while the house grew silent around him. Evans would be snoring in his bed behind the kitchen, sleeping off the effects of the flagon of cider Lawrence had spotted on the floor beside his chair. Rose, too, would be asleep by now. The occasional creaking of the boards he put down to the wind, which was howling around the house.

He had risen to throw another log on the fire when he heard the rasp of the door hinges. He looked up, his eyes narrowing as he peered through the gloom.

'I thought…about what you said.' Rose moved across the room. She had left off the enveloping wrap, and the diaphanous folds of the nightgown glistened in the candlelight, outlining every curve of her body—she appeared to float towards him. 'One night. Then we will go our separate ways.'

Lawrence still could not believe it was not a dream, until he reached out and felt her warm flesh beneath his hands.

'You are quite sure about this?'

A smile trembled on her lips.

'Quite sure.'

As he dragged her into his arms Rose tilted her face up, inviting his kiss. His mouth ground over hers, savage, possessive, and her mind reeled, but with excitement, not alarm. She threw her arms around his neck, her lips parting to allow his tongue to search her mouth, flickering and teasing. She leaned into him, revelling in the feel of his hard, aroused body pressing against her. There was too much cloth between them. She unwound her arms from around Lawrence's neck and began to unbutton his waistcoat. It was shed without a break in their deep, passionate kisses and she moved on to those tight buckskins.

Breathing heavily, Lawrence broke away, but only long enough to divest himself of his clothes. At last he stood before her, naked and golden in the firelight, his body as muscled and perfect as any Greek statue.

'Rose?'

She raised her eyes to his and slowly gathered up the gossamer folds of the nightgown, lifting them in one smooth movement. As the fine silk whispered over her head she heard another sigh, almost a groan, from Lawrence. Before the nightgown had left her hands and fluttered to the floor he had his arms around her, pulling her to him. He lowered her gently down onto the thick rug where the heat from the fire enveloped them. Her arms were still above her head and he reached out to catch her wrists, imprisoning them with one hand while the other explored her breasts. She writhed beneath his touch, uttering a little moan of pleasure when his circling fingers were replaced by his mouth. He gently teased and nibbled and sucked until she was gasping for breath, but even then he did not stop, but added to her exquisite torment by trailing his free hand down over the soft plain of her stomach, his fingers delving onwards, circling and stroking until her legs parted and her hips tilted invitingly. The long fingers continued to devastating effect; she groaned and twisted, pushed against his hand, crying out as wave after wave of pleasure burst over her. As the ecstatic spasms ceased Lawrence folded her in his arms and held her close.

'Oh.' She made her shuddering whisper into his shoulder. 'I had forgotten. *Thank* you.'

A soft laugh shook him. She felt it reverberate against her cheek.

'It was my pleasure.'

She struggled to sit up, smiling at him. She said, her voice warm and husky with passion, 'And this is mine.'

Gently she pushed him onto his back, smoothing her hands over his shoulders and across his chest. The dark smattering of hair caught at her fingers as she trailed them around the hard nipples. He reached up and removed the clips from her curls, so that when he pulled away the confining ribbon, her hair cascaded down to rest upon his naked body. Rose moved her head, dragging the silky tresses across the taut muscles of his stomach. He arched his back, eyes closed. Rose climbed over him, leaning forwards to kiss the fine line of his throat while the tips of her breasts rubbed against his skin and he groaned louder, his hands reaching for her, easing her into position so that he could thrust into her. It was Rose's turn to arch as she felt him inside her, sleek and hard. She moved against him, following the dictates of her body while his hands on her hips kept her firmly anchored over him. Excitement was building again, but this time it was centred on his pleasure. She held him deep and warm inside her, her body stroking and caressing until his grip tightened around her waist. He held her fast; she was powerless while he thrust into her hard and fast and she cried out, control swept away as he took her to new heights. One final thrust, a gasp, and they clung together until the last wonderful tremor shuddered through their bodies and they collapsed, sated, to lie in each other's arms before the dying embers.

Lawrence kissed her and carefully smoothed the damp tendrils of honey-brown hair back from her brow.

'Well, madam, was it as you expected?'

'Much, much better.' She snuggled deeper into his arms, smiling.

'And there's more.' He sat up and reached for his shirt. 'Put this on.'

'Why?' Obediently she allowed him to throw it over her head. She pushed her arms into the voluminous sleeves while he stepped into his buckskins. She watched him throw on his flowered waistcoat, marvelling at the way it accentuated the firm muscles of his stomach and arms. He reached down to pull her to her feet.

'I am taking you to bed, my love, but you will recall that the passages between here and the bedroom are unheated and I would not have you catch a chill.'

She could not resist reaching out and resting her hand against his naked chest.

'Will you not feel the cold?'

'No.' He swept her up into his arms. 'I shall have you next to my heart.'

He lowered his head to give her a fierce, savage kiss full of triumph and possession. Her body still glowing from their union, Rose wound her arms about his neck as he carried her to the bedroom.

A cold, rosy dawn illuminated the window. Rose stretched, feeling the warmth of Lawrence's sleeping form against her back. Her body felt wonderfully full, satisfied, and she could not help smiling into the semi-darkness. Their lovemaking in the bedroom had been even better than that first, astonishing coupling in front of the fire. Lawrence had proved himself an expert lover—she should not have been surprised, given his reputation, but his gentleness and the way he had sought to put her pleasure before his own had been a revelation.

It would make parting all the more difficult.

Rose eased herself away from his sleeping form and out of the bed. The discarded shirt and breeches on the floor brought back memories that sent a delightful shiver down her spine, but it also reminded her that they had left several telltale garments strewn across the drawing room. She reached for Sir Lawrence's brightly coloured dressing gown. She must go to her own room and dress. Then she could send Evans out to check on the state of the track.

When Lawrence awoke he was immediately aware of a feeling of well-being. The early-morning sun was pouring into the room, battering his eyelids. He did not want to open his eyes. He wanted to—

He turned over, but his hands found only cold empty sheets. Had he dreamed last night's events? His body told him not.

Lawrence sat up, blinking. His clothes were still on the floor, but his banyan was gone. Quickly he grabbed his clothes and scrambled into them, buttoning his coat even as he made his way to the guest room. It was empty. With a growing sense of unease he ran down the stairs to the drawing room.

Rose was standing by the window, fully dressed, her travelling cloak folded over a chair, gloves and bonnet resting neatly on the top. She turned as he came in, but the sunlight was behind her and he could not see her face.

'You are up betimes.' He crossed the room in a couple of strides and reached for her. She stepped away from him.

'I have a long ride ahead of me.'

'You are going, then.'

'Yes. Evans has already ventured out this morning and says the pack ponies have been on the move. We have only to make our way to the lane…'

She reached for her gloves, but Lawrence stepped in her way, catching her hands.

'Can we not talk, first? About last night…' She would not meet his eyes and he squeezed her fingers, saying sharply, 'It is customary to observe the civilities, you know, even with your lover.'

A faint shake of her head sent her curls dancing.

'We are not lovers. It was one night.'

'But a very special night, would you not agree?' The faint blush on her cheek gave him his answer. 'When will I see you again?'

'You will not.'

'But—'

She lifted one hand and placed her fingers against his mouth.

'It is better this way. I have to go back to Mersecombe, to my son. There is no place for you in my life.'

Lawrence frowned. Her words were calm, reasoned, but it made no sense to him.

'I want to be part of your life,' he said. 'After last night I want to know you better—'

'No!' She stepped away from him. 'There can only be pain that way.'

'Because of my past? Believe me, Rose—'

'Are you going to promise me you will change? It will not happen.'

'Hell and damnation, woman, how can you—?' Again that tiny shake of her head accompanied by such a sad smile that he bit back his fury. 'Tell me, Rose. Tell me why you are so sure.'

Her blue-grey eyes rested upon him for a long moment, then she turned and walked back to the window. Her eyes were fixed on the snowy scene, but her thoughts were very far away.

'Once a rake, always a rake. I was married to such a man. I met Harry when I was still at school in Barnstaple. He charmed me from the first. Everyone knew his reputation, but he told me it would be different when we were married. I believed him. I was just seventeen when I became his wife, Harry was five and twenty. For a few months I think, believe, he was faithful to me, but then I was with child and he…he began to stay away. Whenever I taxed him with it he would deny it; if I caught him out in his philandering then he would come back to me, repentant, promising he would reform. It was after one such incident that he bought the property at Exford. He said we would make a fresh start, but whenever there was a pretty woman…' She crossed her arms, hugging herself. 'His death was something of a relief. I could continue to love him, but he could no longer hurt me.' She turned back to look at him, her eyes bright with unshed tears. 'So you see why I will not allow that to happen to me again?'

'But I am not like your husband, Rose. I will prove it to you.'

She shook her head, taking out her handkerchief to wipe her eyes. When she spoke again her tone was brisk.

'You can only prove it by living a respectable and chaste life for…I do not know…years. I can see by your horrified look that the idea does not appeal.'

Lawrence watched in silence as she put on her bonnet and gloves. She was going. If he could not come up with some argument within the next few minutes, she would walk out of his life for ever. He tried to think, but his brain refused to work. Mechanically he picked up her cloak and placed it around her. He noted the way her fingers paused in tying the strings when he allowed his hands to rest for a moment on her shoulders.

'So there is nothing I can say.'

'Nothing.'

'What if…' his hands tightened and he turned her to face him '…what if there is a child? I would have a right to know.'

She paled, her eyes dilating, and he braced himself to hold her, should she faint.

'You would, of course,' she murmured, her voice barely above a whisper. 'But there will be no child.'

'How can you be so sure?'

She gently pushed his hands away.

'I can be absolutely sure. That is all you need to know.'

With that she turned and swept out of the room.

Evans was waiting with the horses at the door. He stepped forwards to help Rose to mount, but a word from Lawrence forestalled him. She did not object as Lawrence threw her up into the saddle. He checked the girth, made sure her foot was secure in the stirrup, anything to delay her departure.

'Goodbye.' She leaned down to him, holding out her hand. 'It was very good of you to take us in. I am very grateful. For everything.'

They might have been parting after an innocuous morning call, save for the haunted look in her eyes, from which all the blue had disappeared. He took her gloved fingers, felt them tremble in his grasp.

'If ever you need me—'

She nodded.

'That is kind, thank you, but I have everything I need at Mersecombe.'

'At least say I may call on you—'

'No.' Her fingers gripped his hand and she bent her serious gaze upon him. 'Promise me, promise me you will not come looking for me.' Her grip tightened. 'Please, Lawrence.'

Her eyes demanded an answer. He nodded.

'I give you my word.'

'Thank you.' She released his hand and straightened in the saddle.

It was a dismissal. There was nothing for it but to step back.

'Very well. I wish you Godspeed, madam.'

'And I wish you every happiness.'

A final smile, a final look from those slate-grey eyes, then she turned away, to ride out of his life for ever.

Lawrence knew that if the pack ponies were moving it would not be long before his servants returned to Knightscote. The scullery boy arrived first, followed by the stable lads. The short winter day was drawing to a close when his butler and housekeeper finally trooped into the house. By supper time the lodge had returned to normal, lights burning in the passages and servants on hand to attend to their master's slightest whim.

'Lord bless us, but why are you sitting in the dark, Sir Lawrence?' Mrs Brendon bustled in, carrying her master's supper on a tray. 'I do hope you haven't been too uncomfortable while we's been away, sir; I see you finished up all the ham, and someone's been using my kitchen, too...'

'Yes—how was your journey?' he asked the question to deflect her attention.

'Well, it could have been worse. Brendon and me got a ride on the carrier's cart as far as the crossroads, and the track was pretty well trodden from there on.' She put her tray down and began to go round the room, lighting candles from a taper. 'Now, sir, that's a game pie I brought back with me from Exford, so I hope it will do until I can get cooking again in the morning!'

'Excellent, thank you.'

'But there's hoof marks leading right up to the door, sir. Have you had visitors?'

'Yes. A traveller on the way to Mersecombe arrived here Christmas Eve. The weather was too bad to go further.'

'Ah, that explains the pots and pans that's been moved in my kitchen.' She nodded sagely. 'I was fair certain it weren't you that had taken to cooking!'

'No. Tell me, Mrs Brendon. You come from Exford way, do you not? Do you recall a gentleman who used to live there, name of Westerhill?'

'Harry Westerhill? Aye, I do. Gennleman, you say? Nothin' but a lecher I'd call 'n. The good Lord carried 'im off a few years back, and a good thing, too. No woman was safe!'

Lawrence pulled a chair to the table and sat down to his supper.

'He had a wife, I believe?' He hoped he sounded uninterested.

'Ah, that he did. Poor little thing. Led her a merry dance he did, what with his women and his gambling. And they say he used to beat her, when he was in his cups.'

Lawrence's hand tightened around his knife. 'Indeed?'

'Oh, he could charm the birds from the trees, could Harry Westerhill, but when he had had a few to drink…' She shook her head, tutting. 'Well, good riddance, that's what I'd say. The poor lady's better off without 'n. Better off without any man, if you ask me. Beggin yer pardon, sir!'

'No, you are right, Mrs Brendon.' Lawrence gazed down at the plate, his appetite quite gone. 'She is better off without any man.'

Chapter Four

'Very well, children, that is all for today. Put your slates on the shelf, please, before you leave.'

A scraping of benches and sudden explosion of chatter announced the end of the school day. Rose began to tidy her desk while the room gradually emptied around her.

'Mama, Mama, Jem wants me to go to the farm with him, to see his pointer's new litter!'

Sam was tugging at her skirts, looking up at her with such a look of hope and trust in his eyes that her heart turned over. She put a hand on his unruly fair hair.

'I am not sure you should. Mrs Wooler will have chores for Jem to do...'

'Nothing very much tonight, Mrs Westerhill, and Sam can help me with those.' Jem twisted his cap between his hands and said haltingly, 'Me mam says she likes it when Sam comes to see us—she likes to hear us laughing...'

Rose imagined Mrs Wooler, only a few months widowed, and she nodded.

'Then of course Sam may go with you, as long as he is home before dark.' Sam's mouth opened to argue and she lifted her finger. 'Before dark, Sam. Promise me.'

With an audible sigh he nodded. The next moment the boys had disappeared and she heard them whooping and laughing as they ran down the steps and off through the village. She stood for a moment, enjoying the silence. She never worried when the two boys were together. Jem was a little older than Sam and built on sturdier lines. He had always protected Sam from the older boys in the village, who tended to bully him, and since Jem had lost his father the boys had become even closer, united in their common plight.

The little schoolroom was situated above the north porch of the parish church, and when Rose was alone the peace of the building settled around her like an old but comfortable cloak. However, it was not enough to keep out the cold and she shivered. With winter approaching it would soon be time to bring out the old brazier to heat the schoolroom. She must remember to speak to the churchwarden about it.

Rose locked the schoolroom door and descended the stone steps built at the side of the porch. She walked slowly through the graveyard, but at the gate she stopped. She should go home, Mama would be expecting her, but to her left the track wound upwards through the ancient woods and on to the moor. Surely there was time for a short walk? A carriage rattled along the high street, distracting her. She quickly turned back, but it was only Farmer Ansell's son in his new gig.

Who else should it be? Rose asked herself. Restlessly she set off up the hill into the woods. She declined to answer her own question. It was nearly ten months since she had seen Sir Lawrence Daunton, but there was not a day that she had not thought of him, nor a morning that she did not wake up and wonder if today he might travel to Mersecombe to find her.

Her short sojourn at Knightscote haunted her dreams. It did no good to tell herself that it was for the best. Upon her return to Mersecombe she had given her family and friends to understand that she had been stranded at some remote farmhouse. It had taken all her tact and skill to persuade Evans to corroborate her tale and for some time she had been torn between hope and dread that Sir Lawrence might turn up and give the lie to her story. When the snows had cleared two weeks later and Evans reassured her that he had made enquiries and learned that Knightscote was now empty once more, she was surprised at the depth of her disappointment. She tried to be glad there was now no possibility of meeting up with Sir Lawrence again, but sometimes, when the children were being particularly troublesome or she was yawning behind her fan at some tedious party, she longed for him to arrive and carry her off.

'Romantic nonsense!'

She uttered the words aloud as she strode along, her skirts dragging on the long grass. Sir Lawrence was not some fairy-tale prince who would carry her off to live happily ever after. He was a rake. A libertine. He

might well run off with her; he might even make her
forget the world for a short while, but then there would
be nights of uncertainty when he did not come home,
tears and recriminations and the certain knowledge that
she would have to share him with every other female
who caught his eye.

'Never!'

She stopped. She had reached the edge of the wood
and she could see the moors ahead of her, the bracken
glowing reddish-orange in the sunlight. She dared not
go further. The sun was already low in the sky and her
mother would be worried, just as she worried about
little Sam.

Rose turned back.

By the time she reached the church again the sun had
gone down and the air was filled with a faint haze and
the scent of wood smoke. She saw a figure at the church
gate, a stocky, thickset man in a brown riding jacket
and tall hat. He was standing at the entrance to the
churchyard, feet spread, hands behind him, as if waiting for someone.

Rose stifled a cowardly impulse to dive into the
bushes and wait for him to go. Instead she fixed her
smile and said brightly, 'Magnus! Have you been waiting for me?'

He swept off his hat, displaying ordered brown curls.

'I had business in Minehead which took longer than
anticipated, so I was too late to catch you in the schoolroom, but since I had come from the high street I knew
I could not have missed you. However, if you had not

appeared in the next five minutes I would have gone home.'

If only she had walked a little further up the track! Rose chided herself for the thought and, to make up for her churlishness, tucked her hand into his arm.

'Well, I am here now, so you may walk me back to Bluebell Cottage.'

'Have you thought what you will wear for the Assembly?'

'Good heavens, Magnus, that is weeks away! I have not given it a thought.'

He gave a ponderous little laugh. 'I would like to be prepared; I want to present you with a corsage to match your gown and you know how difficult it is to find flowers in the dead of winter.'

She had a sudden unreasoning urge to announce she was going to wear the brightest, most vivid scarlet gown she could find. Instead she said, 'How kind you are, Magnus. It will most likely be my midnight blue.'

'What, are you not having a new gown? My sister Althea has ordered another, I saw it this morning. I thought it was the usual practice for all you ladies to have a new gown for every occasion.'

'I am sure it is, if one has unlimited funds!' She immediately regretted her snappish retort and squeezed his arm. 'I beg your pardon, Magnus. I know you were only funning.'

'And you know I would buy you a dozen gowns, if you would let me.' He stopped. 'Let us put an end to this dilly-dallying, Rose. Even without a special licence we could be wed before Christmas.'

'Magnus, I have explained to you why I cannot marry you yet.'

'You are concerned for young Samuel, I know that, and I understand why you cried off in the spring, but to postpone it for a whole year—'

'You have been very patient, Magnus. It is only a few more months.'

'Sometimes I wonder if you have changed your mind, what with the losses I suffered when the *Sealark* went down...'

'That is unjust,' she cried. 'My decision to postpone the wedding was taken months before you lost the *Sealark*. And besides, I would never allow such a misfortune to weigh with me!'

'Of course, and I beg your pardon.' He stopped to press a kiss upon her fingers. 'Forgive me, the whole affair is preying upon my mind—until the insurers pay out for the loss of the ship and the cargo I cannot honour my promissory notes to the crew!' He gave a rueful smile. 'I fear it is making me very bad company.'

'Not at all, I understand your concerns. I am only thankful that more lives were not lost in the accident. But that has nothing to do with my decision that we should delay our marriage.'

'Then it is solely to do with your son.'

'Yes.' Rose was relieved that he did not notice the heartbeat's hesitation before she responded.

He said heavily, 'In my opinion you refine too much upon the wishes of that young man! Once we are married he will soon learn to respect me.'

'But I do not want him to do so out of fear! Be patient, Magnus, please.'

'Well, if you will not agree to our marriage, then at least let me help you open up the mine at Hades Cove. I am sure it is not so unprofitable as you have been led to believe.'

She put up her hand.

'My dear, we have been over this before. My late husband poured a vast amount of our money into the mine. I will not allow you to do the same.'

'But once we are wed it will become my property.'

Rose smiled up at him mischievously. 'Ah, yes, well, *then* you will be master of everything and may do as you please!' She sighed. 'Let us not argue. Tell me instead about your sister's new gown. Is she having it made up in Minehead?'

'No, there is an excellent modiste in Dunster who has all the latest London pattern books. She showed me a drawing. Too many frills and flounces for my taste, but there you are, Althea says it is the latest thing. And you know Althea likes to keep up with fashion.' He chuckled. 'As my sister she knows she must set the standard, even at a little local gathering such as the Mersecombe Assembly!'

Rose smiled absently, her mind wandering to more anxious matters.

'I wonder if Sam is home yet,' she murmured, almost to herself. 'I gave him permission to go to the Woolers Farm, but told him he must come home before dark.'

They had reached the little bridge that led across the

stream to Bluebell Cottage and Magnus stood back to allow Rose to precede him.

'Then I have no expectation of seeing the boy before midnight.'

She shook her head, saying over her shoulder, 'You know that generally he minds me very well, Magnus.'

She had reached the cottage, but stopped as she always did to admire the little rosemary bush growing beside the door before she stepped into the hall.

She allowed Magnus to take her cloak, then turned to smile at him. 'I hear voices. You see, he is home before me.'

Rose walked across and opened the sitting-room door, her smile freezing on her face when she found herself looking into the intensely blue eyes of Sir Lawrence Daunton.

'Sir Lawrence!' Magnus followed Rose into the room, his hearty tone quite at odds with the paralysing shock she was suffering. 'Good heavens, man, what are you doing here?'

'You know each other?' asked Mrs Molland, who was standing with her arm on Sam's shoulder and beaming at Sir Lawrence, delighted to have such a charming gentleman in her house.

'Aye, ma'am. We met at the Pullens' ball.'

Three weeks ago! Rose put a hand on the back of a nearby chair to steady herself. He had been at Knightscote for three weeks and she had not known!

Magnus turned to Rose, saying in a slightly aggrieved tone, 'You may recall, my dear, that upon my persuasion Lady Pullen sent you an invitation, but you chose not to go.'

'And *you* may recall that it fell upon a week-night and I was obliged to be up betimes to open the school-house,' Rose answered coolly. 'If I had accompanied you, it would have meant you returning home at an unseasonably early hour and Althea would not have liked that.'

'No, no, you are right there,' he conceded, pursing his lips and looking a little thoughtful before turning back to Sir Lawrence. 'But what brings you to Merse-combe, sir?'

Rose was acutely conscious that Sir Lawrence's gaze had been fixed on her, but now he shifted his attention to the questioner.

'I heard about the pointer puppies for sale at Woolers Farm.' His eyes flickered across Rose again as he moved his gaze to Sam. 'This young man was there and helped me make my choice. Then, as it was growing dark, I asked him to show me the way back to the Ship.'

'Sir Lawrence allowed me to ride on his horse with him,' declared Sam, his eyes shining.

'It was the least I could do, since you were good enough to guide me. And once we had stabled the horse I thought I should come along and explain why Sam was late…'

'You—you are staying in Mersecombe?' stuttered Rose.

The blue eyes once more rested on her face.

'Yes. I have more business here tomorrow, Mrs…'

'Oh, heavens, where are my wits?' cried Mrs

Molland. 'This is my daughter, sir. Mrs Westerhill. Samuel's mother.'

Should she admit they had met before? Would he say anything? He was bowing, no sign of recognition in his face. Rose tried to think clearly. Perhaps it was coincidence. No. Even her befuddled brain could not believe that. He would not have forgotten her in ten months— would he?

'Sir Lawrence is having first pick of the litter,' Sam piped up. 'Of course they are too young yet and will not be taken from their mother until they are weaned, but Jem says they don't have buyers for them all. Could *we* have a puppy, Mama?'

Sam was looking up at her. She tried to concentrate on what he had said, tried to put out of her mind the fact that Lawrence was here, in her home, filling her sitting room and her senses with his presence.

'Please, Mama…it would be company for Grand-mama!'

The childish logic caused a ripple of amusement.

'I have plenty to occupy me without adding a dog to the family, Sam,' laughed Mrs Molland, ruffling his hair.

'It is out of the question,' declared Magnus. 'If Mrs Molland truly requires a pet, she should consider a little lapdog. You do not have room here for a pointer.'

'We have plenty of room,' put in Rose, angered by his calm assumption of authority. 'But I'm afraid we cannot have a puppy just at the moment.'

The look of disappointment on Sam's face tugged

at her heart and she dropped down beside him, putting her hands on his shoulders.

'This is a bad time of year to bring home a puppy that needs so much exercise, my dear,' she said gently. 'Perhaps next time, when the weather is a little better and you are older.'

His lip trembled, but before he could reply Mrs Molland held out her hand to him.

'We can talk about this more in the morning. Come along now, Sam; bid your mama and our guests goodnight and I will take you up to bed.'

Rose put her arms around him and kissed him, standing at his side as he made his bow.

'Do not forget to thank Sir Lawrence for seeing you home,' Magnus reminded him.

'No, no, you have that the wrong way round,' replied Lawrence seriously. 'Sam showed *me* the way.' He held out his hand. 'Goodnight, Master Westerhill. I am greatly indebted to you.'

'So, what business is it that keeps you in Mersecombe?' enquired Magnus, when Sam and his grandmother had left the room.

The gentlemen were settling into chairs close to the fire, but Rose moved to the window seat, still trying to collect her wits.

'Oh, this and that,' Sir Lawrence responded vaguely. 'I return to Knightscote tomorrow, but I shall have to come back again once Wooler sends word that the dog is weaned.'

Magnus leaned back in his chair. 'You could send your man to collect it.'

'I could, of course, but I enjoy finding my way about.' He added apologetically, 'I fear I have been far too reclusive during my previous visits to Exmoor.'

'I do not see what you need with a dog when you are here for only a few weeks each year.' Rose's statement brought both men's eyes upon her and Magnus was moved to protest. Lawrence held up his hand.

'No, no, Emsleigh, she has a point.' Again she was subjected to that intense gaze. 'I have brought my keeper with me. The dog will be put into his care to be trained up, for use on whichever of my estates we are visiting.'

'Do you plan a long stay at Knightscote, Sir Lawrence?' asked Magnus.

Rose looked down at her hands, desperate to hear his answer.

'That depends. I have made no firm plans yet.'

She dared not look up, afraid of what she might see in his eyes.

'Well, sir, if you are still here at the end of October you should come to the Mersecombe Assembly,' declared Magnus. 'I will be able to introduce you to everyone. Not the highest society, of course, as you are used to in London, but nevertheless it will give you an opportunity to meet your neighbours. It is held at the Ship, so before you leave tomorrow you could take a look at the Assembly Room—I think you will agree it is a fine space for dancing.'

'And will you be attending, Mrs Westerhill?'

Rose jumped as Sir Lawrence addressed her.

'Why…yes.'

'Then, if I am still at Knightscote, I shall look forward to seeing you there.' He picked up his hat. 'I must go.'

Rose jumped to her feet.

'I shall see you out.'

Magnus immediately sat up.

'My dear, you should ring for Janet—'

'She will be helping Mama put Sam to bed.' Rose went to the door. 'This way, sir, if you please.'

The hall was blessedly free of people, but suddenly all the questions that had been flying around in Rose's head disappeared. All she could think of was Lawrence standing at her shoulder.

'Do you know, I am not sure I can recall my way back to the inn?' His low voice provoked in Rose a shiver of aching memory.

'Nonsense,' she retorted. 'You walked here only a short while ago.'

'Ah, but I was distracted by my companion's non-stop chatter. Would you be good enough to walk a little way with me?'

Rose knew she should refuse, but she took up her cloak and threw it around her shoulders. As they stepped outside Sir Lawrence stopped and she saw that he was staring at the shrubs beside the door, illuminated by the lamp from the parlour window.

'Rosemary,' he muttered. 'For remembrance.'

Rose gave a little shrug, trying to ignore the sensation of his eyes boring into her.

'I planted it as soon as I got home. By some miracle it has survived.'

She turned away quickly, hurrying through the garden and across the stream. Once they were on the road Sir Lawrence held out his arm to her and she laid her fingers on his sleeve. Beneath the fine cloth the muscle felt reassuringly solid.

'So you did not marry him on Lady Day.'

'No.'

'Because of your visit to Knightscote?'

'Of course not.' The denial was far too quick, unconvincing even to her own ears. 'My son is not yet ready for a new father.' She added, so he should be in no doubt, 'My opinion of you is unchanged, Sir Lawrence. You should not have come in search of me.'

'I did not. I am here on business of my own.'

'Oh.' Rose bit her lip, trying not to dwell upon her sense of disappointment. 'Well, I am glad of it. I, um, I suppose I should thank you for not mentioning the fact that we have met before.'

'Your mother was clearly unaware of it and I doubted very much if you had told Emsleigh.'

'No indeed.'

'So what did you tell them?'

'They think I was stranded at one of the outlying farms.'

They had reached the crossroads and Rose stopped.

'There.' She pointed. 'The Ship is just around the corner; you can see the glow from the lighted windows on the road.'

'Ah, yes, of course.' He caught her outstretched

hand. 'Thank you. And will you give me permission to call—?'

'No!' She stepped away from him, pulling her fingers free. 'No. We agreed.'

'We agreed nothing. Ten months ago I let you ride out of my life—'

'I told you then it was better if we did not meet again. Nothing has changed.'

'You do not know that.'

Rose desperately wanted to believe him, just as she had wanted to believe Harry every time he promised he would mend his ways. She took refuge in her bitterness.

'A rake reformed?' Her lip curled. 'An impossibility.' She shivered. 'I must go back.'

She pulled her cloak about her and began to retrace her steps.

'So you will not allow me to call upon you?'

Rose stopped.

'No.'

'But you will be at the Assembly?'

She shrugged.

'That is not until the end of the month. I cannot think you will want to stay at Knightscote for so long.'

'I shall be there.'

'I cannot prevent you from attending a public assembly, Sir Lawrence, although I think you will find it dull work.'

She saw the flash of his white teeth in the moonlight.

'We shall see!'

He strode away, whistling, and Rose hurried back

to Bluebell Cottage. How dare he come back into her life? What was he doing in Mersecombe, if he had not come to find her? She had told him they should not meet again and she would hold to that. After all, it was not just her happiness that was at stake if she allowed herself to become entangled with a rake, but that of her son.

Rose returned to the house to find her mother and Magnus waiting for her in the sitting room. Mrs Molland looked up, relieved, as she walked in.

'My dear, we were about to send out a search party!'

'I beg your pardon. Sir Lawrence was unsure of the way, so I stepped outside to—er—point him in the right direction.'

Magnus frowned.

'That was imprudent, Rose. I would not advise you to step out into the dark with any man, but when it is someone of Sir Lawrence's reputation…'

Mrs Molland nodded.

'Mr Emsleigh has the right of it, my love. Sir Lawrence and his circle are constantly mentioned in the London news sheets. You may recall even your aunt has mentioned him in her letters. Rake Daunton! Why, his name is for ever being linked with some society hostess or another. They say he is never seen twice with the same woman on his arm.'

'There has been very little about him this year, Mama.' And she had searched the newspapers more carefully than usual, looking for his name. Rose told herself she was not defending Sir Lawrence, merely trying to be fair and just.

'Perhaps we missed it.' Mrs Molland laughed. 'Good heavens, Rose, Mr Emsleigh will think the society gossip is the only page we read!' She added soberly, 'For all that, I was most grateful to Sir Lawrence for seeing Sam home. That was very thoughtful. And I was most impressed that he should then sit and converse with Sam and me in a very civilised manner. He is most agreeable.'

'I would expect nothing less of the man,' put in Magnus, giving an indulgent little laugh. 'I noticed at the Pullens' ball that he is like a magnet to you ladies. Gambling and flirting is how he spends most of his time in town.'

'I wish he had stayed there,' muttered Rose.

Magnus smiled at her.

'I know. It is a pity that you should meet him, but you need not worry. It is most likely he will return to Knightscote in the morning and we shall hear no more of him. But if he *should* come to the Assembly, I shall make very sure he understands that we are to be married next Lady Day, and if he attempts to go beyond the line of what is pleasing, he will have to answer to *me*.'

Never had Rose known the weeks to drag by so slowly. Her work at the village school occupied her for four mornings of the week, but she spent the rest of the time thinking of Sir Lawrence and wondering if he was still at Knightscote. She had forbidden him to call upon her, but that did not stop the flutter of hope every time there was a knock at the door.

The day of the Mersecombe Assembly dawned cold and wet. Heavy rain fell all morning; although the weather became drier as the day went on the thick cloud shrouding the hills remained, bringing an early dusk. Despite the drear weather Rose experienced a little thrill of anticipation as she walked with her mother the short distance from Bluebell Cottage to the Ship Inn. She told herself it was merely the thought of dancing that excited her; she had no expectations that Sir Lawrence would attend a provincial ball. After all, she could not even be sure that he was at Knightscote—he had certainly made no attempt to see her again.

That was as it should be, she told herself as she followed Mrs Molland into the Ship, but she could not prevent the rough edge of disappointment chafing her spirits when she could not see his tall figure amongst the crowd in the Long Room. Magnus and his sister were already present and came up immediately.

'It is as I feared,' declared Magnus, kissing and retaining Rose's hand. 'A sad crush. All the village must be here, including those who can ill afford it!'

'Fie, sir, they are a very good sort of people, and why should they not enjoy themselves?' Mrs Molland responded, her eyes bright as she surveyed the company. 'I am sure we shall enjoy some lively dancing this evening. Miss Emsleigh—what a delightful gown.'

Althea spread her flounced skirts. 'This colour is called blushing rose. It is all the rage in London.'

'You are quite the most fashionable lady here this

evening,' replied Rose diplomatically. Privately she thought the pink a little bright, for it clashed horribly with Althea's yellow hair and plump red cheeks. In her opinion the gown would also be better for a little less ribbon and lace, but Althea seemed delighted with it.

'You are very kind to say so,' she replied, simpering. 'Especially when it is you, Mrs Westerhill, who is always being held up to me as a model of elegance. Always so...neat.'

She means plain and drab, thought Rose, but she was not offended. Her midnight-blue silk was not new and had only a single row of silver lace around the hem, but it suited her and she had always liked its simplicity. She glanced down at her corsage: three large white camellias pinned to her shoulder. Magnus had delivered it to the cottage that morning and impressed upon her that he had ordered the flowers to be brought down from Bristol at great expense. Since he had gone to so much trouble Rose was obliged to wear it, although she felt it was a trifle ostentatious, more a badge of ownership than regard. She chided herself for her ungratefulness, but the impression remained.

'Of course,' Althea continued, 'as a widow, no one would expect you to wear a new gown on every occasion.'

Mrs Molland was quick to jump to her daughter's defence.

'When one has an excellent figure, like Rose, no one remembers the gown, only how lovely she looks.'

Althea gave a tinkling laugh. She smoothed her gloved hands over her skirts.

'I am sure you must think me very extravagant to buy another new gown. I know Magnus is always complaining that I cost him a fortune.' She giggled. 'My poor brother cannot wait to have me married and off his hands.'

'I do not deny it,' Magnus replied. 'But these things cannot be hurried and he must be a man of excellent birth and good fortune. I am seriously considering taking Althea to London next year.' He took a step closer to Rose. 'When I have a wife to escort her.'

'Oh, London,' sighed Althea, glassy-eyed. 'How I long to be away from the country! Just think of it, parties and balls every night. And we would be able to meet some *real* gentlemen—like the one standing in the doorway!'

The change in her tone coincided with a sudden lull in conversation. Nearly everyone in the room was looking towards the entrance and Rose suspected hers was not the only heart that leapt at the sight of Sir Lawrence Daunton as he walked in. His hair was brushed back from his brow and gleamed like a raven's wing in the candlelight. His black coat fitted so perfectly it might have been moulded to his form, and the pale waistcoat and breeches only added to the sophisticated elegance of the man. She heard Magnus harrumph and mutter, 'Bond Street Beau,' but there was nothing ostentatious about Lawrence's dress. It was simplicity itself and in Rose's opinion he looked magnificent.

'Is he not the most handsome man you have ever seen?' Althea gave an ecstatic sigh. 'We danced together at the Pullens' ball last month. So very much a gentleman—I told him we attend the Mersecombe Assembly, but I never thought he would remember! Magnus, we must go and greet him.'

Magnus nodded. 'If you wish. Rose?'

She stepped away, raising her hand.

'Please, take your sister. Mama and I will go and sit down.' She saw the concern in her mother's eyes and forced a tiny smile. 'It is the heat. It is a little oppressive and I need to save my energy for the dancing...'

Mrs Molland led her to the benches at the side of the room. Rose gave a sigh of relief, knowing that they were temporarily shielded from Sir Lawrence's gaze. Magnus returned shortly after to claim her hand for the first dance and when he led her out she noticed that Lawrence was standing a little way down the line, partnering Althea. She was a little surprised to find Magnus smiling happily upon the couple.

'You do not object to Sir Lawrence dancing with your sister?'

Magnus spread his hands.

'Whatever Sir Lawrence's reputation, he is unlikely to act with impropriety towards my sister. Or, for that matter, towards my fiancée.' He leaned closer and smiled complacently. 'You have been a widow too long, my dear. You have forgotten what it is to have a man's protection.'

Her response was little more than a murmur, lost as the music began. The dancing was lively, but Rose's enjoyment was tempered by the knowledge that the movement of the dance would soon bring her face to face with Lawrence, a moment she longed for and dreaded in equal measure. Magnus was left behind; she made her way through the line, partner by partner, ever closer to Lawrence. Her mouth dried when he held his hand out to her, a challenge in his eyes. But there was understanding, too. He knew how hard it was for her to smile politely and act as if they were mere acquaintances.

The brief, heady moment as he took her hands and led her through the line of dancers was everything Rose had anticipated. Despite her best efforts to remain impartial her heart was singing. She kept her eyes fixed upon the top button of his waistcoat, frowning a little as she tried to concentrate on the steps.

'Why, Rose, are you afraid of me?'

Her eyes flew to his face.

'No.' Her voice was little more than a croak and she was relieved that at that moment he had to release her and move on to the next partner. She whispered, to his departing back, 'I am afraid of me.'

She lost sight of Lawrence as she was swept up by her next partner and carried away, her smile bright, feet tripping lightly through the familiar steps. The dance continued until she was back with Magnus again. The world was righting itself, but her heart was still pounding far too heavily against her ribs. She scolded herself for allowing her peace to be overset so easily.

It would be best, she thought, *if I did not allow him near me again.*

She danced a few more times with older, safely married gentlemen who wanted nothing more than to enjoy a lively dance with a pretty woman, but at the end of each set she kept her attention firmly fixed upon her partner until she was engaged with the next, or she had been returned safely to her mother's side.

She was congratulating herself upon her tactics as she stood by the refreshment table, flanked by Magnus and her mother, when she heard Miss Emsleigh's grating laugh behind her.

'Here they are, sir. I told you we would find them!' Rose looked round to see Althea approaching on Lawrence's arm. He smiled across at her, his blue eyes glinting wickedly.

'At last I have caught up with you, Mrs Westerhill. Would you honour me with this next dance?'

Alarm bells began to clamour in her head.

'Thank you, sir, but I have danced enough tonight.' She tucked her hand into Magnus's arm, indicating she was happy to remain with him.

Magnus beamed, but said magnanimously, 'I assure you I have no objection if you wish to dance one more measure.'

'Sadly, I do not.' Rose's smile took in them all. She said firmly, 'I am sure you will find other, more willing partners, Sir Lawrence.'

The sudden spark of anger in his eyes shook Rose. A tremor of unease ran through her, but she refused to succumb to it and held her smile. He must learn that she was not his for the asking. Lawrence gave a stiff little bow.

'As you wish, madam.'

Althea gave a loud sigh and watched him walk away.

'What a shame. If I had known you meant to refuse,

I would not have told him that I was going to dance the next with Magnus.'

'What?' Magnus raised his quizzing glass. 'Oh, Lord, I had forgotten. Come along then, my dear, we had best take our places.' He gave his arm to Althea and led her away.

Rose heard a slight huff from Mrs Molland.

'What is it, Mama? Why do you look at me that way? I was not uncivil.'

'No-o, but I think you might have accepted Sir Lawrence. He is, after all, a visitor to Mersecombe.'

'But he has a fearsome reputation, Mama. You know what Aunt Jane says of him.'

Mrs Molland frowned.

'Your aunt enjoys gossip, my love. Entertaining as it is to read, it is often grossly exaggerated. We should take as we find. And Sir Lawrence was very kind to little Sam.'

Rose looked away, acknowledging her mother's gentle rebuke with a slight flutter of her hand.

'I…I did not want to encourage him, Mama.'

'One dance in a public assembly! What harm could that do?' Mrs Molland shook her head.

Rose did not reply. Everyone in the room was aware of the identity of the elegantly dressed gentleman and Rose knew that there were those present who loved gossip just as much as her Aunt Jane. If they had the slightest reason to connect her name with Sir Lawrence, then her reputation would be in jeopardy. She was the widow of one womaniser and any goodwill would quickly evaporate if she was seen to encourage the advances of another, far more notorious rake!

From then on the evening descended into a game of cat and mouse. Rose studiously avoided Sir Lawrence. When he drew near to the refreshment table she made sure she was at the far end of the room; later, when she was sitting with her mother and she saw him approaching, Rose quickly excused herself and slipped away into the crowd. Her behaviour was making him angry; he might continue to smile as he made his bow to this person or that, but the set of his jaw and the slight narrowing of his eyes told Rose that his temper was on a tight rein. It made her even more determined not to go near him again that evening.

The Assembly drew to a close. The musicians packed away their instruments and the crowd began to disperse. Rose collected her wrap and returned to the ballroom. There was no sign of Sir Lawrence.

'Mr Emsleigh has offered to take us up in his carriage, is that not kind of him?' Mrs Molland gave Rose a gentle nudge.

'Mmm? Oh, yes—yes indeed. Thank you, Magnus.'

He looked down at Rose, who had her sturdy leather half-boots in her hand. 'My dear, there is no need to put those on if I am taking you in the carriage.'

Rose hesitated. Her mother and Althea were already waiting by the door. She waved at them.

'It will not take me a moment. You may all go on; I shall join you as soon as I am done.'

She sat down and tugged off her dancing slippers. Really, Magnus was so irritating. All very well for him to declare that she only had to step into the carriage, but she knew full well that the stairs brought them down to the side door of the inn and the coach would only be able to pull into the yard or to wait in the street. Either way they would have to walk on the dirty cobbles and she had no intention of risking her last pair of good dancing slippers. Angrily she took her time over lacing her boots. They could easily have walked. It was only a step to Bluebell Cottage, but if Magnus was determined to coddle her then he must wait.

The rooms were almost empty when at last Rose made her way to the door. The servants were already blowing out the candles, filling the air with thick, pungent smoke that swirled like grey mist in the deepening shadows. Quickly she hurried down the wide staircase. Noise from the inn filtered up to her, but the stairs had been designed to carry those attending balls and routs directly to and from the Long Room, keeping them separate from customers drinking in the taproom.

She reached the door and stepped out. To her right the Emsleighs' carriage was waiting in the yard, but even as she looked that way a hand shot out and gripped her arm, jerking her roughly into the shadows. She found herself pinned against a hard, unyielding chest, her cheek rubbing against the fine wool of an evening coat. Rose raised her head to protest, but immediately a dark head swept down and her lips were captured in a savage, familiar kiss.

Rose went weak with relief as she recognised her attacker. How could she not know the feel of those strong arms around her, the arresting mouth that worked on hers in such a demanding way? She was in Lawrence's arms, where she had so often dreamed to be. For a few moments she clung to him, her body compliant, ready to surrender, then she recovered her senses and pushed against him. She was powerless to free herself, his arms were like iron bands holding her fast, but he released her mouth, moving his lips to her ear.

'I do believe you have been avoiding me, Rose.'

His voice was low and warm. Desire stirred. She closed her eyes, steeling herself to reply.

'Have you not been avoiding *me* these past weeks?'

'Ah. So you noticed that.' There was a purr of satisfaction in his voice. 'I had not meant to come here tonight, but the temptation to see you again was too strong. Why would you not dance with me?'

He was holding her very close, his cheek rubbing against her hair as her body leaned into him. Her heart was jumping in her throat, making speech difficult.

'I...I did not wish to dance. I did not want to be near you.'

'You enjoyed being near me last Christmas.' His teeth nibbled gently at her ear and she bit down hard on her bottom lip to counteract the pleasure curling and growing inside her. 'You called it an idyll.'

'We knew it would not work. We agreed...'

'We agreed that you were coming back here to marry Emsleigh. That has not happened.'

'Single or wed, it makes no difference.'

She put her hands against his chest, determined not to give in.

'No?' The single word was so low, so quiet, yet her body reacted; her breasts grew taut, almost painful as they pushed towards him, aching for his touch. He traced one finger down her cheek and drew it gently along the line of her jaw. Rose closed her eyes. She stopped trying to push him away and instead her fingers clutched at his jacket. This was madness. She could hear voices calling her. She looked up, trying to see his face; Lawrence had pulled her into a shallow alcove where the shadows were deep and black, adding to the unreality of the situation. The temptation to give in to him was almost irresistible. He was a devil to torment her so!

'No,' she managed at last. 'Go back to Knightscote, Sir Lawrence. Better still, go back to London. I'll have none of you.'

'Too late for that, Rose. What if I tell your friends how you came calling upon me last Christmas Eve?'

She caught her breath in dismay.

'You would not do that. I would be ruined!'

She felt the heartbeat's hesitation before he replied.

'No, I will say nothing, but if you continue to avoid me quite so blatantly people will begin to wonder why you shun me. It is only a matter of time before tongues begin to wag.'

'You expect us to meet as…as indifferent acquaintances?'

'We must, unless you wish to be something more…'

'No!' She hissed out the word, panic adding urgency. 'Oh, will you not go away and leave me in peace?'

His arms tightened. He said angrily, 'Do you think I like this situation any more than you?'

'Then leave, sir. My life is here. I cannot do so.'

'No more can I, at least not yet!'

It was as if the words had been forced out of him. Rose frowned.

'Why should that be—what keeps you here?'

He did not reply, and into the silence came the clatter of boots on the stair. She heard Magnus saying irritably, 'She is not upstairs, nor in the retiring room. Where can she be?'

Rose tensed. Any moment he might turn towards the shadows and discover her. The dark shape that was Lawrence drew her closer. He whispered in her ear.

'Your friends are looking for you. You must go.' His lips brushed her cheek. 'The next time we meet at least treat me with some semblance of civility. I am going to be around for a good while yet, Rose, so you had best get used to it!'

Lawrence gave Rose a little push and she stepped out of the shadows.

'Rose! What in heaven's name—!'

Magnus came hurrying towards her, his breath clouding on the frosty air.

Quickly she moved to meet him.

'I…I dropped my fan…' She waved her hand, implying that it had skittered into the darkness. A quick peep showed her that the alcove was empty.

'Well, never mind that now, let us get you home and out of this cold.'

He guided her to the carriage and she climbed in beside her mother.

'Goodness, you are shivering,' declared Mrs Molland. 'You should have left your fan, my love. We could have walked up and retrieved it in the morning.'

'Well, well, no harm done,' declared Althea, her hands tucked snugly inside her swansdown muff. 'Tell Lewis to drive on, Magnus. The sooner we have dropped Rose and Mrs Molland at Bluebell Cottage, the sooner we can be home.'

Magnus jumped into the carriage and almost fell into his seat as they pulled away, the lamps of the inn yard momentarily lighting up the carriage.

'My dear, whatever have you done to your corsage?'

Magnus's cry caused Rose to glance down. Her cloak had fallen open to reveal the neckline of her gown and on her shoulder were the sorry-looking remains of the three camellias, crushed flat against her gown.

Magnus was muttering about the inordinate cost of obtaining such delicate flowers and guiltily Rose pulled her cloak together to hide the damage.

'Oh, my,' giggled Althea. 'They look well and truly ravished!'

Rose sank her teeth into her bottom lip and stared miserably out into the night.

Ravished was exactly how she felt.

Chapter Five

From the deepest shadows Lawrence watched the Emsleigh carriage drive away, the horses' hooves ringing on the cobbles. Hell and damnation, he should never have come here tonight. He thought savagely that if George Craven had not been in such a fix he would never have come back to Exmoor at all.

Craven had come to him in London, when Lawrence was enjoying a solitary dinner at White's.

'Daunton, my friend. I have been looking for you all over.'

'Good evening, George. Come and join me,' Lawrence greeted him with the wave of his fork.

'Heard you were in town,' said Craven, sitting down at the table, 'but you have not shown your face in any of your usual haunts.'

'Turned over a new leaf, George.'

'Aye, so it would appear.' Craven grinned. 'The ladies are bemoaning the absence of Rake Daunton from their drawing rooms. What have you been doing with yourself in town?'

'Visiting my man of business.'

'Dull work!'

'Aye, but necessary. I spent the spring touring my estates in Surrey, and I have been in Hampshire for the past month, at Daunton, putting everything in order. Hadn't realised just how run-down the place had become. Once my business here is ended then I shall be going back. I dare say I shall make my home there.' He shot a sideways glance at his friend. 'Does it surprise you, George, that I can give up town life so easily?'

His friend shook his head.

'I always thought you would, one day.'

'The devil you did!'

'You forget, Lawrence, we've known each other for ever. You always loved Daunton, but you began to avoid it when it became linked with marriage to my late, lovely, lamented sister. Never could quite bring yourself to make that final commitment, could you, Lawrence?'

'Damn you, George, you know I always intended to go back.' He pushed his plate away, his appetite gone. 'We agreed we would wed when she was one and twenty, not before. But if she had only said the word I would have come back—'

'No need to blame yourself, old friend. Belle wanted the marriage even less than you.' He met Lawrence's amazed gaze with a rueful smile. 'I never thought much of it at the time, but she said to me once that she thought she would have liked to be a nun and dedicate her life to good works.'

'Well, if you think of the way she lived, in the end that is what she did.' Lawrence sighed, running a hand through his hair. 'What must she have thought of me? I positively flaunted my indiscretions—I never denied any scandal, no matter how outrageous or untrue.'

George shrugged.

'As for that, she knew better than to believe a half of what she read in the newspapers.'

Lawrence sighed.

'I still think I treated her abominably. I am surprised you did not call me out, George. I deserved it.'

'Devil a bit, I could hardly pull caps with you over your behaviour when I was kicking up every sort of lark myself!'

'No, it is good of you to say so, but I am ashamed of how I behaved towards your family. I wish I could make it up to you.'

'Perhaps you can.' George signalled to the waiter to bring them another bottle.

Lawrence frowned at him across the table. 'I heard you had some pretty bad losses recently. What was it, cards? Hazard?'

Craven shook his head, saying glumly, 'I wish it had been! No, I decided I should be doing something more prudent with my money. Prudent, hah!' Craven emptied his glass and refilled it. 'I underwrote a merchant ship, sailing out of Bristol. Hadn't even cleared the Channel before she foundered, ship and all the cargo lost.'

'A disaster, then.' Lawrence sat back. 'Many lives lost?'

'Only one. The bosun was lost overboard as the crew

took to the boats. The rest were picked up by a passing vessel and brought safely ashore.'

'Fortunate that there were enough boats on board to take them all.'

'Aye, wasn't it,' muttered George Craven. He scowled. 'And how thoughtful of the owner to issue promissory notes to his crew, in case the ship should miscarry.'

'You suspect foul play?'

'Aye, and so do my fellow underwriters. We haven't paid out yet, and don't intend to do so until more investigations have taken place.' He leaned forwards. 'Which is why I have come to you, Daunton.'

'Me?' Lawrence laughed. 'I am no investigator!'

'We sent an agent to Bristol to talk to the crew, but very few of them were local, and those he did find would not talk to him. So he went to Somerset to find the captain, but he came up with nothing.'

'Then it seems a hopeless case. You will have to pay up.'

'But you do not understand!' George Craven banged his fist on the table, causing several of the other diners to look around. He chewed his lip for a moment. 'I was greedy, I admit it. I was convinced there could be no risk. It was high summer, the journey a routine sailing from Bristol to France, albeit with a bigger cargo than usual, a valuable one, too: the best English woollen cloth, fine linen, porcelain and pewter—' He gave a bitter laugh. 'What could possibly go wrong? I agreed to underwrite more than I could readily afford. If I have to pay out, I shall be ruined.' He looked up. 'I shall have to go to my father, and the only way he will be able to pay my debts will be to sell the Hampshire estate. It would kill my mother, I think, to leave the house she has lived in all her married life.'

'Do you want me to loan you the money?'

'No, no, I could not ask you for such a sum.'

Lawrence shook his head.

'Then I do not see how I can help you, my friend.'

Craven leaned closer.

'You have a property on Exmoor, do you not? The ship's owner has a house there and Captain Morris lives nearby. Why, man, they are practically your neighbours. It is possible they will let something slip to you.'

Lawrence shook his head.

'I'm sorry, my friend, this is not my line of work. I have no plans to go back there.'

'I'd go myself, but you know what it is like in these areas, any stranger is looked upon with suspicion. But if you were to go, well, no one would think anything of it.' George reached for the bottle and refilled their glasses. 'The bosun's family live on that coast, too, near a small village called Mersecombe. These are seafaring people, Lawrence; you could talk to them, see what they think of the ship foundering. If there is the least chance that this was no accident, I want to know about it!'

Lawrence lifted his glass, staring at the ruby-red contents.

'I haven't been to Knightscote this year,' he murmured, almost to himself.

'Then it is time you did, my friend,' declared Craven.

'What could be more natural than that you should visit the place now, with autumn coming on?'

Lawrence paid him no heed. He was picturing an exquisite little face with large blue-grey eyes that smiled up at him so trustingly. He had given his word to Rose that he would not seek her out and, despite the fact that she was constantly in his thoughts, he would abide by that. She would be married by now to her dull and upright tradesman. She might even be with child.

The idea wrenched at his gut, but suddenly he needed to know. To learn that Rose was happy and content in her new life would be painful, but nothing to the uncertainty that tortured him now. He sat very still, his hands clasped about his wineglass. What if he had business in Mersecombe, and they met by chance?

He raised his eyes to look at his friend.

'Very well, George. I make you no promises, but I will look into this case for you.'

How Lawrence regretted that momentary weakness. To return, to see Rose again and find her every bit as alluring as he remembered had only brought back the memories he had spent the summer trying to suppress. She wanted nothing to do with him and to observe her tricks and evasions at the Assembly only rubbed salt into the wound.

Lawrence had planned to stay at the Ship overnight, but he now decided he would prefer to ride back to Knightscote. He strode into the inn and gave instructions for his horse to be saddled.

'You'll never be travelling at this time o'night, sir!' declared the landlord.

'Why not, there's a moon. You need not worry.' Lawrence reached into his pocket for his purse. 'I shall pay you for the bed, even though I won't be sleeping in it!'

Twenty minutes later he was trotting out of Mersecombe and making his way up over the moor towards Knightscote. The clouds had given way to a clear sky and a sharp frost now glittered in the moonlight, turning the world silver-grey. The bitter night air nipped at his cheeks, but he was glad of the icy chill; it cooled his anger and for the first time in hours he could think clearly.

He had been a fool to go to the Assembly. He was no further forwards with his investigations and he had suffered the humiliation of being snubbed. It was a novel experience. During his years in town he had never been rejected by any woman. The stricter chaperons might keep their innocent young charges away from him, but they could not prevent the young ladies from casting longing glances in his direction. He had been so sure that Rose would at least dance with him. He had anticipated the thrill of it; to anyone listening they would be talking upon unexceptional topics, but their carefully coded words would refer to their time together at Knightscote. Even now he could imagine her eyes smiling into his, sharing the joke.

He shivered. She had spent the evening running away from him and when at last he cornered her she had refused to dance, had avoided all contact with him, until that last stolen kiss in the darkness. Then she had responded to him, albeit reluctantly.

For the first time in his adult life he doubted his ability to charm a woman. Perhaps Annabelle had never been as enamoured of him as he had believed: he remembered how incredulous he had been when Rose had suggested that his fiancée had preferred her single state. Perhaps she would have married him, to please her parents, to fulfil the contract that would combine two great estates. He would never know. He had never asked her, they had never *talked*. It was too late now to help Annabelle, but he would show Rose that there was more to him than smooth words and careless flirtations.

With a sigh he looked up at the cloudless night sky. The deep blue reminded him of Rose's gown. Heaven knew he had seen the back of her flowing skirts often enough as she spent the evening moving away from him.

'You are nothing but a fool,' he told himself angrily. 'She has told you she wants nothing more to do with you so you had best let be.'

He squared his shoulders and straightened in the saddle. Tonight had been a mistake. He would not go out of his way to see her again.

Rose huddled in her corner of the carriage, thankful that she was not expected to contribute to the discussion of the night's events. She was still shaken by being so roughly accosted by Sir Lawrence. That she had angered him was plain, but why did he not go away and leave her in peace? What reason could he have for lingering in Mersecombe, if he had not come to seek her out? She wondered if she had spoken this last thought aloud, for she heard Magnus say, 'Dashed if I know why the fellow showed up tonight. I know I told him of the Assembly, but I never really expected him to take me up on it. To my knowledge he has never before ventured away from Knightscote on his visits to Exmoor.'

'Well, I expect him to call upon me at Emsleigh House very soon,' replied Althea.

Magnus chuckled.

'I am not surprised, for you were making eyes at him all evening, you naughty puss. Well, if he calls, I suppose I shall have to invite him to dinner one night.'

'*You* are not deterred by his reputation with the ladies, sir?' asked Mrs Molland.

'Pho! I confess I was a little wary of the fellow to begin with, but I saw nothing in his manner to alarm me. He made no attempt to flirt with anyone tonight. I dare say his reputation is much exaggerated. Sir Lawrence is a rich man and as such his every move in town attracts attention. And if he wishes to fix his interest with my sister, well, his birth is impeccable and with his wealth I would have no hesitation in welcoming him as a brother-in-law!'

Rose shifted uncomfortably in her corner. She had seen Althea's attempts to capture Lawrence's interest and did not think they were successful, but what if she was wrong? In their last few moments together Lawrence had intimated that it would be necessary for them to meet. What if he was trying to fix his interest with Althea? Rose shivered. The idea was preposterous. Wasn't it?

Rose was glad to open up the little schoolroom the next morning. She needed to keep her mind away from the Assembly. To see Lawrence again had awoken all the memories she had tried so hard to bury, and when he had pulled her roughly into his arms and kissed her in the black shadows at the edge of the inn yard, her emotions had rioted out of control. She wanted him so badly that it hurt.

If she had been living in a fairy-tale world, she thought she would have given in to the demands of her body—and her heart. She could have danced with Lawrence, her infatuation clear for all the world to observe. The evening would have been one of unalloyed pleasure as they laughed and danced and talked together. But this was not a fairy tale. Any hint of impropriety and she would lose her position as teacher here in Mersecombe. Although it did not pay much, it provided a boost to her meagre savings and, more than that, the post carried with it the respect of the village. That meant a lot to her, not only for her own sake but for her mother's, and for Sam. It was very hard for him, growing up in Mersecombe without a father—he must not feel ashamed of his mother.

And what about marriage? Not that it had been mentioned, but nevertheless the question gnawed at her. Marriage to Sir Lawrence would give her respect, would it not? But only until some other pretty face lured him into infidelity.

'I do not know why you are even bothering to consider such things, Rose Westerhill,' she muttered savagely as she put out the slates ready for the morning lesson. 'You are not of his world. It is not marriage that he is likely to offer you!'

The door opened to admit the first of her pupils and she forced her mind back to the present. This was her world now, until she married Magnus in the spring. She found she was not looking forward to the event with any great enthusiasm, but Magnus represented security for her and for Sam. She would miss teaching, but she was sure she would find plenty of things to occupy her day as wife of one of the richest merchant traders in the area.

She looked up as Sam came in with Jem, chattering noisily. Rose frowned and gestured to them to sit down. In the schoolroom she tried to treat Sam like any other pupil, which was why she allowed him to wait at the cottage until Jem came by and the two of them could walk to school together rather than dragging him out of bed an hour earlier to accompany her.

Dear Sam. Everyone said he looked like her with his thatch of blond hair and blue-grey eyes, but she constantly saw his father in him, in the tilt of his head, his ready smile and charm of manner. As Magnus's wife she would be able to give Sam the education he deserved. He would grow up a gentleman, able to make his way in the world. She might not love Magnus, but she esteemed him. He would make a dull but faithful husband, she was sure, and that was all she required.

'Sir Lawrence. You've come to collect the puppy, I suppose.'

The woman holding the door open was no more than thirty, but a harsh life and her recent widowhood had etched lines in her face that made her look much older. Lawrence gave her his most charming smile.

'Good day to you, Mrs Wooler. I have indeed.' He held up the basket. 'And I thought you might find a use for these.' He was rewarded by the flush of pleasure on the woman's worn face.

'Oranges! That's very generous of you, Sir Lawrence.'

She stood back and signalled to him to enter, as he had known she would.

'They arrived yesterday from the hothouses on my Surrey estate, but I cannot use them all myself.'

A grey-haired lady was waiting for them in the sitting room, smoothing her gnarled hands over her apron.

'Here is Sir Lawrence, Mother Wooler, come to fetch the bitch he's chosen,' announced the younger woman. 'And look at what he has brought us.'

'I can see.' Old Mother Wooler smiled at him, gracious as a duchess. 'You will take a glass of fruit wine with us?' She indicated a chair at one side of the hearth and sat down opposite him. 'My husband is still out in the fields, sir, so you may have his place and welcome.'

The younger Mrs Wooler carried a glass of wine to them and stood, nervously clasping her hands together.

'I wonder—would ye mind waiting 'til our Jem has come in before you takes your pup, Sir Lawrence? He shouldn't be so very long…'

'Now, Maggie, Sir Lawrence is a busy man and can't linger on the whim of my grandson—'

'No, no, I should be delighted to wait,' put in Lawrence. He took the smallest sip of the overly sweet fruit wine. 'I take it Jem is still at the schoolroom?'

'Aye, learning his letters, good as gold,' replied the old lady proudly. 'Reads to me a passage from the Bible every night, he does. He'll not go to sea to earn his living, like his dad, God rest his soul.'

'You must miss your son a great deal, ma'am.'

'Aye, we do.' The old woman lifted the corner of her apron to wipe her eyes.

'He was on the *Sealark*, was he not?' said Lawrence gently.

'Aye, she sank out there in the Channel. Fire broke out, they said, and Ruben was lost in the confusion to get the men into the jolly boats.' She was silent for a moment, her thoughts far away, then with a visible effort she smoothed out her apron. 'Still, I'm thankful that we still have Abel. Losing two boys to the sea would have been too much to bear, although we wouldn't be the first around here to do so.' She reached out a hand to her daughter-in-law. 'But it was a good day when Ruben married his sweetheart and brought her here to live with us. We've been able to comfort each other, ain't that so, Maggie?'

'It is, truly, Mother Wooler. And it's good for Jem to be here, where he has his grandfather and uncle to teach him how to go on.' Maggie Wooler gave a tired little smile. 'It's a sad thing for a boy to lose his father.'

'Aye. I feel sorry for the poor little Westerhill boy, growing up with only his mother and grandma for company.'

'But that will change in the spring, Mother, when Mrs Westerhill marries Mr Emsleigh.'

Lawrence quickly brought the conversation back to its original course.

'So you intend to stay here with Jem, do you, Mrs Wooler?' The widow looked at him blankly. He added gently, 'Once the insurers pay out...'

'Oh, you mean the note that Mr Emsleigh gave us?' She shook her head. 'That money is going away for Jem.' She put the wine bottle on the hearth and hurried out of the room.

Her mother-in-law watched her go.

'Poor dear,' she muttered, shaking her head. 'Four months it's been and she still can't quite believe Ruben's not coming back. But at least Jem is provided for. It ain't as if we need the money, after all,' continued the old lady. 'The farm provides enough for us, and now we have Abel back working here we shall do very well.'

'I am still very new to this area,' remarked Lawrence. 'Is it common practice for shipowners to give these notes against the ship sinking?'

'Never happened before that I know of, but my son Abel might tell 'ee different. All I know is that when Ruben came in and told us that everyone sailing on the *Sealark* would get a payout if the ship miscarried I couldn't think but that it was a good thing. Not that we wouldn't rather have Ruben back with us, but forty-five guineas is a goodly sum. The note was left with Maggie, of course, to do with as she will, and it's her decision to put it aside for Jem.'

'Forty-five guineas?' Lawrence's brows went up. 'A good sum indeed.'

'Aye, Ruben was bosun, see, so gets more.' The old woman nodded. 'Abel only gets thirty, but that's not to be sniffed at. I'd wager 'tis more than the poor school-teacher gets in one year. Not that she ain't worth a great deal more, her being a lady born.'

Since the conversation had come back to Rose, Lawrence could not resist a question.

'Did you know her family, ma'am?'

'Nay, sir, she was from Barnstaple way, but I was born in Exford, where she and her husband lived, so I knows more than most.'

She sat back in her chair and drank her wine with every appearance of relish. She finished her wine and turned her bird-bright glance upon him.

'More wine, Sir Lawrence?'

He leaned down to pick up the bottle.

'Allow me, Mrs Wooler.'

As he had suspected, once she had a full glass she was ready to talk again.

'I don't say anything in front of the family,' she said. 'I wouldn't like the lady to think her business was common knowledge in Mersecombe, but you're a man of the world, sir, and I guess you've seen men like Wester-hill before, them as can't resist both the bottle and a pretty face. He was a bad 'un.' She scowled, shaking her head. 'Me sister's midwife in Exford and she believes it was 'is doing that made Mrs Westerhill lose 'er baby. Poor dearie. Ill for weeks, she was, and the doctors said the damage was such that she would never have more children. She insisted that she lost her footing and fell down the stairs, but m'sister said she'd never seen such bruises, and she was with her when Westerhill came in, crying for forgiveness. Forgiveness—tch! I know what I'd have given 'im!'

Lawrence maintained a mask of polite interest as he listened to the old woman, but inside he was raging against Harry Westerhill. It was as much as he could do to prevent his hands clenching into fists at the thought of what he would like to do to such a man. He wanted to go and find Rose, hold her close and promise that he would never let anyone harm her again. A cold hand twisted at his stomach. She would refuse to listen to him, of course, especially after the way he had treated her at the Assembly. Was it any wonder that Rose did not believe he could change? The distant thud of a door and a sudden flurry of noise interrupted his thoughts. Old Mrs Wooler gave a dry chuckle.

'Ah, that's our Jem home now.'

It was not one boy but two that erupted into the room. Sam Westerhill stood expectantly beside his friend, cap in hand and looking so much like his mother that Lawrence had to clamp his jaw closed to prevent himself from remarking upon it.

'Just in time,' announced the old lady. 'Sir Lawrence is here to take his pup, so you had best go and say your goodbyes.'

'Yes, Grandma.'

Lawrence stood up.

'Come along then, Jem—show me the way!'

Lawrence and the boys crossed the yard to one of the smaller outhouses. Jem carried a lantern, for although the sun had not set, the shadows were lengthening and they would need its light once they entered the barn.

'How will you get her home?' asked Sam, skipping along beside Lawrence.

'I have a basket.' Lawrence sidestepped across to the gig and reached into the footwell. 'There, that will be more than sufficient, do you not think?'

'She'll be snug enough in there.' Jem nodded.

He unbolted the door to the outhouse and held up the lamp. The pointer bitch and her puppies were cosily tucked on to a pile of straw in one of the wooden stalls, sleeping peacefully. She raised her head as Jem moved forwards, alert for any danger to her offspring. Lawrence held Sam back.

'We had best wait until she knows we mean no harm.'

A board had been propped across the entrance to the stall to prevent the puppies from escaping; once Lawrence was confident that they would not alarm the mother he allowed Sam to step over. He followed, being careful not to tread on any of the small bundles of liver-and-white fur that were now moving around the floor. Lawrence identified the puppy he had chosen, a well-grown, healthy bitch with liver-coloured patches across her head.

'May I hold her?' asked Sam.

Lawrence glanced an enquiry at Jem, who nodded.

Sam picked up the wriggling, squirming bundle. The puppy lifted her head and licked at his nose.

'She is very lively.' Sam giggled. 'I hope you know how to look after her.'

'Well, I shall give her to my keeper to train,' said Lawrence apologetically. 'He is much the best person to do so.'

'She'll be a good gun dog, sir,' said Jem, kneeling beside the mother and tickling her ears. 'She comes from very good stock.'

Sam gave a very loud sigh.

'I wish I could have a dog. I would look after it and teach it to mind me, then when it was bigger it would come about with me and protect me from the bigger boys.'

'Oh, do they trouble you?' asked Lawrence.

Sam shrugged. 'Sometimes, if Jem is not with me.'

'They mean no harm,' said Jem. 'It is the way, to pick on those of us who have no father.' He looked up. 'Abel is teaching us to box.'

'Very useful,' said Lawrence gravely.

'Jem is very handy with his fists,' added Sam, proud of his friend's achievement. 'But Abel says I'm too small yet to punch properly.'

Lawrence ruffled his hair.

'It is not always about your size, young man. There are few tricks you can use to give you the advantage.'

'Really?' Sam looked up, his eyes shining. 'Would you teach me?'

'Stow it,' muttered Jem, frowning. 'You can't ask Sir Lawrence that, he'll think you im…impertinent.'

Lawrence laughed.

'Do not look so anxious, Jem, I am not at all offended, and, yes, Sam, I would happily show you a few things you can do to protect yourself. But not tonight, for I must get my new puppy back to Knightscote.'

'I still wish I could take her home with me.' Sam hugged the puppy even closer.

'These are working dogs, Sam.' Lawrence scooped up another of the puppies that was trying to escape and put it back on the straw. 'I doubt if your mother or grandmother go out shooting.'

'No.' Sam sighed. 'But Mama does like to go for long walks!'

'Anyway, we have buyers for them all now,' said Jem. 'By this time next week they will all be gone.'

'Is your house very far away from here, Sir Lawrence?'

'It will take me the best part of an hour to get there. Are you worried that the puppy will be cold? There's a folded cloth in the basket, you see, and I shall throw a rug over it while I am travelling.'

Sam giggled again as the puppy tried to bite his chin.

'I think she is my favourite,' he said.

Lawrence bent down until he was level with Sam and the puppy.

'And if she was yours, what would you call her?'

Sam frowned in concentration.

'I would call her… I would call her Bandit, because her markings look like a mask!'

'Then that shall be her name,' announced Lawrence with a smile.

Sam stared at him.

'Oh, that's…th-thank you, sir!'

As Sam stammered out his gratitude for this honour they heard footsteps on the cobbled yard.

'Sam, are you in there? Come along now, it is time we were going!'

Lawrence jumped to his feet and turned in time to see Rose enter the barn. In the dim lamplight the mulberry-coloured cloak and bonnet accentuated the delicate tone of her skin. Her cheeks were flushed and her eyes sparkled, as if she had relished the walk uphill to the farm.

'Oh, Sir Lawrence!' Instantly the sparkle was replaced by wariness. 'Mrs Wooler said I would find the boys here…'

'They are helping me collect my new acquisition.'

'This is Bandit.' Sam stepped forwards, holding up the puppy for his mother to see. 'She is Sir Lawrence's new puppy and he let me give her a name!'

'He—he did? That was very good.' Rose was looking everywhere except at Lawrence. Who could blame her if she was uneasy in his company? He cursed himself for allowing his anger to get the better of him at the Assembly. She held her hand out to her son. 'Give Sir Lawrence back his puppy now, Sam. We must go home.'

'So you found them!' Old Mrs Wooler wheezed in, wrapped in a heavy shawl. 'Oh dear, oh dear, sir, you have straw all over your clothes. Will you step into the house again and I'll have Jem fetch a brush for you…?'

'No, no, ma'am, thank you. I must be going.' He carefully took Bandit from Sam and placed her in the basket. 'Thank you for your help, Master Westerhill.'

'Can I carry the basket to the carriage for you, sir?'

'Sam!' Rose reached out her hand again. 'Come along, young man. It is time we were going home.'

'Oh, but please!'

They were being shepherded out of the barn by Jem, who was anxious to settle the mother and her remaining puppies for the night.

'I have no objection to him carrying the basket,' said Lawrence mildly.

'Now, isn't it a fortunate thing that Sir Lawrence has his gig?' declared Mrs Wooler. 'I am sure he would be happy to drop you and your boy off at your cottage, Mrs Westerhill.'

'Ooh, yes! If you please, sir!' cried Sam.

'Oh, no, there is no need—'

Lawrence cut through Rose's protests.

'It is on my way, Mrs Westerhill. It would be very discourteous of me to drive past you.' Rose looked around, shifted from one foot to another and glanced down at Sam, who hovered expectantly. 'Young Sam may sit in between us and hold the basket,' murmured Lawrence helpfully.

'There now, Mrs Westerhill. What are you waiting for?' Mrs Wooler took Rose's arm and began to walk her back towards the gig. 'Let us get you up in that seat and Sir Lawrence will have you home in a twinkling.'

Rose capitulated, but she ignored Lawrence's hand and nimbly climbed up into the carriage. Lawrence lifted Sam onto the seat and placed the basket with its precious cargo in his lap. He pulled out the carriage rug.

'I think this is big enough to cover your legs, the basket and your mother—'

'I will do that.' Rose quickly batted away his hands as he tried to tuck the rug around her knees.

'As you wish.'

Once he had said all that was necessary to Mrs Wooler, Lawrence jumped up into the gig and set off down the winding lane.

'Are you warm enough, ma'am?'

'Perfectly, thank you.'

Sam was settled happily beside him, but Rose was sitting tense and rigid on the far side of the gig. Her silence weighed heavily between them.

He said abruptly, 'I am ashamed of my behaviour towards you last night.'

'I will not discuss this in front of my son!'

'I have no intention of *discussing* anything, but I must apologise and there is no reason why the boy should not hear me.' He glanced down at Sam. 'I was very uncivil to your mama, and I humbly beg her pardon, and yours. A gentleman should always respect and protect a lady, Sam, remember that.'

'Yes, sir.'

'Very well.' Even in the gloom he knew Rose was glaring at him over Sam's head. 'We will say no more about it, if you please.'

Lawrence wanted to say much more about it, but now

was not the time. Instead he remarked, 'The Woolers are good people. They had only the two sons, I believe?'

'Yes, Ruben and Abel.'

'And both wanted to be sailors rather than follow their father on the farm?'

'Yes, but I think the death of his brother persuaded Abel to give up the sea.'

'Jem says Ruben was the best sailor ever,' put in Sam. 'He sailed across Mersecombe Bay to Sealham Point once, and put ashore there. He carved his name on the rocks. Jem's going to show me.'

'Oh, no,' said Rose quickly. 'You are not to go out sailing with Jem. You know his mama will not allow that.'

'I know *that*,' replied Sam. 'She is afraid he will drown, like his poor papa. No, Jem says at low tide we can walk around the cliff to Sealham Point.'

'But not in winter,' Rose replied. 'It is not to be thought of until the weather improves.'

'But, Mama—'

'It would be a pretty miserable journey when it is this cold,' observed Lawrence.

'Oh, we would not mind that,' said Sam.

'But your mother would,' Lawrence replied quietly. 'You are the man of your household, Sam. She would worry for you and you would not want that, would you?'

'No, of course not.'

'And Jem, too, is needed on the farm. He will be expected to earn his keep, now his father is not there to provide for him.' Rose sighed. 'They must miss Ruben very much.'

'They do.' Sam nodded. 'Abel says that when he gets his money from Mr Emsleigh, he will have a stone carved with Ruben's name and put up in the church.'

'It is fortunate that Emsleigh gave them those promissory notes. Do you know why he did so, ma'am?'

'Why should you ask me that?' Rose sounded surprised. 'Magnus does not discuss his business with me, but it is the nature of the man to take care of those in his employ. That is why he took out the insurance.'

'If he is to pay the whole crew, it will amount to quite a sum.'

'That merely shows Magnus considered the risks so very slight.'

Lawrence said nothing, giving his attention to guiding his horse through the near-darkness. He had his own ideas about why Emsleigh had offered his crew that money, and why he had taken out such a high insurance on his cargo, but his suspicions were so far unproven. Should he share them with Rose and put her on her guard against Emsleigh? Would she believe him? He doubted it.

'I am surprised to find you driving a common gig, Sir Lawrence. A little beneath your touch, I would have thought.'

The gentle teasing in her voice decided it. She was thawing towards him and he would do nothing to jeopardise that.

'It is not my usual carriage, but perfect for these roads.' He grinned as they bounced over a particularly stony section and Rose grabbed the side-rail. 'I would not risk my racing curricle here.'

Sam looked up.

'You have a curricle? Ooh, I should like to see it.'

'Alas, it is in London.'

'Then how do you usually travel when you are here?' the boy asked.

'On horseback.'

'I like horses,' Sam declared. 'Evans is going to teach me to ride, one day, when I have a pony of my own. Then I shall ride up to Knightscote to see Bandit, if I may.'

'We must see what we can do about finding you a pony,' said Rose. She was smiling, and when Lawrence glanced at her she even met his eyes for a brief moment.

'*Pax*?' he murmured.

The dim light made it difficult to read her expression, but he was encouraged by the slight nod of her head. She turned away again, peering into the distance.

'Bluebell Cottage is just ahead of us, sir, and my mother is in the doorway, looking out for us.'

Lawrence drew up at the gate and Mrs Molland hurried to the little bridge to meet them.

'There you are at last, Rose. I was beginning to worry, with it growing so dark. Good evening, Sir Lawrence. How kind of you to bring Sam and my daughter home safely.'

'It was my pleasure, ma'am.' Lawrence handed the reins to Sam. 'Hold him steady for me, while I help your mother to get down.'

He smiled at the boy's obvious delight and left him concentrating hard on holding the reins, knowing all the time that nothing short of a pistol shot across its ears would make the nag between the shafts move an inch.

Watching such skilful handling of her son, it was only when Sir Lawrence stood at the side of the gig that Rose realised she should have climbed down earlier. Now she was obliged to put her hand in his. The memory evoked by his touch made her freeze and in that brief moment Lawrence took charge. Releasing her fingers, he put his hands firmly around her waist and lifted her out of the carriage. She expected him to prolong his hold and was prepared to protest, but as soon as her feet touched the ground he released her. Rose was obliged to grab hold of his coat as her knees gave way.

'Steady!'

He caught her again. There was something supremely comforting about the feel of his arms around her. The deep breath she took to calm herself had quite the opposite effect, for it carried with it the distinctive fragrance he wore and her wayward mind conjured up images of lying naked with Lawrence before a roaring fire. The shrieking of the hinges as Mrs Molland opened the gate was like a sharp rebuke for indulging in such memories. Rose quickly disengaged herself.

'I beg your pardon. I lost my balance. I must be a little cold from the journey.'

'Then let us get you indoors,' declared Mrs Molland. 'Samuel, come along, my dear.'

'A moment, Grandmama.' Sam secured the reins and scrambled down onto the road and made a very creditable bow. 'Goodnight, sir, and thank you for allowing me to name Bandit. Perhaps we might be able to come to Knightscote and see her one day?'

'Perhaps.' Sir Lawrence put a hand on his shoulder. 'Now, sir, take your mother indoors before she catches a chill!'

'Yes, come along, Sam.' Rose held out her hand to him.

'We did not have time to talk properly at the Assembly,' said Mrs Mollard, closing the gate. 'I wanted to invite you to come and take tea with us.'

Standing behind her mother, Rose shook her head vehemently, but Lawrence chose to ignore it.

'I would be delighted, Mrs Molland. I shall call the next time I am in Mersecombe.'

'Now you have your puppy I would have thought your business in the village was at an end,' said Rose, frowning at him.

'Oh, no, I expect to be riding this way often in the next few weeks.'

Rose detected a hint of laughter in his words and her eyes narrowed. Was he teasing her again? She said coolly, 'I am obliged to you, sir, for bringing Sam and me home, but we must not delay you any longer. You will not want to keep your horse standing in this chill wind. Samuel, come with me now.'

She caught Sam's hand and almost dragged him up the path.

'Well,' declared Mrs Molland, following behind, 'that is the second time Sir Lawrence has been of assistance to us. Did he come upon you in the lane, my love?'

'No, he was at the farm,' muttered Rose. 'Do hurry, Mama, it is far too cold to tarry out of doors.'

'Grandmama, he let me give his puppy a name,' cried Sam. 'And he let me carry her basket!'

'Did he now? Come inside and you can tell me all about it…'

The door closed firmly upon the little family and the voices were lost. Lawrence grinned to himself as he drove away. Rose was thawing towards him and now Mrs Molland had invited him to take tea. Mrs Rose Westerhill might not like the idea, but he had been given another chance to show her he could behave like a gentleman and he was going to take it!

Chapter Six

Rose knew he would call. Much as she knew it would be better for her peace of mind if she never saw Sir Lawrence Daunton again, she could not deny she was curious to know just what was keeping him at Knightscote. That he had no intention of removing from the area in the near future she learned from Sam, who came home after spending the day with Jem to say that Sir Lawrence had been at Woolers Farm again.

'Oh? Is there something wrong with the puppy?'

'No, he said Bandit was very well and that his keeper is very pleased with her.'

'You spoke to him?'

'Of course. We are friends.'

He was smiling happily and Rose's heart ached with love for her son. Sam was a quiet boy who did not make friends easily and normally she would have been delight-ed to hear these words, but she could not help thinking that Sir Lawrence had won Sam's confidence after only a few meetings whereas Magnus, who had known Sam for more than two years now, was still treated with a grave reserve, despite his efforts to befriend the boy. Sam continued to chatter away, sublimely unaware of the heartache he was causing his mama.

'Sir Lawrence wanted to see Abel, but he wasn't there. Jem's mama told Sir Lawrence that Abel had gone to Minehead with old Mr Wooler—which was odd, because I thought I saw Abel in the barn when I arrived—but Sir Lawrence said it did not matter, and he took me up on his horse and we rode around the paddock. Sir Lawrence says I will be a—a bruising rider when I have my own pony!'

'I hope he has not been filling your head with extravagant nonsense,' declared Mrs Molland, coming into the room in time to hear this last remark. 'Evans has more than enough to do looking after two horses already—'

'Oh, no, Grandmama, I told Sir Lawrence that we cannot afford a pony for me until Mama marries Mr Emsleigh—' He broke off, frowning. 'What? Should I not have said that?'

'No, love.' Rose brushed his unruly hair back from his face. 'We should not tell strangers our business.'

Sam's brow cleared.

'Oh, if that is all—! I told you, Mama, Sir Lawrence is not a stranger, he is a *friend*! Oh, and, Grandmama, he said to tell you he would call upon you tomorrow!'

Rose would have delayed her return to Bluebell Cottage the following day, but Sam was determined that they should hurry home together and he tugged insistently at her hand all the way along the high street. He was a little disappointed not to see the gig or Sir Lawrence's bay mare standing outside the cottage when they arrived, but this was soon explained by Janet, the maid, who explained as she opened the door to them that Sir Lawrence was with the mistress, and that Evans had taken his horse to the stables out of the cold.

Thus prepared, Rose was able to greet Sir Lawrence with tolerable composure.

'Rose, my dear.' Mrs Molland came over to kiss her cheek. 'You will see that the kettle is filled and ready to set on the fire, and the tea tray has been set ready for you to begin as soon as you wish.'

'And how is Bandit, sir?' enquired Sam, making a hasty bow. 'Has she settled in, is she eating well? How—?'

'She is growing very fast.' Sir Lawrence threw up his hands to stem the flood of questions. 'She also has a predilection for chewing shoe leather, a habit that my man is even now trying to break.'

'How big is she?' demanded Sam. 'Up to my knees yet? I *wish* I could see her. If only she were not so far away. If only I had a pony I could ride there myself!'

Rose stiffened, but after a fleeting look towards her Sir Lawrence merely smiled and said, 'I shall be sure to give Bandit your regards when I get back.'

'Sam, my love, I do think you should go upstairs and change your coat,' said Mrs Molland, shepherding her grandson towards the door. 'Janet will help you wash your face and hands, then you may come back and have a little cake with us.'

Rose gave her mother an anguished look, silently begging her not to leave them alone, but Mrs Molland appeared not to notice and she went out, closing the door behind her.

Almost a year ago they had been so easy together, but now an uncomfortable silence cloaked them. Rose's nerves were on edge. Even when he was sitting down Sir Lawrence dominated the room. It was as much as Rose could do to sit still, her hands clasped tightly in her lap. There was so much she wanted to say to him, so much that could never be spoken.

In an effort to break the tension Rose picked up the kettle and put it on the fire. She searched her mind for some innocuous remark.

'Is your business in the area completed now?'

'Business?'

'At the Assembly you said you could not leave.'

He looked surprised.

'I said that? I fear I misled you. I am here purely bent upon pleasure.'

'Not mine!' Rose uttered the retort unthinking and she quickly sat back down, blushing.

'No,' he said quietly, 'I am aware of that.'

He stood up and began to pace the little room, coming so close she could feel the air move as he passed her.

'However, there is a little…matter that I would like to discuss with you, if I may. It concerns Sam. I would like to help him.'

'Why should you want to do that?'

'He is a delightful boy.' He could have said nothing more designed to please her, but his next words provoked panic. 'I would like to be better acquainted with him.'

'That is not possible. You—' She ran her tongue around her lips, forcing herself to speak. 'You are not a…a suitable person for him to know.'

He winced at that.

'Very well—but I should still like to help, and he does not need to know I had any hand in this.'

Immediately she was wary.

'Go on.'

'I was in Barnstaple the other day and happened to look in at the auction. I bought a pony.'

Rose jumped up.

'Sir Lawrence, I—'

'It is for my godson,' he continued, talking over her. 'I know the previous owner, a country gentleman whose own children have outgrown the animal. She is beautifully mannered and will suit my little godson perfectly when he is older. I did not want to miss the chance to obtain such a gift so…I bought her.' He turned his rueful smile upon Rose, who tried to ignore the tug of attraction it inspired. 'The only problem is what to do with her until then. She needs to be ridden or I fear she will soon forget her manners. I know it was your intention to find such a mount for Sam and I wondered if you could help me out. I need someone to make use of the pony until such time as my godson is old enough to ride her.'

'I cannot imagine any sensible person asking you to stand godparent to their child,' said Rose, momentarily distracted. 'Unless you have reformed.'

The disturbing twinkle appeared in his blue eyes. A familiar ache curled low in her belly. She swallowed hard. She wanted him now as much as ever.

'I *am* reformed. I told you I would do so, though you have yet to believe it. And my cousin is exceedingly sensible, although I cannot deny that she is very fond of me, which may have clouded her judgement when it came to choosing a godfather for her child. Well, Mrs Westerhill, will you help me out of my dilemma?'

She was not fooled by his innocent look.

'How old is your godson, Sir Lawrence?'

'Oh, he must be all of eighteen months, by now.'

Rose's lips twitched. She said gravely, 'It will be some years, then, before he will be able to appreciate your gift.'

'And until then I need someone to look after the mare. I will of course pay for her stabling.'

'That would not be necessary, I am not a pauper!'

His blue eyes captured her gaze and held it. At last she dragged her eyes away. She left her chair and walked towards the window.

'I cannot accept,' she said at last. 'I would be under such an obligation to you.'

'The obligation would be all mine.' He moved towards her. Rose kept her eyes averted, but her spine tingled, knowing he was behind her. His breath was on her cheek as he murmured, 'Please, Rose, why should the animal be eating its head off in my stable when Sam could be learning to ride?'

She continued to stare out of the window, not daring to turn and face him. The air was charged with danger, like an electrical storm crackling about them. Rose tried to fight off the heady recklessness that was creeping under her skin. She should have nothing to do with Sir Lawrence if she truly wanted to forget him. And yet, how could she deny Sam this opportunity? A small voice of reason argued that it was madness. Magnus would certainly say so.

As if reading her mind, Lawrence murmured, 'Perhaps you should ask Emsleigh before you make a decision.'

Her chin went up.

'I do not need to consult him on such a matter!'

'No?'

The challenge was blatant.

'No.' She stifled the voice of reason and turned to face him. 'Very well, Sir Lawrence. We will look after this pony for you.' His lips curled in a slow smile that turned her insides to water. She struggled to continue. 'Your groom may bring the animal to the stables. If there is any communication regarding the arrangement, it is to be conducted through Evans. I want nothing more to do with the matter.'

'Nothing?'

'No. And…and I will explain the matter to Sam, if you please, but not today.'

'As you wish.'

He was still smiling at her and she turned away again, knowing that if he touched her the thin control she had over herself would slip away and she would melt into his arms, as she had dreamed of doing almost every night for the past year.

Sam saw nothing amiss in the idea of Sir Lawrence lending him a pony, but Rose was obliged to explain more fully to Mrs Molland, who was inclined to question Sir Lawrence's motive.

'I think it was an impetuous purchase,' said Rose, avoiding her eyes. 'Once he had bought the pony he had to do *something* with her until his godson is old enough to make use of her.'

'It does seem extremely generous of him, to loan the animal to us,' mused Mrs Molland. 'Forgive me, my love, but have you thought that he is perhaps trying to buy his way into your affections—as Aunt Jane might say, to have his evil way with you?'

Rose summoned up all her will-power to give a light-hearted laugh.

'Heavens, Mama, what a nonsensical notion!'

'No, it is not. You are young and pretty—'

'I am a widow and about to marry another man. Believe me, Mama, Sir Lawrence knows he would be wasting his time to set out lures to catch *me*!'

'Would he, though?' Rose found herself blushing at the knowing look in her mother's eye. 'The fact that you allowed the kettle to boil quite dry when I left you alone with him tells me you are not as immune to Sir Lawrence as you would have me believe.'

'We were discussing the pony, Mama, nothing more. And perhaps I should take *you* to task for leaving us alone in that shameful manner!'

'Well, I think Sir Lawrence is quite charming,' replied her mother, unabashed. 'If I was twenty years younger, I know I would enjoy being alone with him!'

'Mama! You are quite…quite outrageous. The more so when you know I am betrothed to Magnus, and very happily so,' she added defiantly.

'Then a few moments' *tête à tête* with Sir Lawrence Daunton should not have discomposed you.'

'It did not do so!' Rose felt the blood heating her cheeks and hurried on. 'Besides, I have already told him that he must deal with Evans—I will not have him use the animal as an excuse to call upon me. It…it is a perfectly sensible arrangement, to our mutual benefit. Nothing out of the ordinary at all.'

Mrs Molland looked sceptical.

'Well, whatever Magnus will say about it I don't know.'

Rose had wondered that herself, but when Magnus called at the cottage a few days later he said jovially, 'I have just bumped into Sam, who tells me he has a new pony. This is very sudden—you did not tell me you were going to buy him one?'

Rose said airily, 'No, it—it was rather sudden. I—er—had the opportunity to obtain the perfect mount for Sam.'

'Well, you know what you are about, my dear, but I

would have thought keeping another animal would be too much of an expense for you.'

'Having two horses in livery already, we were able to negotiate a very good rate for a third,' put in Mrs Molland, with perfect truth.

She neatly turned the subject and exchanged a look with Rose that confirmed them as co-conspirators. There was a tacit understanding that Magnus need not be told.

Sam was delighted with his new pony and spent every spare moment at the stables. A period of clement weather enabled him to be out of doors every day and by the end of the first week the groom reported that Sam was making good progress, and showing an aptitude for riding. When Rose went to watch a lesson for herself, the happiness shining in her young son's face made her heart swell and she felt a wave of gratitude towards Lawrence.

She had seen nothing of him since his visit to Bluebell Cottage—it was as they had agreed: the loan of the pony was not to make any difference to their acquaintance. It was certainly much better for her peace of mind, yet she found herself wondering if he was still at Knightscote. Would he inform her if he went away? Her mind went round and round the question, but came up with no satisfactory answer; in the end she determined to put all thoughts of the dangerous rake out of her mind and concentrate upon her own life, and the forthcoming dinner at Emsleigh House.

It was a long-standing engagement; Mrs Molland

had received the invitation from Althea Emsleigh several weeks ago and had told her daughter she was not at all deceived by its honeyed tones.

'The invitation really comes from Magnus. Althea considers us very poor company. You, a schoolteacher, and me, an ageing widow!'

'But she must be charming to us for her brother's sake.'

'And you should be charming to her,' retorted Mrs Molland. 'She will be your sister-in-law soon and you will have to share a house with her.'

'Heavens, yes,' replied Rose, much struck. 'She will not enjoy having to make way for me as mistress of Emsleigh.' A dimple appeared. She said mischievously, 'I wonder how quickly we can find her a husband?'

Magnus sent his carriage to Bluebell Cottage on the day of the dinner and the two ladies waved goodbye to Sam as they set off in style. That morning they had seen the first snowfall of the winter. It was very light, but it dusted the tops of the walls and the thatched roofs of the village and covered the surrounding hills with a blanket of white that glistened in the wintry sunset. They reached Emsleigh House just as the short winter's day was fading into night and thankfully hurried indoors.

They paused in the hall to divest themselves of their wraps. From her previous visits to the house, Rose knew that the drawing room lay at the top of the wide flight of stairs that swept upwards in front of them. She was surprised, therefore, to hear voices coming from Magnus's study, which was situated off the entrance hall. As she handed her cloak to the waiting footman the study door opened and a portly gentleman in a brown suit and bag-wig stepped out.

'I am very sorry to hear that your insurers have not yet paid up, Emsleigh,' he said, looking back into the room, 'but I have to tell you that unless I get my money soon I shall be forced to take action.'

The impassive butler was already shepherding Rose and her mother across the hall. Althea appeared at the top of the stairs to greet them, resplendent in blue shot silk decorated with pink ribbons.

Rose glanced back over her shoulder as she heard the front door bang.

'Who was that man?' asked Rose

'Oh, *him*.' Althea pouted and shook her head. 'Pray take no heed. He is merely one of Magnus's creditors. He rode all the way here from Minehead to dun us! Horrid little man. I do not think we should deal with him in future. Is that not so, Brother?'

Magnus had left the study and now ran lightly up the stairs to join them.

'Good evening, Mrs Molland, Rose. I am sorry you had to witness that. A little untimely business.' He ushered them into the drawing room and closed the doors. 'But now we may be easy. You know everyone, I think?'

Rose regarded the assembled company. There were no surprises: the local magistrate, Sir Jonas Pullen, and his wife; the local vicar, Mr John Wilkins, and four other couples from Minehead thought worthy to dine at Emsleigh House.

'You will note, Mrs Westerhill, that we are at present an odd number.' Althea took Rose's arm and led her across to a sofa. 'But we are acquainted enough now for you to know I would never arrange anything so awkwardly! We have another gentleman coming to make up the numbers. We shall have eight couples sitting down to dinner. What do you say to that?'

'I wonder that you should put yourself to so much trouble when you have your Winter Ball in less than two weeks. I applaud your energy, Miss Emsleigh.'

Althea simpered and waved a hand.

'Oh, it is nothing. I have been my brother's hostess for so long now it is second nature to me to organise these things. But we digress. I was asking if you could guess who I had found to make up the numbers?'

Rose spread her hands.

'I have no idea, Miss Emsleigh... Mr Truelove, perhaps?'

'Truelove, the attorney?' Althea threw back her head and gave a little trill of laughter. 'Dear me, no. No one so provincial. It—but I do not need to tell you, because I think this is he!'

Rose's spirits fluttered erratically. Althea's words had aroused her suspicions and she was not surprised when she heard the butler's sonorous announcement.

'Sir Lawrence Daunton!'

Rose watched Althea fly across the room to greet him. Was it her imagination or did all the ladies in the room sit up a little straighter when he came in? Certainly he looked very elegant, his simply cut black coat moulded to his frame and his dark hair brushed back from his handsome face. Althea was guiding him around the room, ensuring he knew everyone, but keeping a proprietary hand on his arm. Rose knew they would have to speak and she drew herself up. She must not blush, or show any signs that they were other than the merest acquaintances.

I can do this, she told herself as Althea and Lawrence approached. *We mean nothing to each other.*

She schooled her features into a cool, distant smile.

'Mrs Westerhill.'

She tried not to be disappointed that he did not reach out for her hand and gave her only a slight nod of recognition, or to feel bereft when he turned away immediately. The greeting he gave Mrs Molland was much warmer. Quickly Rose moved across the room to join Magnus. There would be no sighs, no longing looks. She was no fainting schoolroom miss, but a grown woman. Not by the flicker of an eyelid would she betray how much Lawrence's presence affected her.

'Ah, Rose.' Magnus held out his hand to her. 'Mr Wilkins and I were agreeing that you are in high bloom tonight, my dear.'

'Why, thank you, sirs. And you, Mr Wilkins—how do you go on? You were suffering from a slight cough last Sunday.'

'I was. I hope it did not detract too much from my sermon. But it is quite cleared up now, ma'am, thank you.'

Rose smiled as she listened to him conversing with Magnus. She liked the Reverend John Wilkins. He was a mild-mannered man who worked hard for his parishioners and, despite a slightly distracted air, he managed the funds for the village school very efficiently.

'…and that is something I wanted to tell you, Mrs Westerhill.' He turned his kindly gaze back to Rose. 'I think I have found someone to replace you at the school.'

'So soon?' Rose was startled.

'I asked Mr Wilkins if he knew of anyone who could take over from you, my dear,' Magnus explained. 'There will be plenty to do before the wedding. You will not have time to be schoolmistress as well.'

'It is but a few mornings a week—'

'Mornings that you might be spending with me,' declared Magnus, squeezing her fingers. 'You must see why I am eager for your replacement to arrive.'

'The lady in question is a distant relative of mine, fallen upon hard times and in need of a position.' Mr Wilkins coughed, his eyes shifting to Magnus and back again. 'When Mr Emsleigh mentioned the matter to me…'

'Of course I do not expect you to give up your post immediately,' said Magnus. 'I thought she might work with you for a little while, learn how you do things.'

Rose suspected he was trying to smooth her obviously ruffled feathers. She bit back a sharp retort and instead asked Mr Wilkins when his relative would be arriving.

'I expect her here any day now,' replied the vicar, patently relieved at her mild response.

'Then you must bring her to the schoolroom as soon as she is settled in. I look forward to meeting her.' She allowed Magnus to lead her away, saying quietly, as soon they were out of earshot, 'Really, Magnus, I do think you could have discussed this with me.'

'I beg your pardon, my dear, it quite slipped my mind.'

'Just as it slipped your mind to tell me you had been to Hades Cove.' It gave her some satisfaction to note his startled look. 'Mrs Ansell told me she had seen you riding there on Wednesday—you know full well the track down to the cove winds around the hill overlooking Mersecombe. You cannot expect to use it without someone seeing you.'

'Of course not. I had business in Lynton and decided to look at the mine on my way home. Surely you do not object.' He gave a soft laugh. 'I hope you do not plan to charge me with trespass.'

'Of course not, Magnus, but I would like to be kept informed of matters that concern me.'

He raised her hand to his lips.

'Neither the school nor the mine will be your concern for much longer, my dear. When you are my wife all these little problems will be lifted from your shoulders. Now, shall we lead the way into dinner?'

The meal was long and protracted. Lawrence was seated at the far end of the table, next to Althea. Mrs Molland was also placed near him and both ladies seemed to be enjoying his company far too much. Rose had been given the place of honour next to Magnus, but although she conversed happily with those around her, she found herself wondering what Lawrence was saying to keep both ladies so well entertained. Her eyes strayed far too often to the far end of the table and it was an effort to attend to her neighbours. She could acquit Althea of malice—after all, she knew nothing of their previous acquaintance—but it was still painful for Rose to have to sit and watch her flirting with Lawrence.

'What an exciting few months lie ahead of us,' declared Lady Pullen. 'We have your ball here to look forward to, Mr Emsleigh, and then, in the spring, there will be the wedding.' She turned her gracious smile upon Rose. 'You must be looking forward to that, my dear. You can become a lady again.'

'I enjoy my work at the school,' replied Rose. 'I shall be sorry to give it up.'

'You will be far too busy to miss it,' Magnus assured her.

'Will I? What do you envisage me doing, Magnus?' Rose turned her direct gaze upon him, smiling to soften the challenge in her words.

'You will adorn my house and accompany me when I am obliged to make social calls.'

Rose wrinkled her nose.

'Really, Magnus, I think sometimes you want merely a pretty ornament to hang upon your arm.'

He reached across and pinched her cheek.

'A pretty, witty ornament, my dear!' Those around them laughed, but Rose found nothing to amuse her in the idea.

'I am sure, as my wife, there will be plenty of charitable work to amuse you,' offered Magnus.

'Talking of charity,' put in Mr Wilkins, 'I was in

Minehead yesterday and bumped into a sailor there, from Bristol. He was one of the crew from the *Sealark*. He tells me he is still waiting for his money.'

Magnus frowned. He said shortly, 'He will get that as soon as the insurers send me payment for my losses.'

'They haven't paid out yet?' Sir Jonas leaned forwards, his voice carrying the length of the table. 'I thought it was as good as settled. They had the affidavit from every crew member months ago, attesting to it being an accident. What are they waiting for?'

'London investors,' declared his neighbour. 'You would have been better advised to use the insurers in Exeter, as I do.'

'Easy to say so now, Norris,' Magnus responded.

He tapped his glass and the butler rushed to refill it.

'But why do they delay?' asked Rose, frowning slightly. 'Surely there can be no question that it was an accident.'

'None at all, my love,' said Magnus. 'Pray, put it out of your mind. There is nothing for you to worry about.'

'Of course there is!' declared Mr Norris, who had imbibed rather freely and was now in a boisterous mood. 'Mrs Westerhill was expecting to marry a rich man, Emsleigh. If the insurers don't pay out, you'll have the creditors hammering on the door—'

He broke off as he received a hard jab in the ribs from his wife.

'Pray ignore my husband, Mrs Westerhill. His humour is sometimes quite out of place.' She glared at her husband, who returned his attention sheepishly to his dinner.

This altercation had claimed everyone's attention and an awkward silence had settled over the whole table. At the far end, Althea gave a little laugh.

'Well, I am sure I cannot wait for our Winter Ball. I do hope the weather will improve—what say you, Sir Lawrence, does this early snow mean we shall have a hard winter this year?'

Sir Lawrence was thoughtfully watching Magnus, and Althea had to repeat her question before he turned to answer her. The tension eased as a general murmur of conversation began again. Magnus addressed an innocuous comment to Mr Wilkins and good humour was restored.

'Whatever you say about Althea Emsleigh, she keeps a good table,' remarked Mrs Molland. 'Such a pity about Mr Norris! The man never could take his drink.'

The ladies had left the gentlemen to their wines and were gathered once more in the drawing room. Rose followed her mother to a sofa near the fire. She glanced around to make sure they were not overheard.

'But do you think he is correct, Mama? That Magnus will be ruined if the insurers do not pay out? After all, there was that man in the study when we arrived…'

'Good heavens, child, Magnus Emsleigh is one of the richest men in the county! No, no, I am sure there is nothing to worry about; it was merely Mr Norris joking at someone else's expense! Do not let him make you uncomfortable.'

The ladies settled down to while away the hour or so until the gentlemen joined them. Rose began to relax.

She had been in Lawrence's company for several hours and survived. They had not been close enough during dinner to converse and she was hopeful that they could continue to avoid each other for the remainder of the evening, by which time she would be quite used to his company. That, of course, would stand her in good stead for their next meeting, when she did not doubt that they would be able to greet each other with polite indifference.

Her conviction was somewhat rocked when the gentlemen came in and she found her eyes immediately seeking out Lawrence, wanting him to look at her, yet such was her contrary nature, when he did so she immediately turned to join in an animated conversation with her neighbours.

Magnus pointed out that the pianoforte and harp stood ready, should any lady wish to entertain them.

'You are all so diffident,' declared Althea. 'I shall start, then!'

She sat down at the harp and began to pluck at the strings. A polite hush fell over the room. Lawrence moved silently towards Rose.

'Do you play, Mrs Westerhill?'

'The pianoforte, a little.'

'Do not be so modest, Rose,' said her mother in a loud whisper. 'She plays very well, Sir Lawrence.'

'Then I should very much like to hear her.'

Rose gave a little shake of her head. To sit at the pianoforte, inviting everyone to look at her—giving

Lawrence every excuse to look at her—she could think of nothing worse.

'I do not intend to play tonight.'

She was immediately sorry for her sharp tone. Lawrence's brows went up, but it was impossible to apologise without drawing more attention to herself. She was on edge when he was so close and she could only begin to relax again when he moved away to sit beside Lady Pullen.

Althea's performance was warmly applauded and she crossed over to the pianoforte, calling to Lawrence to come and turn the pages for her. Rose watched him standing beside Althea, bending to catch something she said, sharing a smile with her. It took her a little while to realise that the hard, angry knot in her stomach was jealousy. She breathed deeply, her fingers clenching and unclenching in her lap. So much for her resolution!

'Bravo, my dear!'

Magnus's utterance caught her attention and with a little jolt of surprise she realised Althea had finished. She put her hands together in appreciation of the music, although she had not attended to a note.

'Now,' Magnus continued, looking about him, 'who will be next…Rose?'

'Thank you but, no, not tonight.'

'Pray show us what you can do,' he urged her. 'I know you play very prettily; I have heard you perform at Bluebell Cottage.'

Rose smiled and shook her head.

'Do not put her to the blush, Brother,' said Althea sweetly. 'To amuse oneself on the little box piano at

home is all very well, but it is very different to playing
properly on a Broadwood.'

Mrs Molland drew in a hissing breath. Rose put her
hand on her mother's arm to prevent her from leaping
to her defence.

'Of course it is,' she agreed cordially. 'However, now
you mention it, I have been practising a rondo by Mr
Mozart and confess I should like to know how it sounds
on such a fine instrument.'

Rose walked across to the piano and sat down.
Lawrence stepped closer.

'Do you have music, ma'am? May I turn the pages
for you?'

She shook her head, the light of battle in her eyes.

'Thank you, I have no need of music for this piece.'

With that she spread her hands out over the keys
and began to play with such gusto that an immediate
silence descended over the room. It gave her immense
satisfaction to see the shocked look upon Althea's features. Poor Miss Emsleigh, she rarely visited Bluebell
Cottage so she was not to know that the piano was one
of Rose's main pleasures, or that she spent many hours
practising.

Rose ended her performance with a flourish and sat
back. Magnus led the applause, beaming delightedly at
her before looking around the room as if to invite his
guests to appreciate just what an accomplished bride
he had chosen.

'Exemplary,' murmured Sir Lawrence. 'I have rarely
heard anything finer. I can think of no better set-down
for our hostess.'

He had been standing by the piano, watching her, throughout her performance, but Rose had been so caught up in the music that she had barely noticed him. Now his words reminded her of her situation. With a strained smile she shook her head at him and slipped away.

The musical entertainment continued, but Rose could not enjoy it. She was angry that she had allowed her irritation to get the better of her. She had suffered Althea's barbed comments before and had always allowed them to pass unchallenged, but tonight was different. It had been Rose's intention to stay in the background and be nothing more than a spectator for the evening, but her display upon the pianoforte had drawn everyone's attention. With dismay she saw that both Althea and Lawrence were watching her, dark resentment in one glance, warm admiration in the other.

The evening dragged on. The tea tray was brought in and Althea dispensed cups of black Bohea to the guests who milled around the room, talking and laughing. Rose carried a cup of tea to her mother, but could not settle. She wanted to go home, but Magnus would not call the carriage for a good hour yet, and she did not wish to draw even more attention to herself by requesting to leave early. Instead she touched Magnus's arm and drew him aside.

'Is there somewhere I may sit quietly for a little while, Magnus?'

'What is it, my dear, are you unwell?'

'A severe headache, but I am sure it will ease presently, if I can only be alone.'

Immediately he guided her out of the room.

'There is a good fire in the library,' he said. 'Shall I send Althea to you, or your mother?'

'No, no, I would not upset your party, Magnus. I shall do very well alone, thank you.'

They slipped out of the room and Magnus led her away from the public rooms to the library. It was a large, imposing chamber, almost divided in two by the bookshelves that jutted out into the room. On this side of the divide a marble fireplace and two armchairs provided a degree of comfort. Beyond, a large mahogany desk filled the centre of the floor, its surface bare of any ornament. Magnus used his study for working; this room was merely for show, neither the desk nor the leather-bound tomes, purchased by the yard from a Bristol bookseller, intended for anything more than ostentatious display.

Magnus settled her in one of the chairs beside the fire.

'No one will bother you here. I shall come back again in a little while—'

'No, there will be no need for that.' She gave him a weak smile. 'I have taken enough of your time. Go back to your guests, Magnus, and I will join you very soon, I promise.'

She watched him walk away, her smile fading as he left the room. Guilt ripped at her conscience; she was betrothed to Magnus, yet even here, in his house, her thoughts, her attention, constantly turned to Lawrence.

Their brief liaison had lasted only two nights, but the pain of separation was as strong now as the day she had ridden away from Knightscote. It was like a raw, angry wound that would not heal.

'Oh, will it never end?' The words were dragged out of her and she dropped her head in her hands.

As if conjured by her own longing she heard his voice, full of concern.

'What is it, Rose? Are you ill?'

She lifted her head. Lawrence was standing with his back to the door, his blue eyes fixed upon her.

'How did you know where to find me?'

'I saw you leave—you did not look well. Then Magnus came back alone...'

She hunted frantically for her handkerchief.

'Please go.'

'I want to help.'

She wiped her eyes, ashamed that he should observe her weakness. Glancing up, she saw that he was still watching her.

'Talk to me,' he said quietly.

Rose jumped up and began to pace up and down. She sought around for some ladylike term to do justice to the pain inside. There was none.

'Damn you,' she uttered vehemently. '*Damn you*, Lawrence Daunton! You were not supposed to come back into my life. I was managing very well without you.'

This was not quite true, but Rose had no intention of admitting the gnawing loneliness she had felt during the spring months. Angrily she kneaded one fist into the palm of the other. 'I thought I could play this game. That we could meet as strangers, friends even, but it is not possible. I cannot relax in your company—you make me discontent with my lot in life!'

'This does not have to be your lot, Rose.'

She shook her head, hardly attending to him.

'I have worked *so hard* to forget you. My world was ordered and—and calm. My future was assured. Then you come striding back, overturning everything I have worked for, winning my son's regard—'

'I did not plan that.'

'No? And what about the pony?'

A sudden smile softened his features.

'Blame Sam for that! Little monkey, when he chattered away to me, saying you could not afford a mount for him, I could not help myself.'

'And thus he gave you a means to tempt me, to put myself into your debt.'

'No! I would never use Sam as a way into your affections!'

His vehemence surprised her.

'Nevertheless I am constrained to be obliged, when I would rather have nothing to do with you!'

'Do you think you are the only one suffering?' he flashed. 'To be near you, but unable to talk freely, unable to cherish and protect you—'

'We agreed it could never be—'

'No—*you* said it could not work. You had married one rake and would not risk your happiness with another. But I am no libertine, Rose. I was wild, yes, and I allowed rumours to circulate. But I am a changed man. Ask any of my friends in town—write to that wearisome aunt of yours who passes on to you all the gossip! They will all tell you I have not looked at a woman this year. My friends have waited in vain for me at the gaming tables. I have spent most of my time upon my estates, adding new buildings, improving the land—at first I did it out of anger, my only thought was that I would show you I was not the feckless character you thought me! Then, as the months went on, I found I enjoyed it, much more than the social round I had become locked into. I faced up to the truth that I had never wanted to marry Annabelle and had stayed in London merely to avoid the fateful day. I had misbehaved, flaunted my string of mistresses in front of her, hoping that she would realise I would not make a good husband and cry off. She never did. I was afraid to marry her; I did not want to be imprisoned in her world of dull domesticity.' He exhaled slowly. 'It was a dreadful thing to discover about myself, Rose, that I was too much of a coward to tell her the truth. I truly thought it would break her heart. Looking back now, I think she wanted the match as little as I. If only—! I bitterly regret it now, but there is nothing I can do to change the past. But *you* can change your future. You say you are not content with your life—then change it, Rose. Break off your engagement to Emsleigh!'

'You know I cannot.'

He grabbed her arms.

'Why not? Are you afraid of what everyone will say?'

'No!' She pushed her hands against the solid,

unyielding wall of his chest. 'That is not the reason. I chose Magnus because he is everything you are not: correct, dependable, solidly upright. He will be a perfect father for Sam.'

'Are you sure, Rose? Are you sure Emsleigh is the upright, honest gentleman you think him?'

'Of course. He has never given me any reason to doubt that.'

'But you don't love him.'

Rose bit her lip.

'That is not a requirement of our marriage.'

'Then it is doomed to fail.' He pulled her closer, but as he went to kiss her she turned her head away. Her heart was pounding so hard it was a constant drumming in her ears. 'Your blood is on fire when I touch you,' he muttered, his lips grazing her neck and causing her to tremble. Her head went back as his kisses left a burning trail upon her skin. 'If you must marry, let it be me!'

'You—you are asking me to marry you?' she said raggedly. 'When you have just admitted you lived for years in London rather than succumb to—what did you call it?—dull domesticity?'

'There would be nothing dull about our marriage.' The dark desire in his eyes sent a shudder through her. 'I would be a good husband, Rose, if you will give me a chance to prove it.'

She closed her eyes, scalding tears welling up.

'Yes, you have behaved yourself for the past ten months, but that is not a lifetime!' She choked back a sob. 'Harry was a model husband for the first year, until

Sam was born, but then he reverted to his old ways. I cannot—will not—risk that happening again.'

He sighed. 'One can never guarantee what life has in store. Sometimes you have to take a risk.' His grip tightened on her arms. 'Sometimes, you have to follow your heart. You have to trust me, Rose.'

With a tremendous effort she freed herself, shaking off his hands to say angrily, 'I do not *have* to do anything! You ask too much of me, sir, when all I ask of you is that you leave me alone!' She covered her face with her hands. 'Please,' she said softly, 'please, just go away.'

'Is there nothing I say will convince you that I have changed for good?'

She shook her head.

'Only time will tell us that, Lawrence, and that is something I do not have.' She drew a long, steadying breath and said resolutely, 'I am marrying Magnus in the spring.'

She spoke slowly, her words falling heavy as lead between them. Lawrence watched her, his face pale and impassive, but the muscle working in his jaw told her just how tense he was.

'So, I have my answer,' he said at last. 'This is goodbye.'

'Yes.' She put her hands to her cheeks. 'This year has been the most miserable I have ever spent. You c-cannot know how much I regret taking the wrong turning last winter.'

A wry smile twisted his lips.

'I am very sorry if you think that. I have come to

believe your arriving at my door was the finest thing that ever happened in my life.'

With a final, clipped little bow he turned on his heel and walked out. In the silence she listened to his footsteps fading away. He would leave, she knew it. He would hurry down the stairs, there would be a flurry of activity as one footman hurried off to fetch his coat while another dashed to the stables to order his horse.

Go after him. Tell him you have changed your mind.

The insidious voice in her head teased her with views of a halcyon future where they would live in wedded bliss. She folded her arms across her stomach. Better to conjure the images of her marriage to Harry Westerhill: the arguments, the blows, the long waking nights knowing he was lying in another woman's bed. And even if she could endure all that, Lawrence would expect an heir. How was she to tell him that she could have no more children?

Chapter Seven

Lawrence groaned and turned carefully in his bed. His head hurt dreadfully, but he knew he could not blame Emsleigh's wine for that. He had returned to Knightscote in the early hours of the morning and settled down to contemplate his future with a bottle of brandy. To see Rose in such distress tore at his heart. When he had first learned that she had postponed her marriage to Emsleigh he had begun almost unconsciously to hope that she might have changed her mind about him, but that now seemed impossible. She was determined to marry Emsleigh, to provide Sam with a respectable father. Aye, that was the bitter irony—if Lawrence's suspicions were correct, then Magnus Emsleigh was anything but respectable: he was responsible for sinking the *Sealark* to claim the insurance and inadvertently responsible for Ruben Wooler's death. Lawrence could not ignore that, nor could he share his suspicions with

Rose. But he could not let her marry Emsleigh while he suspected him of such villainy. He had to discover the truth.

A week later Lawrence was forced to admit that his investigations were not going well. He had sought out Captain Morris, but he had told him nothing more than the agent had already gleaned from the crew members: a fire had broken out in the hold and they had been forced to abandon ship. The accounts were all the same—too much so for Lawrence's liking—but since they all held notes of hand from Magnus Emsleigh, promising them various sums once the insurers had paid out, it was unlikely any one of them would admit to anything different. The only person who seemed troubled was Abel Wooler, brother of the drowned sailor. Lawrence had spoken to him on several occasions and had the distinct impression that he was hiding something.

Lawrence decided that he would go and see Abel once more. If he stuck to his story then there would be nothing for it but to return to London. He would have to tell George Craven that the insurance claim must stand.

And that would leave Rose free to marry Magnus Emsleigh. The thought irked him, but if he had nothing stronger than his own suspicions, what right had he to object to a marriage that would give Rose and Sam a secure and comfortable life?

Riding to Mersecombe did much to raise Lawrence's spirits. There were still signs of the early snow on the high ground and a biting wind cut at his cheeks as he galloped across the moor. It was a little warmer down in the valley, where the steeply wooded hills provided some shelter, and he slowed his hectic pace. Lawrence tried to convince himself that the sudden twisting in his gut as he rode past the church was due to the brandy and not the fact that Rose would be there, taking lessons in the little schoolroom.

'Good day, Sir Lawrence.'

The soft greeting interrupted his thoughts and he brought his horse to a stand. Mr Wilkins, the vicar, was standing at the edge of the road with a soberly clad woman at his side. He introduced her as Mrs Reed, a distant cousin.

'I am taking Mrs Reed to the schoolroom: she is to be Mrs Westerhill's replacement.'

'Ah, yes.' Lawrence nodded, said all that was proper and rode on.

Another reminder that Rose was to wed Magnus Emsleigh.

Lawrence clenched his teeth. Dear heaven, he would be glad to quit this place! As he rounded the bend in the road he spotted a figure on the road before him—it was Abel Wooler, heading for the Ship Inn. Well, perhaps fortune was favouring him at last.

He stabled his horse and entered the inn, pausing to allow his eyes to grow accustomed to the dim light. The inn was deserted and he soon spotted his quarry, sitting at a table near the fire.

'Good day to you, Wooler. Will you take a drink with me?'

The man looked up. His eyes were wary, but he nodded.

Lawrence called for ale and drew up a stool.

'How is the pointer bitch?'

'She is doing well,' Lawrence replied. 'Growing apace. You've sold all the other pups now?'

'Aye, they've all been taken.' Abel paused while the serving maid brought a heavy blackjack to the table and filled two tankards with frothy ale. Lawrence gave her a handful of coins and asked her to leave the blackjack on the table.

Abel raised his tankard to Lawrence, taking his time to savour the drink before saying in his slow drawl, 'Somehow I don't think 'tis dogs you wants to talk to me about.'

'No. I wanted to ask you again about the *Sealark*.'

'I've told you all I knows, Sir Lawrence.'

'But have you? Doesn't it seem odd to you that Emsleigh should entrust such a valuable cargo to his least seaworthy ship?'

Abel shrugged.

'Summer. He didn't expect it to suffer heavy weather.'

'And the fire? Tell me again how it broke out.'

'No one knows.' Abel took another long draught. 'There's a lot of tar on a ship, Sir Lawrence. Fires 'appen.'

'So everyone says. I've read the crew's accounts— those that could be collected. It took some time to gather them, with the crew scattered far and wide. Some have even set sail again.' Lawrence paused. 'Seems strange to me that Morris should sign up his crew in Bristol. He usually finds his crews locally, does he not? From Barnstaple or Minehead.'

Another shrug.

'So how did you and your brother come to sign up?'

'Cap'n Morris told Ruben about it. Ruben told me.'

'So Morris would not have taken you if your brother had not mentioned it?'

Abel said quickly, 'I never said that.'

Lawrence refilled the tankards.

'Some of the crew's accounts say the fire was the bosun's fault.' He saw the flash of anger in the other man's eyes, but it faded again and he merely shrugged.

'It's easy to blame the dead. They can't defend themselves.'

'But the fire could have been started deliberately.'

'To what end?'

'To scuttle the ship,' said Lawrence. 'After the cargo had been safely unloaded.' He paused, watching Abel closely. 'There would be a reward, you know, if the cargo was to be recovered.'

'You think if you get me drunk I will confess everything to you?' Abel's slow grin appeared. He shook his head. 'It will not happen. There's nothing to confess.'

'But you must admit it looks suspicious: Emsleigh has debts to pay, takes out a large insurance on his cargo—'

'Sir Lawrence, you are a gentleman, we've done business together. More than that, our Jem has taken a shine to 'ee, and you've paid for these drinks. All those things stop me from punching your daylights out for suggesting I might not be telling the truth!' Abel glowered at him. 'I have already signed to say we did all we could to save the ship. What would happen to me if I was to change my mind? My word against my fellows—that would do no good. Besides, if—and I'm not saying it was deliberate—*if* it was discovered that the *Sealark* was scuttled, then Jem would not get the money that was promised to his dad. I couldn't do that to the boy.'

Lawrence was about to argue more when a soft, distressed voice called from the doorway.

'Abel—Abel, are you there? Have you seen Jem?'

Both men swung round. Maggie Wooler was hurrying across the taproom with Rose close behind her. One look at Rose's face and Lawrence was on his feet.

'It's Jem,' said Maggie. 'He's not been to school.'

'Sam is missing, too,' added Rose. 'When they did not arrive at school I thought they had gone back to the farm. Mrs Reed was with me, so I left her in charge of the children and walked up to fetch them.'

'But they wasn't with me,' cried Maggie, wringing her hands. 'They've run away somewhere.'

Lawrence turned to Rose.

'What about the pony?'

She shook her head, eyes shadowed with worry.

'I checked the stables; Evans has not seen them.'

'Gone—?' Abel stopped. He slowly shook his head. 'Nay, he wouldn't.'

'What is it?' cried Maggie. 'What are you thinking, Abel?'

He rubbed his chin.

'Well, you know what today is, Maggie.'

'Aye, it's Ruben's birthday.'

'An' I remember, last time young Sam was up at the farm with us, he was telling Jem how on *his* father's birthday he and Mrs Westerhill went off to lay flowers on the grave in Exford.'

'But Ruben has no grave,' said Maggie.

'No,' muttered Abel. 'Just his initials carved at Sealham Point.'

Rose looked aghast. 'But they cannot have gone there. The tide…'

'Jem knows the tides; he'd reckon they could walk there and back before the tide came in and cut them off,' said Abel. 'But I'd wager it will have taken 'em longer than they thought to get to Sealham Point. The tide will have turned. They'll be stuck there now.'

'If they haven't been washed out to sea!' cried Mrs Wooler, lifting her apron to cover her face.

'Nonsense, Maggie, our Jem has more sense than that. He'll have seen that they can't get back and will be sitting it out on the rocks.'

'But it will be dark by the time the tide goes out again.' Rose tried to speak calmly, but could not prevent the quiver in her voice. 'They will not be able to see their way back. Th-that means they will have to wait until the morning…'

Abel stood up. 'I'll row across the bay and collect them. There'll be an onshore swell for an hour or so yet. It won't be too hard.'

'Let me come with you,' said Rose immediately.

'Nay, ma'am, I will not take thee, unless ye can row.

An extra pair of oars would be useful, but everyone I know is already at sea, making the most of the daylight.'

'I'll go with you,' said Lawrence. His lips quirked at the incredulous look his words received. 'I suspect rowing on an English river is somewhat different to the open sea, but I'd like to help.'

Abel looked at him for a long moment, as if weighing him up.

'Very well. I'll be glad to have 'ee, sir.'

'What should we do?' asked Rose, following them to the door. 'Should we come down to the jetty…?'

'No,' said Lawrence, 'I suggest you both go to your homes. We could be wrong, you know, and the boys might already be home.' He watched the play of emotion on Rose's face. She wanted to argue, to do something more useful than sitting at home and waiting. He touched her arm. 'Don't worry, we'll bring them back safely.'

She swallowed. 'Very well.' She laid a hand on his sleeve as he turned to follow Abel out of the inn. 'Be careful.'

The soft words and the look that accompanied them cheered Lawrence as he followed Abel along the winding lane that led out of the village and through the fields to the shore. There were no signs of activity at the water's edge, only a few beached boats and the fishing nets spread out to dry. Abel headed for an upturned rowboat and with Lawrence's help it was soon on the water.

For a while they rowed in silence, the only sounds

the scrape and splash of the oars, but Lawrence was aware that Abel's eyes were upon his back.

'Well,' he said over his shoulder, 'I am out of practice, but what do you think?'

He heard his companion chuckle.

'Aye,' said Abel in his deep, slow drawl, 'you'll do.'

They made good progress across the bay. Lawrence glanced over his shoulder at their destination, the ragged cliffs of Sealham Point, and his blood ran a little colder when he saw the white spume of the waves crashing against the rocks.

'I can't see them…'

'Jem'll know better than to stand on this side o' the Point,' said Abel. 'You can scramble up away from the waves on t'other side, and that's where we're going; we can bring the boat real close there.'

Lawrence put all his efforts into rowing as Abel guided them safely around the point to approach the shore from the south. At last his companion gave a grunt of satisfaction.

'There they are.'

Looking round, Lawrence saw two small figures waving from a rocky shelf some way up the cliff. They began to scramble down as the boat nosed its way towards them. He tried not to think of the jagged rocks just below the surface. Abel concentrated on keeping the boat steady while Lawrence reached out a hand to help first Sam and then Jem jump across.

'Little fools,' said Abel once both boys were safely on board. 'Forget the time, did you?'

'We was late settin' off,' stammered Jem, his teeth chattering. 'We never meant to—'

'We can discuss that later.' Lawrence shrugged himself out of his greatcoat. 'Put this around the both of you.'

'What about you, sir, won't you be c-cold?' asked Sam, his face pinched and white.

Lawrence grinned.

'I don't think so; I am working so hard at the rowing that it's keeping me warm.'

'Ah, an' it's time to be rowin' again, sir, if we're to get these nippers home!'

The two men pulled hard on the oars to bring the little boat away from the treacherous rocks and as they moved into clear water Lawrence had time to observe the rugged coastline with its towering cliffs. A little way south of Sealham Point was a cleft in the hills, a valley so deep and narrow that the shadowed woods looked almost black, save for a ragged clearing that ran like a scar along one side, a little way above the waterline.

'What is that?' He nodded towards the cliffs, his hands too busy with the oars to point.

'What? Oh, that's Hades Cove,' offered Jem, looking back.

'And the rocky outcrop? It does not look natural.'

'Tedn't natural,' Jem affirmed. 'It's the old drift-mine. They used to bring out the iron ore and load it onto the ships. You can still see the small jetty there, in the cove. No one uses it any more.'

'It belongs to Mama,' piped up Sam, buried deep in Lawrence's greatcoat.

'Really?' Lawrence rested on his oars and stared at the cove. 'But it's not used now, you say?'

'Tedn't been used for years.' Jem nodded. 'The ore ran out.'

'But ships could still get in there?' asked Lawrence.

'I suppose so.' Jem shrugged. 'As long as they had a pilot that knows the waters...'

'Stop yer gabbin', Jem!' Abel ordered him roughly. He leaned forwards to address Lawrence. 'I'd be obliged to 'ee, sir, if you'd give yer attention to getting us home. It'll be a lot harder to make progress once the tide turns!'

Lawrence swung round, but Abel had his head down, concentrating on rowing. With a shrug Lawrence accepted the rebuke and applied himself once more to the oars.

Rose quickly returned to the schoolroom where she found Mrs Reed had everything under control.

'You may safely leave me to finish up today,' she said, giving Rose's arm an understanding pat. 'The children are no trouble and I am sure you would prefer to be at home until you have news of your son. And if you need me to come in tomorrow, you only have to send word to the vicarage.'

So Rose made her way to the cottage, where she joined her mother in pacing up and down and staring out of the window at the deserted lane, knowing all the time there could be no news for hours yet. The short winter's day came to an end and Rose put a lighted lamp in the window. Janet prepared meals, but they were returned hardly touched.

'Surely they should be back by now,' she said, unable to settle. 'What if they cannot find them?' She shivered. 'What if they have capsized…?'

'Patience,' said Mrs Molland. 'The sea has not been particularly rough today and Abel Wooler is an experienced seaman. We will hear soon enough. The time would pass quicker for you if you had some occupation.'

An involuntary smile tugged at Rose's mouth. 'Like you, Mama? You have had your sewing on your lap for a good hour, but I have not seen you set a stitch. Besides, I have not been idle; I have built up the fire and brought down dry clothes and a blanket for Sam when he comes in. He is sure to be wet and cold.' She glanced at the clock again and exclaimed, 'Oh, what could have possessed them to go off like that? I shall give him *such* a scolding when he returns!'

Mrs Molland put up her hand, an expectant look upon her face. Voices could be heard in the hall and the next moment Sir Lawrence walked in with Sam in his arms.

'Here he is.' He handed the boy to Rose. 'Wet, cold and tired, but unharmed, I think.'

With a little cry Rose hugged her son tightly.

'It was as we thought,' he added, easing his shoulders. 'They had gone to Sealham Point to see where Jem's father had carved his name on the rock. It was some sort of tribute to him on his birthday, but they misjudged the tide.'

Rose nodded, distracted. She carried Sam over to

the fire, where Mrs Molland was waiting to help her undress him.

'Thank heaven you are safe!' Rose's fingers trembled as she struggled with the buttons of his coat.

'I do beg your pardon, Mama,' muttered Sam. 'I never meant to be away so long. Jem said we'd be there and back before school ended.'

'And did you think I would not worry if you did not turn up at school?' demanded Rose. 'Naughty boy, I do not know what you deserve for such a trick—perhaps we should have left you on those horrid rocks all night!'

'Hush now, he has learned his lesson,' soothed Mrs Molland. 'And you are making a sad mull of undressing him, Rose. Give him to me.'

Realising she was far too tearful and shaken to be helpful, Rose left Sam to his grandmother's care. As she turned she saw Sir Lawrence heading for the door.

'Don't go!'

He stopped at her words. Rose went towards him, saying shyly, 'Will you not stay? I am sure Sam will want to thank you.'

He glanced across to make sure the others were not attending.

'I thought I was not a fit-and-proper person?'

She flushed. 'Did I say that? I beg your pardon! Please, do not go just yet. I—we would like to hear what happened.'

It was not until he gave a little nod that she realised she had been holding her breath and, with some difficulty, she invited him to sit down.

Within the warm glow of the fire he briefly relayed

the tale. Mrs Molland blanched as he described how Abel had guided the little boat into the shore, and Sam took her hand.

'Do not be afraid, Grandmama, Jem and I were safe enough up on the rocks.'

Rose smiled.

'You can see he has come to no harm, Mama. I have no doubt he will want to go out on his pony tomorrow, as usual.' She tried hard to look severe. 'Although I do not know whether we should allow him such a treat…'

'Mama, you would not stop me riding, would you?' Sam looked horrified. 'Not when I have told you how very sorry I am for making you worry?'

'No, not this time,' she relented, unable to withstand the pleading look in his eyes and her heart still full of relief that he was safe.

She turned to Lawrence. 'He is doing very well. Evans says he has a natural aptitude for riding.'

'I never doubted it.'

After a slight hesitation Rose said, 'You could come to the paddock tomorrow morning and watch him.'

'Better than that,' said Lawrence, 'if it is a fine morning, why do we not go up on the moor?'

'Ooh, yes, sir, if you please!' cried Sam, clapping his hands.

Rose shook her head. 'I do not think…'

'Oh, please, Mama,' Sam beseeched her, his eyes shining. He added, with a flash of inspiration, 'It will be Sir Lawrence's reward, for rescuing us!'

They all laughed at that.

Rose said slowly, 'I *should* like to go riding, I have

not been out for over a week and my poor mare will be growing horribly restive.'

'You have not forgotten we attend the Emsleigh ball tomorrow night?' put in Mrs Molland.

'We shall be back in plenty of time for that,' said Rose, throwing caution to the winds. 'Very well, sir, Sam and I will ride out with you tomorrow!'

The assignation made, Sir Lawrence took his leave, but by the time the maid returned after showing him to the door Rose was having second thoughts about the morning. To ride out with him, even with Sam and Evans in attendance, would be sure to cause comment, and she was certain Magnus would not approve.

'I must catch him,' she muttered, snatching up her shawl. 'I must tell him I have changed my mind.'

Rose rushed out onto the path, but there was no sign of Lawrence, only the black outline of a lone rider clip-clopping up the lane towards her. She was about to make her way back indoors when she heard her name.

'Magnus.' She peered through the darkness at the rider.

'I heard from Wilkins that Samuel had run away so I came to see if there was any news.'

'He is here now, and safe.' She could not prevent herself giving him a wide, relieved smile. Rose waited for him to tie his horse to the gatepost and accompany her inside. 'He walked to Sealham Point with Jem Wooler and they found themselves stranded by the tide. Thankfully Jem's uncle guessed where they would be and rowed out to rescue them.'

'Indeed?'

He followed her into the sitting room. Sam was standing before the fire, concentrating on fastening the last buttons of his clean jacket.

'Well, young man, what do you have to say for yourself?' Sam jumped as Magnus addressed him sternly, but he was given no chance to speak as Magnus pressed on, hands clasped behind his back and glaring down at the little boy. 'You have given your mama a great deal of anxiety. What were you thinking of, to run off without a by your leave, to miss your schooling and take off on such a foolish venture? I am surprised your mother has not spanked you for your disobedience. You would have been well served if you had been left to shiver on the rocks all night!'

Rose had said very much the same thing, but to hear Magnus utter the words roused her in defence of her son. She stepped forwards, as if to shield Sam.

'Thank you, Magnus, he is well aware that he has done wrong and he has already begged my pardon.' She glanced down at her son, noting the mutinous look about his mouth. 'Mama, perhaps you will take Sam away. Janet can find him a little supper and then he should go to bed.' She bent to kiss him, murmuring, 'Run along. I will come up to tuck you in shortly.'

Rose waited until they had left the room and turned back to Magnus, who said heavily, 'You are too soft with the boy, Rose. I would thrash any son of mine who was so disobedient.'

Rose fought down a sharp retort. Instead she said quietly, 'In the main Sam minds me very well. He has had a fright, and that, I think, will do him good.'

'He should be at school.'

'And so he will be, when he is a little older.' She put out her hand. 'Please, Magnus, let us not fight. I have been in such a worry today. You cannot imagine how relieved I was when Sir Lawrence brought Sam back.'

'Oh?' Magnus's brows snapped together. 'What has Daunton to do with this?'

'He was with Abel in the Ship when Maggie Wooler and I called. He rowed across the bay with Abel to collect the boys.'

Magnus stroked his chin.

'I wonder what he was doing with Wooler?'

'I have no idea. All I know is that when he heard Sam was in trouble he offered to help.' Rose clasped her hands tightly together. And they were going riding tomorrow. To cry off would seem very churlish, when he had been such a good friend.

'So Daunton brought the boy back,' Magnus continued. 'Did he mention me, or ask you any questions about me?'

Roes blinked.

'No, why should he?'

'Oh, no reason.' He seemed to shake off his thoughtful mood and reached out for her hands, smiling. 'I am glad little Samuel is returned unharmed, and partly for my own very selfish reasons. If he was hurt, it might have prevented you from coming to the Emsleigh ball tomorrow night.' He squeezed her fingers. 'Are you sure I cannot persuade you to stay at Emsleigh House after? There is no school for you to teach the following day, and you know we have rooms and to spare.'

'Thank you, Magnus, but no. Mama and I will come home, as we agreed.'

'Perhaps it is for the best.' He drew her into his arms. 'If you were to stay under my roof, I might be tempted to pre-empt our wedding night!'

Rose stood passively while his lips met hers, waiting for the tremor of excitement, the unfurling of desire deep in her belly that she had experienced when Lawrence had kissed her, but there was nothing. In fact, she had to steel herself not to pull away. Magnus raised his head, a crease wrinkling his brow at her lack of response.

'I know what it is.' The frowning look vanished, replaced by a kindly smile. 'You are tired and distracted by Samuel's little escapade. I shall leave you to rest then, for I want you in your very best looks tomorrow night!'

Sam was up early the following morning, none the worse for his adventure. Rose was relieved and amused to see him so eager for his riding treat and she allowed him to go off to the stables with Evans to saddle up the horses, promising to join them once she and Mrs Molland had broken their fast. When she did at last reach the stable yard, Rose was surprised to find Lawrence had arrived before her. He was standing in one corner, showing Sam how to make his small hands into very serviceable fists. They looked up as she approached.

'I hope you are not teaching my son any bad habits, Sir Lawrence.'

'On the contrary, I have been showing him how to defend himself.'

Sam's face cleared when he saw that Rose was smiling.

'Sir Lawrence has been teaching me to box, Mama. Extra things to the punches Abel has been showing Jem.'

She raised her brows.

'Goodness, have I been so very long?'

'Not only this morning,' replied Sam in the tone of one explaining something to a simpleton. 'He showed Jem and me some moves the other day, up at the farm.'

Rose was not sure she was pleased to hear that, but Evans brought her mare out at that moment and she decided to let the matter drop.

'I hope you do not object,' said Lawrence, helping her to mount. 'When Sam mentioned to me that some of the bigger boys bully him, I thought it might help.'

Rose's doubts eased a little.

'If it gives him more confidence then I am very happy,' she replied. 'As long as it does not turn *him* into a bully.'

'Very little chance of that.' Lawrence looked across the yard to where Sam was scrambling up into the saddle. 'His manners do you credit.'

He could not have said anything better to Rose. Praise of her son always raised her spirits and she trotted out of the yard, convinced that they would spend a very agreeable morning.

A bright, wintry sun beamed down upon the little party as they rode through the village, Sam proudly putting his pony through its paces with Evans riding beside him.

'Playing chaperon?' queried Lawrence, nodding towards the groom.

'Yes, if you like.' An involuntary smile curved Rose's lips. Indeed, she felt she had not stopped smiling since rising from her bed that morning. This excursion in Sir Lawrence's company was not only a treat for Sam.

They rode up onto the moor. A chill wind was blowing in off the sea, scouring the hills and blowing away any warmth they might have gained from the bright winter sun.

'Bracing,' declared Rose, taking a deep breath.

They trotted along, taking care to keep Sam close, until they reached a stretch of open ground. After a nod from Rose, Sam allowed the little pony to dash off, Evans following closely behind. Lawrence put his hand on Rose's bridle.

'Wait. Let them get ahead of us and we can enjoy a good gallop to catch up.' Rose tightened her grip as her mare snorted and sidled. 'She's eager to go,' observed Lawrence. 'Is she fast?'

'Yes, there's a touch of Arab in her.' She leaned forwards to pat the mare's glossy neck and added wistfully, 'I wish I had more time to ride her. I suppose I should not really keep the horses; they eat into my savings, but riding is my one indulgence.'

'Then why not,' said Lawrence, 'if it means so much to you?'

Rose was going to add that she could only afford to keep the mare because her circumstances would change when she married Magnus, but somehow she did not want to mention that. Instead she laughed and said teasingly, 'You speak as someone who has never had to go without.'

'That is not true. I have gone without a great deal this past year.'

Colour rushed to her cheeks. The serious look in his eyes stirred a fluttering panic in her chest. Swallowing hard, Rose gathered up her reins.

'I think Sam is far enough ahead now—shall we go?'

Thankfully Lawrence said no more, but set his horse to the gallop. Rose was left to follow on and the effort to keep pace with his sleek hunter over the uneven ground took all her concentration. When they caught up with Sam and Evans, Lawrence drew rein and addressed her in such a relaxed, matter-of-fact manner that it was easy for Rose to respond in kind, and to persuade herself that his earlier comments had not been a reference to his alleged reformation of character.

With everyone in good spirits the little party set off again.

'It is like riding on the top of the world,' cried Sam, sitting up in the saddle and gazing across the moor to the wooded hills beyond.

Lawrence laughed. His glance slid to Rose.

'Well, are you glad you came?'

Meeting his eyes, she could not help but return his smile.

'Very glad, thank you.'

'Mama, Evans says that path leads to the mine at Hades Cove.' Sam was pointing towards an overgrown track leading away to a wooded combe. 'Can we ride down there? Please.' He added the last word plaintively after reading a refusal on his mother's face.

Sir Lawrence consulted his watch.

'We *do* have time. And I, too, should like to go down there. We saw the mine when we were rowing back from Sealham Point.'

Rose demurred. 'I cannot think it would be of interest.'

'But, Mama!'

Lawrence put up his hand, saying quietly, 'We shall not go there if your mama objects, Sam.'

'I do not *object*, exactly,' said Rose, 'but there is nothing to see. I have not been there for years, but I believe it is boarded up now and wildly overgrown, with only ruined buildings, spoil heaps and the remains of a few rusted wagons to be seen.'

'I can think of nothing more likely to appeal to a child.'

Lawrence's boyish grin made her chuckle.

'Children of all ages, perhaps! Very well, if you wish to ride down to Hades Cove, let us do so!'

They wound their way down into the combe, leaving behind them the bracken and stunted gorse bushes and plunging into dense woodland, their path carpeted with fallen leaves. At one point the track took them through a wide clearing and they could look down on Mersecombe spread below them, before dropping down into the trees again.

'Someone has been this way recently,' observed

Lawrence, who was following Evans along the narrow track. 'The grass has been trampled down in places.'

'That may have been Magnus; he visited the mine not long ago,' said Rose.

'Is he in the habit of coming here?'

'No, we rode here once, shortly after we met.' She added ruefully, 'I was out of reason cross with him when I learned of this last visit. It was very foolish of me; after all, it will all become his once we are married.'

'Did he say why he had come?'

She waved one hand in a dismissive gesture.

'He believes Hades Mine could still be profitable. I do not. When my husband was alive we paid for the best surveyors and engineers to report, but Magnus thinks he knows better.' She stopped. To air such opinions was disloyal to her future husband. With a faint, apologetic smile she relapsed into silence.

Finally they emerged from the trees and followed the path onto a windswept promontory. Rose brought her horse to a stand.

'Here we are. And, as you can see, it is nothing but a ruin.'

She looked about her sadly. They were on a narrow, grassy shelf of land near the bottom of a steep, wooded combe. Below them was nothing but bare grey rock leading down to an equally grey sea, which tossed and eddied in the narrow cove at the mouth of the combe. The small promontory had once been a hive of industry, but only a few bleak ruins remained. The walls of a small hut were still standing, but its roof and windows had long since disappeared. Spoil heaps were now green mounds and the entrance to the mine shaft was covered by heavy planks. An overgrown track ran down steeply to the cove, where an old jetty was still visible, but near the mine the track ran along the edge of the shelf with a sheer drop to the churning grey sea below. Rose called to Sam to be careful and Evans said gruffly, 'Don't 'ee worry, ma'am, I'll look after him.'

She watched for a moment as her groom followed Sam towards a wooden truck that lay at a drunken angle, one wheel broken off and the rails that had carried it lost beneath the weeds. The only sound was the cry of gulls overhead and the faint rush of the sea.

'A desolate place,' remarked Lawrence, dismounting and coming over to lift her down.

She dropped into his arms, trying not to think of his hands on her waist, the familiar fresh scent of his skin. Her heart thumped so loud and erratically she was sure he must hear it.

'And dangerous,' she said, referring not only to the physical hazards of the area. Flushing, she stepped out of his grasp, struggling to control her wayward thoughts. 'Thankfully it is some distance from all the main byways, and no one comes here. I should never forgive myself if a child should be injured in the mine.'

'Unlikely,' said Lawrence. 'It appears to be well boarded up.' He went across to the opening for a closer inspection. 'Yes, it is remarkably well secured.'

'I am pleased to hear it.'

'You say your husband bought the mine?'

Sir Lawrence came back and proffered his arm. With

only a slight hesitation Rose placed her fingers on his sleeve.

'Harry could never resist a bargain. He thought Hades Mine would bring us wealth beyond our dreams. He won it from a man in Barnstaple. They had been playing at dice and his partner offered Harry the mine in lieu of the money he owed him. Harry was so pleased with himself when he came home with the deeds.'

'You were not so happy?'

Rose did not answer immediately, but at length she said in a low voice, 'I had only recently given birth to Sam; I knew very little about mines, but I thought it odd that a man should part with something supposedly worth a fortune for a gambling debt of a hundred pounds.' She turned her frank gaze upon him. 'What would you do if someone offered you such an exchange?'

'That depends upon who was offering it.'

'A fool, a spendthrift…almost as big a wastrel as my husband—I beg your pardon.' She began to hunt for her handkerchief. 'I should not have spoken so. I should be over this by now.'

Lawrence took her shoulders and turned her to him. Cupping her face in his hands, he smoothed his thumbs gently over her cheeks to wipe away the tears.

'You are angry and rightly so. From the little I have learned—not from you, you have been very discreet, but to be left thus, with a young son to raise—it must be very hard for you.'

'It is.' She moved away from him and finished wiping her eyes. 'I only want what is best for Sam.'

'And you think marrying Magnus Emsleigh is the best you can do?'

'He is a good man and will provide Sam with the father he needs.'

His blue eyes were fixed on her face, holding her gaze. Rose's pulse quickened; she felt again the strength of the bond between them. It was much more than the hot, urgent desire stirring inside her: it was a sense of meeting a kindred spirit, someone to share her hopes, her fears—someone to laugh with. If it were not for Sam, would she take a chance and throw in her lot with Sir Lawrence Daunton? Would she give in to the temptation to enjoy his company and his lovemaking, until some other woman caught his attention? All this ran through her mind in the space of a moment, swiftly followed by the memory of the pain she had suffered with her husband. Not merely physical, that had been minor compared to the torture of knowing she was no longer first in his affections. Even in her company his mind had been elsewhere, longing to be back with the laughing beauties who would pander to his every whim and not burden him with the day-to-day responsibilities of looking after his family. That had been bad enough, but she was shocked now to find that the affection she had felt for her husband was nothing to the love she felt for the man now standing before her.

Lawrence watched the play of emotion crossing Rose's face. He guessed something of her confusion and was tempted to tell her his suspicions about Magnus Emsleigh, but he knew how it would sound. She would think it merely the accusations of a jealous rival. She still did not trust him. A shudder ran through her and she stepped away from him, dropping the lashes to veil her thoughts.

Stifling a sigh, he let her go; it seemed a year of living blamelessly was not enough to convince her that he was in earnest. She pulled up the collar of her riding jacket.

'It grows colder. I do not want to keep Sam out in this wind for too long.'

Confidences were at an end. Accepting that, Lawrence nodded.

'Very well. Stay here with the horses while I persuade Master Sam we have to go back. It may not be easy; he has found an exciting world to explore.'

He was rewarded with a faint smile; until he could prove that it was Emsleigh who was not the fit-and-proper person he appeared to be, Lawrence realised he would have to content himself with that.

Rose and Sam returned from their outing much refreshed, but although Sam was eager to recount everything to his grandmother, Rose was more reticent. She had seen the speculative look in her mother's eye when she had announced she was going riding with Sir Lawrence; she would not add to the conjecture by admitting how much she had enjoyed herself, and instead turned her mother's thoughts to what they should wear to Emsleigh House that evening.

As she made her preparations for the ball, Rose was increasingly thankful that she had refused to allow

Magnus to send his carriage for them. She did not want to be under any more of an obligation to him and since her ride out that morning this feeling had intensified. On the journey back from the mine she and Lawrence had talked only of commonplace subjects, but she had rarely enjoyed herself more, and it was not until he had taken his leave of her that she realised she had never thanked him properly for bringing Sam back from Sealham Point. She considered writing to him, then decided she would seek him out at the ball that evening. The little surge of pleasure she experienced at the thought gave her pause, and she began to question whether she could really marry Magnus, knowing she could never love him. If not, then she must tell him, and soon. And she thought it would be easier to make a decision if she was not enjoying the comfort of his elegant chaise.

In the end they were taken up by Farmer Finch and his wife in their ancient but stately carriage. The good-natured farmer and his lady were very vocal in their excitement at being invited to Emsleigh for the Winter Ball.

'Very good of Emsleigh, it is,' pronounced Mr Finch in his lazy, rolling drawl. 'Once a year he invites all his neighbours to Emsleigh House to eat, drink, dance and be merry until the morning!'

'Aye,' chuckled his wife. 'Not at all high in the instep is Mr Emsleigh, for all his money. And he dresses as fine as any London beau, don't you agree, Mrs Westerhill?' She gave Rose a playful dig in the ribs. 'He'll make you a fine husband, my dear, you mark my words. And don't you go putting him off for another year, else you might find some other lady will come along and snabble him up.'

'Just what I have been telling Rose myself, ma'am,' agreed Mrs Molland. 'She needs to make up her mind and stick to it.'

Rose peered through the darkness, trying to see her mother's expression. The words were more than a casual remark, she was sure. Mrs Molland had never tried to influence Rose about her marriage, saying that she would be happy to have her daughter and grandson live with her for ever, but now Rose wondered if Mama was anxious to see her settled.

'Aye, and then p'raps you'll set yourself to finding a husband for that sister of his,' put in Mr Finch. 'Not that *that* will be so easy, since she thinks herself so far above her company.' He laughed. 'Lord, but this ball must be a sad trial for her, poor woman. She'll be worrying all evening that one of her brother's clodhopping guests will walk mud onto their carpets!'

They laughed at this, but Rose could not be comfortable at talking in such a way of Althea, even though she might share their opinions. She was relieved when her mother neatly turned the subject, asking Mrs Finch about the health of her latest grandchild, and they finished the journey listening to the harrowing story of little Jacob's continuing bouts of croup.

At Emsleigh House Rose and her mother alighted and followed the Finches into the hall, which was already crowded with laughing, chattering guests. They made their way up the wide curving stairs to the first landing, where the partition doors between the two reception rooms had been folded back to make one huge ballroom heated by roaring fires in the two hearths and hundreds of candles burning in the glittering chandeliers. Althea came up to greet them.

'So glad you are come,' she said, laying her hand on Rose's arm. 'You are amongst the very few people here that I can bear to talk to!' She leaned closer. 'I really do not know why Magnus insists upon inviting so many *common* people—even his tenants!'

'But it has always been the custom for the foremost landowner in the area to hold the Winter Ball,' explained Mrs Molland. 'And who should do it, if not Mr Emsleigh?'

'Well, there is *that*,' agreed Althea, somewhat mollified, 'but why should we have them all in the house—could he not hold a dance in the barn?'

'That would avoid having clodhopping farmers in your house,' murmured Rose, sharing a mischievous look with her mother.

'Yes, it would,' agreed Althea. 'But there it is; Magnus wishes to be thought generous.' She added, brightening. 'At least we have more gentlemen here this year, including Captain Morris, who has just arrived.' She dropped her voice. 'He was captain of the *Sealark* on her last journey, you know, but such good manners, no one would think him a sailor!'

Althea tripped away as more guests arrived, leaving Mrs Molland to shake her head after her. Rose soon spotted Lawrence talking with a group of gentlemen in one far corner. She wanted to go immediately to speak to him, but the music started and Magnus came to claim her hand for the first dance.

No matter, she told herself. *Before the night is out I will thank him for rescuing Sam.*

And I will tell him I misjudged him.

Rose blinked. That had not been her original intention at all, but suddenly it was important to set things right with Lawrence.

The ball was noisy but good-natured. Magnus strutted around the room full of cheerful goodwill, reminding Rose of a genial monarch with his subjects. Althea was more regal, but less genial, except when she stood up to dance with Lawrence. Then she was all smiles. Rose tried not to allow her eyes to follow them around the room. Her body was still singing from the morning ride. During the day she had relived every look, every word they had shared. She felt so alive, her skin tingling with the anticipation of being close to Lawrence again. However, as the evening wore on it became clear that Lawrence was not going to ask her to dance with him.

It is your own fault, she chided herself. *You asked him to leave you alone and that is what he is doing.*

Her spirits were dampened, but she was not wholly downcast. She herself did not lack partners and was content to bide her time until she could find the opportunity to speak to Lawrence. She was reluctant to approach with so many people around him, especially Althea, who was constantly at his side. Rose watched them dancing together and when the music ended he relinquished her hand to Captain Morris, one of the few gentlemen present that Althea thought sufficiently elevated to partner her. The two men exchanged a few words, then Lawrence bowed and moved towards the door.

Rose saw her chance. She casually walked into the card room and out again by another door that led onto the landing. As she had hoped, Lawrence was outside the supper room, talking to Mr Ansell. They broke off their conversation as Rose approached. She greeted them with a shy smile and turned to Lawrence. She was a little nervous now the moment had come—what if he should reject her?

'Sir Lawrence, I wonder if I might have a word with you?'

'Aye, take him, ma'am,' exclaimed Mr Ansell with a jovial laugh. 'I've just offered to buy his hunter and been refused, so I want nothing more to do with him. He is all yours, Mrs Westerhill!'

Lawrence smiled, but she detected a wary reserve in his eyes. She ran her tongue over her dry lips.

'Sir Lawrence, I wanted to say—'

A group of laughing young people came hurtling out of the supper room and Rose broke off. Sir Lawrence caught her arm and pulled her back out of the way.

'Perhaps we should find somewhere we may talk undisturbed.'

Rose nodded and led him away from the ballroom to an unlit corridor.

'The library is at the end of this passage, we will go there,' she murmured, blushing at her own temerity. She was glad he did not tease her. Instead he placed a hand beneath her elbow to guide her through the darkness. When they reached the library door she paused for a moment, listening. Reassured by the silence, she turned the handle.

The library was still and silent, illuminated only by the pale light of a rising moon that shone in through the long, unshuttered windows. Rose slipped inside and Lawrence followed, softly closing the door behind him. She heard the click as he turned the key in the lock.

'There. Now we can be sure we will not be disturbed.'

What now? As they had progressed along the dark corridor, moving further from the noisy ballroom, Rose had been aware of a nervous excitement growing within her. Lawrence's hand on her arm had been warm, possessive. The heated blood pulsed around her body, heightening her senses. Alone with him in the darkness, all her wayward mind could think of was making love to him. That had not been her intention in bringing him here, but she acknowledged that she wanted him, with every fibre of her being. She remembered being here with him once before. Then he had pulled her into his arms. Now she wanted him to do the same, but instead he remained out of arms' reach, a still and silent shadow. With an effort she dragged her mind back to the original purpose of the meeting.

'I—I wanted to thank you.' Rose swallowed, trying to clear the nervous constriction in her throat. 'For rescuing Sam.'

Her voice sounded abnormally loud in the heavy silence. She moved away, hoping that by putting some distance between herself and Lawrence she could control her unruly desire. She heard Lawrence's voice behind her, deep and resonant in the darkness.

'It is Abel Wooler who deserves your thanks. He knew where to find the boys and had the experience to row out to Sealham Point.'

She nodded. She had reached the desk and she stood before it, staring out of the window at the moonlit gardens.

'I realise that and spoke to him this afternoon. He knows how grateful I am. You l-left last night before I could thank you and this morning...' she faltered '... this morning I was very remiss in not telling you how much I am in your debt.' She clasped her hands together, determined to finish her confession. 'I—I wanted to say I may have been wrong. A-about you...'

Her heart was thudding so hard it was difficult to talk and her nerves were stretched to breaking. She heard no sound, but something made her turn around. Lawrence had come up behind her. He was standing so close she had to look up to see his face, but the shadows were too deep for her to read his expression. They were only inches apart and the sheer force of his presence enveloped her. Silence lay heavy around them; they were cocooned in their own little world.

Rose remained perfectly still. She knew she had reached some momentous point in her life: one false move, one wrong word, could mean disaster.

'You do not know how long I have wanted to hear you say that.'

The words were so soft that at first she thought she had imagined them. Lawrence reached out and ran the backs of his fingers over her cheek. She closed her eyes and leaned her head against his hand.

'You do not know how much I want it to be true.'

His fingers stroked across her chin and slipped around her neck. Obedient to the gentle pressure of his hand, she took the little step necessary to cover the distance between them, lifting her head for his kiss. The first touch of his lips was as gentle as a whisper, but it fanned the flames of the desire she had kept buried for so long. With a little cry Rose threw her arms around his neck, kissing him with a burning passion that was beyond all rational thought. He responded immediately. His arms tightened about her, lifting her off the floor as her mouth yielded to the demands of his kiss, their tongues tangling and exploring. She felt the hard edge of the desk behind her knees and Lawrence pushed her gently back onto its smooth surface. Aching desire pounded through her body, heating her blood, heightening all her senses. She arched against him as he trailed kisses down her neck and across the soft swell of her breasts, her skin burning wherever his lips touched it. Lawrence was leaning over her, pressing her down on the desk, his mouth seeking hers again for another bruising kiss. He gathered up her skirts and she felt his fingers on her thighs. Obedient to the pressure of his hands, she twined her legs about him, gasping as those wickedly long fingers played havoc with her senses, touching and caressing her until she was aching from the sweet torture he was inflicting. He continued to play her while his free hand opened the flap of his breeches. Excited anticipation ripped through her when she

felt his flesh hard upon her own. She pushed against
him, exultant, as he entered her. They moved together,
harder, faster, until Rose lost control of her body while
he worshipped her with his. She bucked and trembled
as they shared a shattering climax, clinging tightly to
Lawrence until the last, ecstatic spasm had finished and
they were left gasping and exhausted.

Lawrence relaxed against her, but Rose held him
close, savouring the wondrous, other-worldliness of
their union. She was unwilling for it to end, reluctant
to make the transition from carefree paradise to the real-
ity of their situation. At length he eased himself away
and Rose sat up. She reached for him, pulling him back
so she could lean against his chest, feeling the thud of
his heart against her cheek. After a few minutes she
raised her head and turned to look out of the window.

'Rose? What is it, love?' He caught her face in his
hands and she heard the concern in his voice.

'I would like to slip away from here now, just you
and me.'

A gentle laugh rumbled in his chest.

'If we were not on the first floor we could climb out
of the window and run off, but there is no help for it, we
must go back to the ballroom. And I fear we must do so
very soon.' He stepped away from her and straightened
his clothing while Rose did the same, silently marvelling at the strength of passion that had overwhelmed
them. This total loss of control had shaken her to her
core. Never before had she felt so vulnerable: she had
bared her soul and put herself completely at the mercy
of one man. She needed to be alone, to examine her

feelings and make sense of them. Her thoughts were still in turmoil and it was an effort to think rationally.

'I am not sure I can go back,' she whispered. 'Everyone will know...'

'I promise you they will not.' He pulled her to her feet and held her hand as they crossed to the door. Cautiously he looked out into the darkness beyond. 'Come, there is no one in sight.'

They slipped out of the library and made their way back towards the public rooms. Rose held Lawrence's hand, drawing comfort from those warm fingers wrapped around hers. She needed to think over what had happened to her in the library, to discuss it with Lawrence, but it was not possible, not yet. She must keep her new-found happiness hidden until she had found a way to explain everything to Magnus. Thoughts and emotions continued to crowd in upon her she walked beside Lawrence. They had almost reached the lighted corridor leading to the ballroom when Rose spoke again.

'Do I look very dishevelled?'

'Not in the least. You look adorable.'

The glow in his eyes made her blush all over again, but she tried to ignore it and shook out her skirts before taking his arm to walk out into the light. They passed several couples making their way to the supper room and Rose was amazed that they did not stop to stare at her. She felt that she was somehow transformed into a completely different person. She stole a peep up at Lawrence. He looked perfectly at ease, although she thought his smile looked a little brighter and there was a definite glow in his eyes when he caught her glance.

'You must tell Emsleigh you cannot marry him,' he murmured as they reached the ballroom.

'Yes, but not tonight.'

'Of course not. We have much to talk about. I will call tomorrow.'

He squeezed her arm and Rose's heart gave a little flip of nervous excitement. Explaining to Magnus that she could not marry him would be painful, but once it was done she would be free…

'So there you are, Sir Lawrence!' Althea's high voice intruded. 'I have been looking everywhere for you, sir. I was hoping you would partner me for the next dance.'

'Alas, Miss Emsleigh, I cannot do that.'

She looked from Lawrence to Rose, whose new-found happiness was shining in her eyes.

'Have you been flirting with Mrs Westerhill?'

'I would never flirt with her.'

The warm smile he bestowed upon Rose was not lost on Althea, whose eyes now positively flashed.

'You have paid her far too much attention tonight.'

Lawrence shook his head.

'No, Miss Emsleigh, I—' He broke off as Magnus came up.

'Daunton, unhand my fiancée, if you please.' His curt, cold tone brought a guilty flush to Rose's cheeks. Had he guessed where they had been, what had occurred? She felt so changed, so altered, it seemed impossible that Magnus should not notice it. He ignored her and continued to stare at Lawrence, unsmiling.

'Captain Morris tells me you have been making enquiries about the *Sealark*.'

Lawrence made no move, his expression did not change, but he grew very still. Rose's initial relief was replaced by consternation. She did not understand the sudden tension that surrounded them. The air was thick with danger.

'Yes,' Lawrence said coolly, 'I spoke to him about it.'

'You are an agent for the insurers.'

Rose laughed.

'That is absurd, Magnus—'

'Yes, I am.'

Lawrence's answer cut across hers and at the same time he gently removed her hand from his arm. He was distancing himself from her and Rose did not know why.

Magnus drew himself up, eyes narrowing.

'You have inveigled your way into my house to spy on me!'

'By no means,' replied Lawrence evenly. 'You will recall that you invited *me*. Although I admit I am guilty of not telling you why I had come to Knightscote.'

Magnus glared at him. 'And have you discovered anything amiss, sir?'

There was a pause no longer than a heartbeat before Lawrence answered.

'No, I have not. As yet.'

'And nor will you. So you may go back to your masters and tell them to pay me what is owed! And you will leave my house. This instant.'

'No!' cried Althea. 'Magnus, no harm has been done; he has found nothing to incriminate you. You cannot throw him out.'

Lawrence inclined his head.

'Perhaps it is best that I leave now.' He held out his hand to Rose, but Althea grabbed his sleeve.

'I will not let you go. You must stay!'

'Miss Emsleigh, please,' said Lawrence gently, 'this is not wise.'

He tried to remove her fingers from his coat, but she only clung tighter.

'No, you shall not walk out on me.'

'I'm afraid I must.'

'No! You cannot!' Her voice rose hysterically. 'I am carrying your child!'

Until that moment Rose had not been aware of the chatter around them, but she noticed immediately when it stopped, replaced by a shocked silence. Lawrence looked stunned.

'That is impossible,' he said quietly.

'What is this, Althea?' Magnus turned to his sister. 'What are you saying?'

'The first night we met, at the Pullens' ball. I w-was flattered by his attentions, s-swept away…' She was crying now, her hands twisting together. 'I allowed him to take me outside for a little air and…'

Lawrence shook his head. He disengaged himself and stepped away from her.

'You are mistaken, madam.'

Althea put up her chin.

'I will force you to marry me,' she said triumphantly. 'I will not let you abandon me!'

Magnus put his arm about her shoulders.

'Impossible. That such a man should be my brother—! No, no, my dear; were he as rich as Croesus I could not allow that.' He lifted a hand and summoned his footmen. 'You, sir, will leave my house immediately. And you will have nothing more to do with my sister.'

'I cannot leave with such a slur hanging over me!'

'A slur? Dear God, as if anyone would doubt it is true. You are well known for your rakish ways, sir, get out of my house.'

'No, Magnus!' Althea grabbed his coat. 'That is not what I want!'

Magnus patted her arm.

'You have nothing to fear, my dear, but whatever the shame, I will not allow you to marry this villain.'

Tight jawed, Lawrence shook his head.

'Rose, do not believe this. I swear I have not laid a hand on her or any woman since I met you.'

She tried to make herself think, but the high, joyous singing that had been resonating through her since they had come back into the ballroom was changed to an anguished scream inside her head. Hot tears burned her eyes, but she was too proud to let them fall. When Lawrence reached out for her, she backed away.

'Rose—it's a lie, I tell you!'

'Do not listen to him,' Magnus urged her. 'He is a libertine, a rogue, not to be trusted.' He raised his voice to address his servants. 'Escort Sir Lawrence from the premises.'

Lawrence gave a snarl of warning and the lackeys stopped, hovering uncertainly at his shoulder.

'Should you not be calling me out, Emsleigh? We could settle this at dawn with swords or pistols, whatever you chose.'

'Yes, that is the way of your sort, is it not?' Magnus curled his lip. 'That may be the custom in town, sir, but not here! Your name is disgraced here, sir, disgraced. You should quit Exmoor.'

'Not until I have proved you deliberately sank the *Sealark* to claim the insurance.'

Magnus laughed.

'Do you think anyone will help you after this? Captain Morris, assist my men to eject this, this *scoundrel*!'

Rose watched, transfixed, as the captain stepped up. Lawrence stiffened, his hands clenching into fists.

'Come, sir,' barked the captain, 'you cannot start a brawl in a gentleman's house.'

Lawrence hesitated, then turned to look at Rose. He was very pale and a muscle was working his cheek.

'Rose,' he said urgently, 'we must talk. You must let me explain—'

With a shudder she fluttered her hand in a small gesture of dismissal. Nothing made sense. The evening had taken on a nightmarish quality. She felt used, betrayed. The servants and Captain Morris stepped closer to Lawrence, but he put up his hand.

'Very well, I will leave—for now.' With a final, blazing look at Rose he turned on his heel and strode out of the ballroom, the crowd hastily stepping back to clear a path to the door.

'Rose?'

Her mother's gentle hand was upon her arm. Magnus was escorting his sobbing sister from the room and Rose was aware of the eyes of the crowd turning upon her. Pride came to her aid. Her chin went up. Lawrence had gone and she wanted to throw herself into the soft, comforting warmth of her mother's embrace, but that must wait. She summoned every ounce of will to force out a few quiet words.

'Take me home, Mama.'

Chapter Eight

Rose lay in her bed and watched the pinky-grey light of dawn creep into her tiny room. She had slept very little and cried even less, the pain in her heart too deep for tears. All night she had replayed the scene at Emsleigh House, trying to find some crumb of comfort, but there was none. Lawrence had not come to Knightscote for her sake; he had been investigating the sinking of the *Sealark*.

It did not explain his kindness to Sam, unless he thought to ingratiate himself with her and provide himself with a little amusement while he carried out his enquiries. If so, it had worked only too well; Rose had abandoned caution and thrown herself into his arms, prepared to count the world well lost. And it was. Her recklessness at Emsleigh House had cost her dear.

Her conscience had troubled her after those precious, snowbound days at Knightscote, but she had salved it by telling herself it had been an aberration caused by the exceptional circumstances. A chance meeting, a moment's happiness before they went their separate ways, never to meet again. Even so she had postponed her wedding for twelve months, unable to face marriage to another man while Lawrence's image was so fresh in her mind. Now she knew she could never marry Magnus Emsleigh, because despite her best intentions, for the second time in her life she had lost her heart to a rake—and how quickly, how cruelly she had been disillusioned.

Althea's outburst had been shocking and it *must* be true; Rose knew only too well Lawrence's impetuous nature—had he not accosted her outside the Ship after the Mersecombe Assembly? To say nothing of their passionate union last night. She had given herself to him, freely, lovingly, and she had been so sure he loved her in return, but she knew now that could not be true. With a groan she turned over and buried her face in her pillow. While her mind might dismiss Sir Lawrence Daunton as a rake and a libertine, her body still ached at the memory of his caresses. She did not know how she would survive without them.

But of course she would survive. She had Sam to think of, and her mother. She must go on, for their sake. Thus, when Janet brought her hot water, Rose dragged herself from her bed and forced herself into her clothes.

Her mother and Sam were already at the breakfast table, and Rose was thankful that, apart from subjecting her to a searching look, Mrs Molland made no mention of the events at Emsleigh House. After the morning pleasantries had been exchanged, Mrs Molland said brightly, 'Evans has hired the gig from Farmer Ansell and is driving me to Minehead today; there are several purchases I must make. Perhaps, Rose, you would like to come with me? You need do nothing but enjoy yourself—it would be purely a pleasure trip for you.'

Pleasure? Rose thought she would never know pleasure again. She shook her head.

'Thank you, Mama, but no. Mrs Reed has asked me to write down my observations upon how the school should be run. However, since there are no classes today, perhaps Sam might like to go with you...'

'No, no, Mama.' This was accompanied by a vigorous shaking of the head. 'You cannot have forgotten that once I have done my chores I am going to Woolers Farm to see Jem.'

Rose looked out of the window; there had been a light snowfall during the night, dusting everything with white, and the walls and roofs sparkled invitingly in the winter sunshine. A brisk walk might clear her head and help to shift the depression that enveloped her.

'Perhaps I shall come with you. I can postpone my writing for an hour or so.'

'An excellent idea,' agreed Mrs Molland. 'It is too lovely a day to stay indoors. And you can take with you the little note I have written for old Mrs Wooler. She suffers dreadfully in the winter months and I promised I would let her have the recipe for a tonic.' She rose from her chair as a movement outside the window caught her

eye. 'Here is Evans now with the gig. Be good for your
mama, Sam, and I shall bring you back a little present.
Rose, is there anything I can get you?'

'Nothing, thank you, but I will walk with you to the
gate and see you off.'

The two women went arm in arm out of the room
and as they walked to the gig Mrs Molland cleared her
throat.

'If you are writing up notes for Mrs Reed, does that
mean you still intend to marry Magnus?' Her grip on
Rose's arm tightened. 'You have no need to tell me that
your affections are not engaged. Indeed, after last night
I should think everyone—'

'Mama!'

She heeded the warning note in Rose's voice and
said merely, 'So, are you going to cry off?'

'I think I must.' Rose bit her lip. 'Was…was it very
apparent that—that Sir Lawrence and I had…formed
an attachment?'

'Crystal clear,' replied Mrs Molland frankly. 'The
only comfort is that his treatment of Althea Emsleigh
has proved him to be a complete rogue and everyone
will regard you with sympathy.'

Rose winced. Her mother patted her arm.

'You do not have to decide about your marriage
immediately. When he took his leave of us last night,
Magnus was most attentive. I do not believe he wishes
to end your engagement. You must consider Sam's
future as well, you know.'

'I do know it,' replied Rose, sighing. 'But whatever
Magnus and I decide, I cannot continue at the school. I

shall send a note to Mrs Reed today, explaining that I shall not be taking any more classes. Perhaps it would be best if I left Mersecombe.'

They had reached the gate and stopped for a moment.

'Consider carefully, my dear,' murmured Mrs Molland. 'You have many years ahead of you.'

Giving Rose a quick hug, she climbed up into the gig and Evans set off down the lane at a smart pace. Rose watched them go. The dark cloud descended even deeper into her soul. She wanted to do nothing except return to her bed, but that was impossible. She must find something to occupy her.

Indoors, Sam was helping Janet to clear the breakfast table, after which he would fill up the log basket in the sitting room. Small tasks, but Rose had insisted that he help out a little in the house and, since becoming friends with Jem and seeing how hard he had to work on the farm, Sam was keen to show that he, too, had a role to play.

Knowing it would be some little while yet before Sam was ready to go out, Rose carried her pens and paper to the little table in the sitting room. She must write letters to the vicar and to Mrs Reed, explaining that she would no longer be teaching at the school. After that, if there was time, she would make a start upon her notes. The letters were quickly dashed off, but when she pulled a clean sheet of paper towards her to write her notes the words would not come. Her mind kept wandering back to the ball.

She felt quite sick when she thought of Lawrence's betrayal—to be investigating Magnus was bad enough, but even that she could have borne, if he had not lied to her about Althea. She had begun to believe that he really had altered, that he was not the libertine she had thought him. Althea's announcement had shown her that her initial conviction had been true. A rake could not change his nature.

The faint sound of knocking at the front door brought her out of her reverie. A familiar deep voice sounded from the hall. With growing dismay she recognised the swift, booted tread outside the door. How foolish of her not to instruct Janet to deny him. Now it was too late to do anything other than rise from the table and school her features into a look of stony indifference.

Lawrence entered the little parlour and stopped just inside the door. The coldness of his reception was almost physical. It hit him like a blast of icy air. Rose stood on the opposite side of the room, rigidly aloof.

'I had to come,' he began. 'We need to talk—'

'There is nothing to be said. Please leave.' Her cold stare was fixed somewhere over his shoulder, her voice as hard as stone. He took a step towards her.

'Rose, please listen to me, I can expl—'

'Oh?' She curled her lip, the words dripping from her tongue like icy water. 'Will you deny that you came here to spy upon us?'

'Not upon you—never upon you!'

She continued as if he had not spoken.

'You sought to put the blame for the loss of the *Sealark* upon Magnus.'

'I did not *seek* to put the blame upon anyone. I merely came here looking for the truth.'

'You have the…the *gall* to talk of truth!'

'I never deceived you!'

'You deceived us all! If I had known you suspected Magnus—'

'You would never have let me near you,' he finished for her.

'What a blessing that would have been!'

'Not for me. I have been living for the moment I would see you again.'

'Do not say that!' She dashed a hand across her eyes. 'I will hear no more of your lies.'

'I have never lied to you, Rose.' He stopped and shook his head. He said slowly, 'Perhaps I did lie, by omission. But if you had asked me, I would have told you I was investigating the *Sealark*.' Lawrence moved a little closer. 'That was not my only reason for coming to Mersecombe.'

'Oh, of course. You wanted a pointer puppy.'

He smiled slightly.

'Puppy be damned. I wanted to see you.'

She ignored that.

'And was Althea Emsleigh one of your *lies by omission*?'

The smile disappeared. He said quietly, 'That is not *my* lie. I have danced with Althea Emsleigh, but nothing more, I give you my word.'

She threw up her hand.

'Do not perjure yourself any further. I wish you would go now.'

She glared at him, full of righteous indignation. She was less than two strides away—Lawrence wanted to cross the space between them and take her in his arms, melting her icy rage with a passionate kiss. But something held him back, a thread as fine as silk, yet stronger than any chain: the fear that she would reject him.

Her eyes were dark and hard as slate, but he read in their depths such pain and rage that it cut like a knife. Unbidden, words rose to his lips. He said simply, 'I love you, Rose.'

She glared at him.

'How dare you talk to me of love?' Her voice shook with fury. 'I w-was silly enough to think— What a *fool* I have been!' She took a long, ragged breath, then said coldly, 'Enough of this. You will go now and never come here again.'

She fixed him with a look of such implacable loathing that further argument died on his lips.

'Very well,' he said at last, 'I will leave now, but whatever you think of me, Rose, you must not marry Emsleigh.'

'What we did last night has made it impossible for me to do so!' she flashed. Her spirits sagged. 'I have proved myself as false as you. I am ashamed.'

'You should not be. We cannot help our feelings for each other, Rose.'

'But what of Magnus? He deserves better—'

'No. He is not the upright gentleman he seems. He sank the *Sealark*—I have a witness who is prepared to tell the truth about that—'

Rose put her hands to her ears. 'Stop it! I will not listen to this. If *you* will not go away, then *I* shall—'

She went to run past him, but he grabbed her arm.

'You will listen to me, madam, or by God I will—'

'You will what?' She confronted him, brows raised, eyes stormy, challenging. 'You will beat me into sub-mission? It would not be the first time I have suffered a man's blows.'

She had not meant to say that—Rose had never admitted it to anyone before and she berated herself as she saw the shock in his face.

'I am not such a monster.' The angry light faded from his eyes and she looked away, unwilling to bear his sympathy. 'Rose—'

'Sir Lawrence, Sir Lawrence, I saw your horse out-side...'

They jumped apart as Sam burst into the room, his innocent face glowing with delight. He skidded to a halt before Lawrence, snatched off his cap and sketched a bow.

'Good day to you, sir. Mama and I are about walk to Woolers Farm—would you like to go with us?'

'Sam, you should not—'

Rose tried to protest, but she was shaking too much to do more than murmur her remonstrance. Lawrence was faster to regain control.

'Alas, Sam, I am bound in the opposite direction.'

Rose said pointedly, 'Sir Lawrence is just leaving.'

Sam's face fell and Lawrence added quickly, 'My business may take some time. I should go now if I am to get back to Knightscote before dark.'

'Is that why you have a lantern strapped to your saddle, so you can find your way home?' asked Sam, wide-eyed.

Lawrence managed a smile and reached out to ruffle the boy's hair.

'No, you scapegrace, I am going exploring.'

'Oh, and what are you going to look for?' exclaimed Sam. 'Gold? Treasure?'

Lawrence's eyes flickered briefly to Rose.

'Something like that.'

'Can I come with you?'

'Not this time. Besides, your friend Jem will be waiting for you.'

'Indeed he will,' put in Rose. 'We must be going, too. Bid Sir Lawrence goodbye now.'

While Sam made his bow she forced herself to look at Lawrence, trying to memorise every detail of his face, while at the same time silently vowing never to see him again. He turned to take his leave of her, the unsmiling look in his eyes making it very plain he understood her thoughts. He made no attempt to take her hand.

'Goodbye, madam. I wish you well, now and always.'

She could not trust her voice to reply and merely inclined her head, jaw clenched, lips firmly pressed together. Lawrence turned on his heel and walked out. The click of the door closing behind him echoed around the room with a sad finality.

'Mama? What did Sir Lawrence mean? Is he going away?'

'Yes, Sam, he is.'

'But he will not be gone for long, will he? We will see him again...'

'Heavens, is that the time? Poor Jem will think you

have deserted him. Come along, Sam, put on your cap while I fetch my bonnet.'

With forced lightness Rose continued to chatter until she had hustled Sam out of the house, then she hurried him along the road at such a speed that he had no breath left to ask more awkward questions.

They had dropped the letters for Mrs Reed and Mr Wilkins at the vicarage and were hurrying along the high street when Magnus drove up.

'Good morning.' He stopped beside them. 'I have just called at your house and your maid told me where you are headed. Perhaps you will allow me to take you up?' He added, as she hesitated, 'There is room for three; neither you nor Samuel will take up much space.'

Rose would have preferred to continue walking, but as she could think of no excuse that would not require lengthy explanation, she merely uttered a quiet assent. She urged Sam to scramble up first and quickly climbed up after him. Magnus gave a little flick of his whip and the carriage pulled away.

'How is your sister?' asked Rose.

'Distraught, naturally, but I cannot wholly forgive her. To make such an announcement, when all the world was there to hear her. Pure folly!'

'Magnus!'

'I am aware I sound harsh and unfeeling, Rose, but however upset she may have been, I cannot condone such a lack of control. I shall send her away, of course— she has an aunt in the north country who will take care of her, but the damage is done: it cannot be hushed up now.'

Rose gripped her hands together so hard they shook.

'Are there no thoughts of…of marriage?'

'Out of the question. I cannot have my sister wed to a man who has shown himself so much my enemy.' He was silent for a moment. 'He tried to turn you against me, too.' She felt his eyes resting on her, but kept her own gaze lowered. He said quietly, 'I fear he insinuated himself into your affections.'

'Magnus, I—'

'Please, Rose, before you say anything more, let me assure you that despite the unfortunate events of last evening, I have not changed my mind: I still wish to make you my wife.'

Rose glanced down at Sam.

'Perhaps this is not the time…'

'Perhaps not, but I must take the opportunity while I can. We are so rarely alone.'

'We have been busy…'

'Not so busy that you could not go riding with Daunton yesterday morning. Oh, yes, my dear, I heard all about that.'

Rose flushed, but before she could respond Sam piped up, 'Sir Lawrence wanted to see how well I can ride his pony!'

'*His* pony?' Magnus raised his brows.

'It is on loan,' she said quickly. 'A gift for his godson. I am merely looking after it for a short while. It was a business arrangement.'

'And you believe that? You are far too trusting, Rose,'

said Magnus heavily. 'I am glad you now know him for the scoundrel he really is.'

'I do,' she said bitterly. 'And can only be ashamed that I allowed myself to be so taken in.'

Sam's head came up.

'Sir Lawrence is not a scoundrel!'

'Hush, Sam.'

'But he's not—'

'That is enough, Samuel,' said Magnus sharply. 'Really, Rose, it is time your son learned his manners.'

'I beg your pardon, Magnus, but—'

'The management of the boy is obviously too much for you. Samuel has been without a father for too long, and you allowing him to be in the company of a villain like Daunton can only make matters worse. Once we are married I shall soon teach him—'

'Sir Lawrence says Mama should not marry you,' exclaimed Sam, enraged by the criticism of his mother and his friend.

'Samuel, that is *enough*!' Rose put her hand on Sam's shoulder. 'One more word and I shall ask Mr Emsleigh to put us down here and I will take you home.' It was an empty threat, for they were already driving through the gate of Woolers Farm, but Sam firmly closed his lips, frowning with the effort to remain quiet. Magnus brought the carriage to a stand in the yard and a young farmhand came out from one of the barns and ran to the horses' heads. Rose waited for Magnus to come around and hand her down.

'Give my regards to your sister.' She smiled at him,

trying to distract him from her son's incivility. 'I shall call upon her shortly.'

'You are very kind.' He raised his eyes to regard Sam, who was scrambling down from the carriage, and after a visible struggle he shook his head. 'I know he is your son, Rose, and your only link with your late beloved husband, but you are far too lenient with the boy. He should be at school, not mixing with the likes of Daunton—'

His words were very quiet, but Sam had excellent hearing. He turned and glared at Magnus.

'Sir Lawrence is my *friend*,' he said pugnaciously. 'He rescued Jem and me from Sealham Point.'

Magnus scowled.

'You will learn nothing from him but bad habits.'

'That is not true. *You* do not like him, but Mama does. He makes her laugh.'

'Sam!'

'It is true, Mama. When we went riding yesterday you laughed and smiled all the way to the mine.'

'The mine?' Magnus gripped Rose by the shoulders, subjecting her to a dark, searching look. 'You took him to Hades Cove yesterday?'

'Yes, I did.' She stepped away, disengaging herself. 'Sam has wanted to go there for a long time, so we rode that way. I think he was a little disappointed that we could not go inside the mine itself.'

'Thank heaven for that!' exclaimed Magnus. 'It was foolish in the extreme to go anywhere near it. Promise me you will not do so again. It is far too dangerous.'

'Sir Lawrence likes danger,' put in Sam, obviously

unimpressed by this cautious attitude. 'In fact, he is going off adventuring today.'

'Nonsense,' said Magnus shortly.

'It is not nonsense,' cried Sam. 'He…he had a lamp, and…and a-a jemmy in his saddle bag!'

'A what?' exclaimed Magnus. 'You cannot possibly know what you are talking about.'

'I do.' Sam gave him a triumphant stare. 'It's an iron bar for opening boxes, trunks full of treasure and…and things. There's one at the stables, Evans showed me. And I saw the end of it sticking out of Sir Lawrence's saddle bag this morning. So you see, I am right. He is an adventurer and the bravest man I know.'

Flinging these words at them, Sam turned and dashed away. Magnus watched him go, a deep frown creasing his brow. Distressed, Rose laid her hand on his arm.

'Oh, Magnus, I do beg your pardon, he should not speak like that to you. Let me bring him back here and make him apologise.'

'What? Oh—no, my dear, let him go. We will take up the matter with him later. I must go.'

Rose watched in some surprise as he leapt back into his seat.

'Will you not come to the house with me? I only came to bring Sam and do not intend to stay long—you could drive me home.'

She had hoped to offer this as an olive branch, but Magnus merely shook his head.

'I have business requiring my attention. I shall call upon you tomorrow.'

With that he raised his whip in salute, turned the

carriage and drove quickly away from the farm. Rose watched him go then walked towards the farmhouse. She found Maggie Wooler waiting for her at the door.

'Jem is feeding the cattle in the barn and I have sent little Sam to help him. I will make sure he sets off for home before it is too dark. I hope you will not object if he gets a little dirty?'

'Not at all. Dirt will wash off and a little hard work will make him sleep.' She reached into her reticule. 'I will not stop, but my mother promised old Mrs Wooler the recipe for a tisane she finds particularly useful against winter chills...'

'Thank you, but will you not step in and give it to her yourself? I know she would like to see you.' Mrs Wooler opened the door wide. 'Poor Mother Wooler has seen no one but me all morning, what with Jem having to do Abel's work as well as his own.'

'Oh, is Abel not well?'

Mrs Wooler shook her head as she led the way through the meandering passages of the farmhouse.

'Nay, he left early this morning, soon after Sir Lawrence came to see him. Said he was off to see Sir Jonas, the magistrate. Wouldn't say why, but I know summat's been botherin' him for a while now.'

'Sir Lawrence was here?'

'Aye.' Maggie Wooler chuckled. 'Gave me the shock of my life when I saw 'im in the yard at daybreak, talkin' to Abel. He must have left his house afore dawn. Didn't think gentlefolk could be about so early—!'

She broke off as they entered the parlour and Rose

went forwards to greet the old lady sitting in a chair by the hearth. Once pleasantries had been exchanged and Rose had handed over the recipe, Mrs Wooler went off to bring in more wood for the fire.

'A good girl, that,' said old Mrs Wooler, as the door closed behind her daughter-in-law. 'All the sorrow of losing Ruben, but she keeps so cheerful. 'Tis hard work for her, lookin' after us all and running the household. But she never complains—even with Abel actin' like the cares of the world are on his shoulders, mopin' and grumbling. Like a bear with a sore head, he was. Then this mornin' he ups and leaves, says there's summat he's got to put right.'

'But he did not say what it was?'

The old woman shook her head.

'I wished he would, for he's not been happy ever since the *Sealark* went down. At first I thought it was the loss of his brother; heaven knows that's grief enough for a man to bear, but I do reckon 'twas more than that. But there, he likes to keep his own counsel, does Abel.' She wiped her eyes with the corner of her apron. 'But for all that he's a good boy. Came to my room this morning to say goodbye, he did. "Don't 'ee worry, Mother," he says to me. "I've a mind to see justice done, but there's those as have promised me our Jem won't lose out." Now what do you make o' that?'

'I am not sure,' said Rose slowly. 'Could it…?' She paused, not really wanting to ask the question. 'Could it be something to do with the insurance money Mr Emsleigh has promised those who sailed on the *Sealark*?'

The old lady sat forwards in her chair.

'Well, I was wondering that meself. Our Abel has always been reluctant to talk about it, apart from insisting that his share would pay for a memorial stone for his brother.' The old woman shook her head. 'Summat very havey-cavey about that whole business, if you was to ask me.'

Despite the roaring fire, Rose felt a chill run down her spine. What was it Lawrence had said? *I have a witness who is prepared to tell the truth about the sinking.* Had he meant Abel?

'Oh, dear God!'

Mother Wooler looked up.

'Is anything wrong, dear?'

Rose blinked. She had not realised she had spoken aloud.

'Y-yes,' she said, rising swiftly. 'I—I have remembered something. I must go home, immediately. Please, give my apologies to your daughter-in-law. I must go!'

With a hasty goodbye she almost ran from the room and out of the house, fastening her pelisse as she hurried through the yard towards the gate. A series of images flashed through her mind: Magnus wanting to open up the mine again; going to Hades Cove without telling her; his anger when he discovered she had taken Lawrence there.

Very soon I shall have proof.

Lawrence's words that morning came back to her, but more worrying, the thing that made her blood run cold, was the way Magnus had dashed away after Sam told him that Lawrence was going exploring with a lantern and an iron bar—the sort of bar one could use to lever nailed boards from the entrance to a mineshaft.

'No.' She stopped, panting. Magnus was no villain. He owned the largest house in the area, was welcomed everywhere. He was on the best of terms with all the local magistrates. He *could not* be involved in anything illegal.

She began to walk on again. Magnus might not have anything to hide, but he had no liking for Lawrence and would not want him breaking into his property.

'Hades Mine belongs to me, not Magnus.' She spoke aloud and immediately a voice in her head answered her. *But you are betrothed and he has long regarded the mine as his property. If he finds Lawrence trespassing there, he will think himself within his rights to kill him.*

Chapter Nine

The boards were hard: bands of seasoned wood firmly fixed into place across the entrance to the mine. Lawrence set to work prising them away one by one. He made slow progress; each board had been secured with several long nails, designed to deter any curious passers-by. He wondered, not for the first time, if he should have brought someone to help him. Had the mine belonged to Emsleigh then he might have done so and risked the consequences, but Rose was involved and he was anxious to avoid casting any slur upon her good name. She was innocent, he would stake his life on it, but if his suspicions were correct and Magnus was using the mine to store the cargo from the *Sealark*, then he would have to persuade Rose to go with him to Sir Jonas. Anything less from her would look like collusion.

At last he had removed enough boards to give him access to the mine and he climbed through the opening.

He found himself in what looked like a large cavern. The ground dropped away gently in front of him and disappeared into darkness. He lit his lamp and set off into the gloom. As he moved deeper the salty fresh air was replaced with a damp mustiness. The tunnel curved, then made a sharp turn to the left, effectively blocking off the last of the natural light. The dim glow of his lamp showed a series of tunnels running off on each side of him, presumably where the miners had dug out the seams of iron ore until each one was exhausted. The first tunnel to his left was very short, barely six feet before the lantern's rays hit the jagged, uneven wall of rock at the end. Lawrence turned to his right and as he swung the lantern around he gave a low whistle. One side of the tunnel was lined with barrels and crates and various packages wrapped in oilcloth, everything neatly stacked against the wall and stretching away into the darkness beyond the lamp's reach. Enough goods, he estimated, to fill the hold of a ship.

Lawrence moved closer and inspected the nearest wooden crate. It bore the name of a Bristol ironmonger. Some of the packages had trade cards attached. It shouldn't be difficult to check back to find out if these goods tallied with those lost on the *Sealark*.

Quickly he strode back to the opening. The winter sun was already low in the sky; as it dipped towards the horizon it blazed into the mouth of the mine in a harsh, blinding glare. Lawrence extinguished his lantern and hooked one leg over the low boards he had left in place, ducking to avoid those above him. As he stepped out and straightened, some presentiment of danger came over him. He bunched his fists, but even as he began to turn a heavy blow caught him on the back of the head and he crumpled, lifeless, to the ground.

Rose went straight to the stables. The young lad looked startled to see her and explained that Evans had not yet returned from Minehead.

'No, and I do not expect him for some hours yet,' she replied, looking about her. 'Can you saddle my horse for me, now?'

The boy hurried to obey and ten minutes later she was trotting out of the village, the voluminous folds of her cloak covering the deficiencies of her walking dress, which was not cut quite so liberally as a riding habit and therefore exposed a rather immodest amount of leg and ankle.

Rose kept her horse to a sedate trot until the houses were left behind, then she dug in her heels and set off at a gallop. The snow lay thicker over the moor, but Rose kept up a fast but steady pace until she reached the track leading down to Hades Cove. She let her horse pick its way more slowly over the rocky path and down into the woods, where no sun had penetrated and the ground was iron hard beneath its white covering.

There were fresh tracks in the snow; one, possibly two riders had come this way. Squaring her shoulders, she moved on, impatient to reach the mine. At last the trees thinned and the little shelf of land was before her, but even before her horse had reached the clearing she saw Magnus dragging something dark and heavy through the snow towards the cliff edge. She jumped from her horse and ran forwards.

'Magnus, no! What are you doing?'

Her heart stopped as she approached and saw that he was pulling at Lawrence's unconscious form. She thought at first that Lawrence had a dark red ribbon twisted across his face, but as she drew closer she saw it was blood trickling from a head wound. It had reached his chin and was soaking into his neckcloth. She stared in horror.

'Have you killed him?'

'Not yet.'

Panic filled her.

'Let him go, Magnus. You cannot commit murder.'

Magnus straightened.

'What is this?' he exclaimed. 'I thought you would be glad to see him gone.'

'I want him out of my life, yes, but not like this.'

There was a groan. Lawrence stirred and began to push himself up onto one elbow.

'Oh, thank heaven!' she muttered.

Lawrence sat up, lifting one hand to his head. Rose dug her teeth into her lip to stop herself from crying when he lifted his fingers away, wet with blood. She dropped to her knees beside him.

'We must get you back—'

'You do not seem to understand, my dear,' drawled Magnus. 'Neither of you can leave this place now.'

He drew a wicked-looking pistol from his belt. Lawrence heaved himself onto one elbow.

'By God, Emsleigh—'

Magnus flourished the pistol.

'Now, now, Daunton, do not try anything heroic or I shall have to use this and at this range I am bound to kill one of you. Hush, now, while I think what I am to do with you.'

Rose frowned.

'What do you mean?'

'He intends to push us both over the cliff,' growled Lawrence, climbing unsteadily to his feet. 'But with only one pistol, one bullet, he cannot overpower us both.'

Magnus shrugged.

'I am an excellent shot, so one of you will die, and whoever is left...' His lips curved into a smile that sent a shiver through Rose. 'A woman or an injured man— either way, I do not see that I can lose.'

'Stop this, Magnus.' Rose put her arm around Lawrence as he swayed. 'He is no threat to you.' A flash of white sail caught her eye and she glanced quickly towards the grey sea. 'There is a ship just coming round the headland. They would hear you if you dared to fire.'

Magnus gave her a pitying look. 'The wind is blowing onshore. Any sound would be carried in the opposite direction. However, they may be watching and I would rather avoid witnesses. We will go back into the mine.'

'I would rather take my chances out here,' muttered Lawrence.

'But it is not your choice,' purred Magnus. He waved the pistol menacingly. 'Quickly now, or I may lose patience and risk shooting you here!'

'Please, Lawrence, let us do as he says,' Rose begged.

She pulled the fichu from her neck and gently held it against the cut on his head.

'Quite the ministering angel,' jeered Magnus.

Rose ignored him and began to half-drag, half-carry Lawrence towards the mine entrance.

'Why did you come?' In between his ragged breaths Lawrence muttered the question.

'Magnus guessed from something Sam said that you were going to explore the mine.'

'And you came to save me?'

'Yes—no!' She gave a little huff of exasperation. 'I did not want to believe he would hurt you.'

He started to laugh, but it ended in a gasp.

'Well, now you know differently.'

'I hope you are not hatching any plots between you!' Magnus's sharp voice brought Rose's head up.

'I think you are the one hatching plots,' she retorted. 'Do I have to remind you that you are on my land?'

'No, my dear, but you will soon see that I have put it to good use. Now get into the mine or I will despatch one of you here and now!'

Her breath catching in her throat, she continued to help Lawrence across the uneven grass towards the mine. It was the longest few yards she had ever taken. The knowledge that Magnus was following with a loaded pistol made her spine rigid with fear. The entrance yawned before her, a narrow black opening surrounded by bleached timbers. She helped Lawrence to climb in, wondering if it was possible to overpower Magnus when he followed them, but as if reading her mind he waved them away.

'Get over there by the wall, where I can see you.'

Once he had climbed through the gap into the shadowy chamber he ordered Rose to light the lantern, but elected to carry it himself in his left hand, while the right maintained a steady grip on the pistol.

Lawrence kept his arm about Rose, but he was no longer leaning heavily upon her and he was walking almost normally as they stumbled further on into complete darkness. He kept the folded muslin fichu to his head, lifting it away occasionally to check if the bleeding had stopped.

At last Magnus told them to halt. He hung the lantern from a hook high on one of the pit props and Rose had the opportunity to observe her surroundings. She had never been inside the mine before. The dim light from the lantern bounced back from the low roof and jagged walls. She found the still, musty air oppressive and fought against her rising panic. To distract herself she glanced at the tunnels on each side of her and suddenly became aware that one of them was far from empty. She moved a step closer. Just discernible on the edge of the lamp's glow were the outlines of the kegs, crates and bundles stacked high against the wall of the mine.

'Is—is this the cargo from the *Sealark*?'

'It is, my dear, thousands of pounds' worth, safely stowed.'

'But…you said it was lost.' She frowned. 'So you *did* scuttle her deliberately.'

'Yes,' said Magnus. 'But not until everything had been offloaded. I have been waiting for the chance to move it, but with the path visible to anyone who happens to be out of doors in Mersecombe I have had to wait—a trail of ponies coming to and from the mine would have caused comment. If only you had agreed to my plan to reopen the mine, my dear, then no one would have thought twice about the activity. It is so galling to have all this valuable cargo and not be able to sell it. And thanks to your friend here I still haven't received the insurance I am due.'

'But you are due nothing,' reasoned Rose. 'This… this is fraud.'

Again that sinister smile lifted his mouth.

'Only if we are caught.'

'We?' She looked at him scornfully. 'I am nothing to do with your schemes!'

'But this is your land,' he reminded her. 'And you are my fiancée.'

'No, that is over. Do you think I can condone what you have done? Have you forgotten that Ruben Wooler lost his life because of your wickedness?'

'That was an accident and his widow will get something.'

'Ah, yes,' said Lawrence. The cut on his head had stopped bleeding and he discarded the bloody fichu. 'Your promissory notes. Very clever—you knew the crew would not speak against you, because if they did they would not get their money.'

'Yes, that's why I sent Captain Morris to Bristol to sign up a crew. I knew we could pick them from far and wide, and afterwards they would all go their separate ways. Pity was, Morris insisted we needed Ruben

Wooler if we were to bring the *Sealark* safely into the jetty at Hades Cove. But Morris should have made some excuse to keep the brother out. I wanted a crew from as far afield as possible; I didn't want them sitting around here after and discussing what had happened.' Magnus turned his cold stare towards Lawrence. 'Don't think I don't know that you have been snooping around the farm, trying to persuade Wooler to testify against me, but he's a close one. He won't talk, because his brother's widow will be forty-five guineas the poorer if he does.'

Rose opened her mouth to speak, but Lawrence gripped her arm. Obediently she kept silent.

Lawrence said, 'He won't need to talk: this cargo is all the proof I need.'

Magnus curled his lip.

'My dear Daunton, surely you do not think I can let you go now?'

'This is the outside of enough, Magnus,' exclaimed Rose. 'You cannot think that I will let you do this!'

'Oh, but you will, my dear.'

'What do you mean?'

He smiled.

'You will marry me and share in the proceeds of my ill-gotten gains—'

'Never!'

'—or I shall have to kill you, too.'

The words were so matter-of-fact that she thought she had misheard him, but as understanding dawned she said slowly, 'You would really *kill* to protect your interests?'

'Of course, if I must.'

Lawrence gripped her wrist.

'You should save yourself, Rose.'

'No. I will stay with you.'

He gave her a little push and said roughly, 'Go on. To me you were nothing but a distraction.' He pinched her arm on the last word. 'Go.'

Rose took a step away from him. She looked at Magnus.

'You would still marry me? Knowing I could ruin you?'

'Oh, I don't think you would do that, my dear. The trappings of luxury are very hard to lay aside.' He held his hand out to her. 'Come, we will go back now and you can put it about that you have decided we will open the mine again. My people can be moving the goods out within the week. We won't attempt to sell anything in this area, of course, although I need to raise some money. I have been dipping far too deep recently, living on credit. I expected the insurers to pay up by now.'

Lawrence shook his head.

'If I do not make my report, I doubt they will ever pay up.'

'Nonsense. Once they are made aware of last night's little scene they will not think it odd that you have disappeared, gone to ground rather than face up to your responsibilities. Your reputation goes before you, Daunton. My sister is just the last in a long line of women you have seduced.'

'By God, Emsleigh, I'll make you pay for this!'

Magnus laughed, the sound magnified and monstrous as it bounced off the walls.

'Empty threats, Daunton.' He held out his hand. 'Come here, Rose, and let us end this—no, don't stand in front of him—!'

The brief moment of diversion was enough. Unsighted, Magnus lowered the pistol. Lawrence hurled himself at him and the two men fell to the ground. Lawrence grabbed his wrist, twisting viciously. The pistol dropped from his fingers and Rose swooped upon it, carrying it safely out of the way.

It was all over in a minute. Magnus was no match for Lawrence's superior strength and Rose heard him cry out, 'Enough, enough!'

Without taking his attention from Magnus, Lawrence jumped to his feet and took the pistol from Rose's shaking hands.

'Well, I think the tables are well and truly turned now,' he ground out. 'Get up, Emsleigh; it is time we took you to the magistrate.'

Magnus stood up, brushing the dust from his sleeve with rough, angry movements. He glared at Rose.

'So he has you in thrall, too. Just like my poor sister.'

'I am under no illusions about Sir Lawrence,' she retorted. 'But I would see justice done.'

'Justice!' Magnus gave a savage laugh. 'After all I have done for Mersecombe, providing alms for the poor, supporting your wretched school—'

'And bankrupting yourself with your excessive spending,' broke in Lawrence. 'Not that the people of Mersecombe know anything of that. You confined your gambling to your trips to Bristol and Bath; I made enquiries there before I came to Mersecombe and found you lost a small fortune in Bath last winter.'

'As did many others!' Magnus threw at him.

'Undoubtedly, but you have been obliged to live on credit since then, have you not? That is why you needed the insurance, to pay your debts.' Lawrence paused. 'I am surprised you did not get yourself a rich wife.'

'I tried,' he retorted bitterly. 'A rich widow, in charge of her own fortune, would have solved all my difficulties. There are any number of 'em in Bath, but they were all so damned cautious, wanting to know the state of my finances!'

'But you had asked me to marry you,' objected Rose. 'We were betrothed.'

His lip curled. 'And what did you have to offer me? A brat of your own and a worthless mine! If I could have secured a woman of sufficient means I would have found some way to break our engagement. But by the time I came back to Mersecombe I had already decided there was only one way to solve my problems. I could still raise enough funds for one last venture, so I loaded the *Sealark* with cargo and took out the insurance. But I needed somewhere to hide the cargo. Hades Mine was the obvious choice. It was an excellent plan.' His malevolent glance shifted to Rose. 'Then you decided to postpone our wedding. Not only that, you would not allow me to open up the mine. Damnation, if you had consented, then no one would have thought twice when they saw pack ponies on the road. I could have moved the cargo out months ago and sold it.'

'I am glad I thwarted you,' said Rose. 'Even if it was unwittingly done.' She shivered. 'Let us get out of this horrid place. We will take him to Sir Jonas Pullen. He will know what to do.'

Lawrence gestured to Magnus to go first, but even as they began to move, footsteps echoed through the tunnel. A high, nervous voice called out and Rose halted.

'Sam!' Her cry was shrill with alarm.

'Mama, Sir Lawrence? Are you here?'

'No, no, Sam, go back!'

'Sam, stop, don't come any further!'

Rose and Lawrence shouted at the same time, their voices bouncing off the walls, distorting into an unrecognisable cacophony of noise. It drowned out any further footsteps, but even as the echoes died away Sam hurtled around the corner, directly into Magnus's arms.

Rose watched in horror as Magnus gripped Sam's shoulders, pinning the boy in front of him like a shield.

'You should have shot me while you had the chance, Daunton.' He cursed as Sam squirmed and wriggled to free himself. 'Be still, Samuel, or it will be the worse for you! Well, Daunton, what do you say now? How good is your aim in this light, with a strange weapon? You have only my head and shoulders to aim for. Will you risk hitting the boy?'

'You know I won't,' said Lawrence, lowering the pistol.

'Very sensible.' Magnus began to back along the tunnel. 'You will both stay where you are. If I see you following us out of the mine, then I will break the boy's neck, do you understand?'

'Mama!'

Sam's distressed cry ripped at her heart

'It's all right, my love, I'm—'

'Get back,' snapped Magnus as Rose reached out for her son. 'He will be safe as long as you do as you are told.'

'Sam, remember what I taught you—about staying safe?' She heard Lawrence's voice beside her, calm and reassuring. Sam stopped wriggling. Lawrence said, 'Do it now, lad. Make it count.'

Sam's little hands clenched into fists and he jabbed his elbow with all his force into Magnus's groin. Magnus doubled up, shock and surprise loosening his grip, and Sam jumped away. Almost immediately a shot rang out and Magnus jerked back against the wall of the mine, clutching at his shoulder.

Lawrence gave a grunt of satisfaction. 'Not bad, even with a strange weapon. How is the boy?'

'Unharmed, thank heaven.' Rose had gathered Sam in her arms and was holding him tightly. 'I think,' she said unsteadily, 'I would like to go home now.'

Rose walked around the little sitting room at Bluebell Cottage, trying not to give in to the anxious thoughts and questions that threatened to overwhelm her. It was late, everyone else had gone to bed, but Lawrence had promised to come back once Magnus was safely locked up and she knew he would keep his word.

Before they left the mine, she had bound up Magnus's shoulder as best she could, then left Lawrence to take him to Sir Jonas Pullen while she took Sam home.

Their arrival had coincided with Mrs Molland's return from Minehead and it was only to be expected that Sam would want to tell his grandmother all about his adventure.

The tale was recounted and revisited many times over dinner. Mrs Molland exclaimed over Magnus Emsleigh's villainy and praised Sir Lawrence's bravery, but she was mildly reproachful of her daughter and grandson for their foolishness in going to Hades Mine at all.

'But if Mama had not gone, then Sir Lawrence might well have been killed,' argued Sam, not at all chastened by the gentle rebuke.

Rose had been at pains to make light of her part in the proceedings and she was a little shocked at her young son's astute grasp of the situation. Her head was still buzzing with all that had occurred and she desperately wanted to be alone, so she was grateful when, soon after they had finished dinner, Mrs Molland declared that she would take Sam up to bed.

'He is far too excited to sleep,' she said when she rejoined Rose in the sitting room some time later. 'I have left Janet with him, and he is telling her of his adventure. He thinks of Sir Lawrence as quite the hero of the hour.' When Rose did not reply she added, 'I think we should invite him to call, that we may thank him properly.'

'We shall see.'

'You are not minded to receive him?'

'I do not deny that he was very brave, but it does not alter the fact that he is a libertine.'

'But perhaps it puts him in a slightly better light.'

'Mama, Althea Emsleigh is carrying his child!' Rose spread her hands. 'What would you have me do?'

Mrs Molland sighed.

'I do not know, but I admit I am seriously disappointed. I had begun to think that Sir Lawrence was just the man for you.'

She had risen then, and gone to bed, leaving Rose to pace up and down and wait for a knock on the door.

It came just after midnight.

'I saw your candle in your window.' Sir Lawrence stepped into the hall. It had started to snow and the shoulders of his jacket sparkled with a frosty dusting. 'How is Sam?'

'Sleeping peacefully. He is very resilient. He spotted me on the hill, riding down to Hades Cove, and decided to follow.'

'And how are you?'

Rose evaded his searching gaze.

'A little tired.'

She led him into the sitting room, where she had banked up the fire.

'I did not expect to be so late.'

He removed his hat and Rose looked intently at him for signs of injury. Apart from an angry graze on his temple there was no sign of the wound he had suffered; the cut itself was covered by his thick dark hair.

'Sir Jonas agreed to put Emsleigh in the lock-up, but insisted upon going back to the mine to see for himself. Abel Wooler was with him when I arrived. He had just finished making his deposition, so Sir Jonas already knew most of the story.' He held his hands out to the fire. 'We replaced the boards across the entrance and he has set a couple of stout fellows to guard it, until the goods can be moved.'

Rose watched him as he gazed silently into the fire. She was looking for similarities with her late husband. Harry had been floridly handsome; there was nothing florid about Lawrence. He was lean and dark with a slow smile that set her pulse racing in a way that Harry's boyish grin had never done. Harry had been incorrigible. Whenever she had confronted him with his latest transgression, be it heavy losses at the gaming table, or another woman, he would always react in the same way: first the denial, then the apology. Time and again he had promised her that this indiscretion would be his last; time and again she had believed him...

Lawrence straightened and turned to look at her, his eyes sombre.

'I am sorry, I should have trusted you. I should have told you I was investigating the loss of the *Sealark*.'

'I thought you had come to Mersecombe to find me.'

'I gave you my word I would not do that. An old friend asked me to investigate the loss of the *Sealark*, to find out if it really was an accident. He is one of those standing surety for the loss, and very reluctant to pay out if it was a fraud.' A wry smile twisted his lips. 'Knowing you were here made me keener to accept.'

'But for all you knew I might have been married!' she challenged him.

He shrugged.

'I knew that, but I needed to know. When I found you had postponed the wedding I thought…I hoped there might be a chance for us…'

Rose put up her hand. She did not want to hear any more of his hopes.

'That explains your frequent visits to the Woolers— you were questioning Abel.'

'Yes.'

'And you befriended Sam to get to me?'

'No—not exactly. If Sam had not been your son, I would have treated him just the same. He is a fine boy.' She turned away, unable to meet his gaze. He said quietly, 'I have changed, Rose. After you left me last Christmas I wanted to prove I could do so—to myself as well as to you. It was not hard to give up the rakehell lifestyle I had been living, but it was harder not to come and find you. When I had an excuse to come back I took it, but returning to Knightscote revived all the memories of those few precious days we shared. It was bad enough in London, constantly thinking of you, wondering what you were doing, if you were happy, but back at Knightscote—I kept opening doors and expecting to see you there. Even riding the moor I am reminded of you—I see your eyes in the blue-grey rocks, hear your laughter in the babbling of the stream.' He reached out for her. 'I cannot bear us to be apart any longer, Rose—'

'Impossible! Please, say no more!' Tears scalded her eyes, but she would not let them fall. She walked away so that he could not see her trembling lip.

'Impossible? No, why do you say that?'

Anger at his insouciance made her turn back.

'What about Althea? Will you still marry her?'

His black brows drew together.

'I have never had any intention of marrying her! If she expected that little outburst last night to persuade me, then I am sorry for it, but she has been deceiving herself.'

Just like Harry.

Hot, boiling fury erupted inside her. If there had been a knife to hand, she would have plunged it into him.

'A rake to the last,' she raged. 'Get out!'

'Rose, I have already sworn to you—I have had nothing to do with Althea Emsleigh.'

'And you expect me to believe that?'

'Yes! Do you think a woman cannot lie?'

'A woman could not lie about such a thing.'

'Perhaps *you* could not, but—'

'Get out! I never want to see you again. Ever.'

Lawrence stared at the rigid figure before him. She was shaking, her face paper white.

'Perhaps, in the morning…'

'No—never,' she spat at him. She put out her hand to clutch at the back of a nearby chair, breathing deeply so that when she spoke again her voice was low and held barely a quaver. 'You will not darken my door again and you will not see or speak to my son. We shall be leaving Mersecombe as soon as I can make arrangements, but until that time it shall be as if you never existed. Do you understand me?'

Lawrence straightened, overcome by a dark, despairing anger. It had been a very long day, his body ached from the blows he had sustained and the cut on his head throbbed painfully. He had successfully concluded his investigation and exposed Magnus Emsleigh for the villain he really was. He shook his head, saying angrily, 'I did not come here to be rewarded, but to be so summarily dismissed is harsh indeed!'

'You have brought it upon yourself.'

'You have made yourself both judge and jury and have found me guilty without giving me any chance to defend myself!'

She shook her head, her hand coming up in a little gesture of denial. Lawrence fought down the angry words that crowded his head. In time she might know that she was wrong, but he had already spent a whole year trying to prove his worth to her. Enough was enough. He scooped up his hat.

'I cannot make you trust me,' he said quietly. 'You have made it perfectly clear tonight that you do not want to try. I know that you have had one bad husband and you came pretty close to taking a second. I understand that. It is enough to make anyone wary, so I shall not trouble you again. But I beg you will remember I am, always have been and always will be your humble servant.'

With a final stiff little bow he turned on his heel and walked out of the house.

Chapter Ten

Rose heard the front door slam, then the silence of the sleeping house pressed in around her. She closed her eyes.

'I was right to send him away.'

She felt the hot tears squeezing out and running down her cheeks. Angrily she brushed them away. She must stop this, she had wasted tears enough. From now on the only man in her life would be her son.

Rose was determined to avoid Lawrence at all costs and when Sir Jonas called upon her the next day she cautiously enquired if she would have to give evidence.

'No, no, I will take statements from you and your boy and that should suffice. Sir Lawrence doesn't see any need for you to go all the way to London.'

'London!'

'Aye. Emsleigh's being taken there now. We arrested

Captain Morris this morning, too, and put him in the same coach. Sir Lawrence is helping my men to escort the pair of them.' He shook his head. 'A bad business, this. When Abel Wooler came to see me yesterday I was much inclined to dismiss him—after all, it was his word against the captain and the rest of the crew. Not only that, but he was accusing Emsleigh of being behind it, one of our foremost citizens! But then Sir Lawrence turned up, and once I had seen for myself the cargo stashed away in Hades Mine I realised there would be a case to answer.'

'What will happen to Abel?' asked Rose, momentarily diverted from her own unhappiness. 'He signed the original affidavit, did he not, to say that the ship and cargo had been lost?'

Sir Jonas pursed his lips.

'Aye, he did, but as Sir Lawrence pointed out, Wooler had just lost his brother and was out of his mind with grief at that time. As soon as he came to his senses he realised the error of his ways and came to me to confess. I have been to see him this morning and told him he'd nothing to fear as long as he has told me the truth.'

Rose looked down at her hands.

'And…will Sir Lawrence be in London for long?' she asked casually.

'Oh, most likely. He told me he means to sell Knightscote—seems this business has given him a dislike for the place.'

'Well, then, that's settled,' she murmured, almost to herself.

* * *

Rose was slightly shocked to feel so bereft and sought for some occupation to fill her day. In the end she decided to accompany Sam to the stables, where he was to go riding with Evans. She changed into her riding habit and was just stepping out of the door with Sam when Janet returned from the market, her basket piled up with food.

'Well, here's a to-do and no mistake,' she announced as they stepped back to let her come in through the gate. 'All over the village, it is. Mr Emsleigh taken off to Lunnon to stand trial and Miss Emsleigh—'

'Yes, Janet, I know.' Rose hastily interrupted her. 'I am going to visit Miss Emsleigh now, to offer her any assistance I can.'

Janet stopped and stared at her, frowning.

'You never are. After what she said—'

'I was very nearly her sister,' Rose reminded her. 'I cannot abandon her in her hour of need.'

'*Her* need!' Janet snorted. 'Why, her maid's been tellin'—'

'I will not listen to gossip, Janet, and neither should you. Come along, Sam!'

Rose grabbed her son's hand and hurried him out into the lane.

'What is wrong with Miss Emsleigh, Mama?' Sam turned his innocent eyes up to her.

'She is being blamed for her brother's villainy,' Rose replied, her cheeks flushed with indignation. 'She has been cruelly used!'

She looked and sounded so fierce when she said this

that Sam dared not say more, and they continued in silence to the stables.

'I beg your pardon, ma'am,' exclaimed Evans, surprised. 'I did not know you were planning to ride out with us and I have not saddled your mare…'

'I only decided this morning that I should like some exercise.' She made sure that Sam was out of earshot and continued quietly, 'I shall have to make arrangements for the pony to be returned to Sir Lawrence, and soon.'

'Will you, ma'am?' Evans looked surprised. 'That'll break the little man's heart.'

The knife inside Rose twisted a little further.

'It cannot be helped. We have imposed upon Sir Lawrence long enough.'

'But I hear Sir Lawrence is gone to London, ma'am. He won't be wantin' the pony sent there.'

'No, so you must write and ask for instructions.' She felt a little guilty about leaving such matters to her groom, but told herself it was best for her not to be involved.

'Very well, ma'am. But until then you'll let Master Sam ride as usual?'

'Yes…yes, I suppose so. And there is no need to say anything to Sam just yet,' she added, quelling another ripple of guilt. 'No point in making him unhappy for any longer than is necessary.'

She waited patiently for her mare to be saddled, but then declined to ride with Sam and Evans up onto the moor—there was a visit she dreaded, but felt herself obliged to make.

* * *

She arrived at Emsleigh House to find the front windows shuttered and the door closed. There was only one nervous-looking groom in the stables and he suggested she should enter the house by the garden door. The butler met her in the hall with the air of one pushed to the limit of his endurance.

'I beg your pardon, ma'am, but we are constantly being pestered by tradesmen and the mistress insisted we should shut up the house.' He gestured towards the stairs. 'Miss Emsleigh is in her boudoir, ma'am. If you wait here, I will announce you—'

A loud hammering on the door interrupted him.

Rose's kind heart was touched at the thought of Althea's distress.

'No need, I will announce myself.'

She picked up the train of her riding habit and looped it over her arm before hurrying up the stairs. She had never been a close friend of Althea, but she recalled being taken to her dressing room on one occasion and hoped she could remember the way. There were signs of disorder everywhere: half-filled trunks stood in doorways, pictures had been removed from the walls and harassed-looking servants were hurrying back and forth.

Rose arrived at Althea's room and gave a soft knock. A muffled sound that could have been 'come in' followed and she entered, closing the door quietly behind her. The room was quite as disordered as the rest of the house, but a number of smashed ornaments in the fireplace suggested that Althea was not in the sunniest of moods. She was pacing up and down, her blond curls jumping and her colour heightened to make her face an unattractive mottled red and white.

'Oh, it's you.' She barely glanced at Rose as she came in. 'Have you come to gloat?'

'Of course not. I came to see if you needed anything.'

'Nothing that you can provide—unless you have a spare fortune I may use to set myself up abroad?' Her lip curled. 'I thought not. I always said it was a mistake for Magnus to offer for you. He could have done much better for himself than an impoverished widow with a brat to look after.'

Rose fought down her anger. Althea was upset and quite possibly frightened.

'Well, it will not come to that now,' she said quietly. 'Will you remain here?'

'With tradesmen hammering on the door for payment day and night?' Althea picked up a teacup from her breakfast tray and hurled it at the fireplace. '*Damn* Magnus for leaving me in this mess!'

'Althea, please, this cannot be good for you—'

'You know nothing of the matter. Magnus has so many debts that everything in this house will have to be sold to pay them.' She began pacing the floor again. 'I have some money, but not enough to live in this style. I shall be able to keep only two servants—three at the most. How could Magnus do this to me? I could *scream* with vexation!'

'My dear, you must try to stay calm,' Rose urged her. 'Think of your condition.'

Althea stopped pacing and stared at her.

'Condition? Oh, that—I am not really breeding.'

'You…you are not?'

'Of course not. It was an attempt to force Lawrence to marry me.' Althea scowled. 'I doubt he can be persuaded to do so now.'

The room started spinning and Rose put her hand on the wall to steady herself.

'Althea, I do not understand… You are *not* carrying his child?'

'No, of course not. Did you really think it was true?' She gave a scornful laugh. 'You must be the only one who believed it!'

'But how could you say such a thing, and say it so publicly?'

Althea shrugged her white shoulders.

'I never intended to do so, until I saw the way Lawrence looked at you. That put me in such a rage. He had never so much as squeezed my fingers, though I gave him every encouragement. La, I was quite disappointed, for he has such a reputation. I had planned to seduce him at the ball, but I soon realised that would not work, and when I saw he meant to leave I announced I was carrying his child. I thought it would be a sure way to give you a disgust of him and to force him into marriage. Only Magnus would not support me. That was a blow, I can tell you. I see why *now*, of course— Daunton was his enemy—but it put me in a damnable position. And I was so remiss I did not think to warn my maid, so when she went to market yesterday and heard them sniggering behind their hands she lost no time in telling everyone she could find that I could not be with child because my courses were as regular as a clock and I have never missed one. Heavens, was ever a woman cursed with such a well-meaning wretch.' She suddenly became aware of Rose's presence and rounded on her.

'Are you shocked? Well, Miss Propriety, if you had not been so caught up in your own petty concerns you would have snapped Magnus up last spring, then he would have been able to send all that cargo to market months ago, and none of this would have happened.'

'Surely you do not condone what he has done?' asked Rose, appalled. 'A sailor lost his life when they sunk that ship!'

'What do I care for that? With the insurance, and the profit from the cargo, we could have settled our accounts and lived very comfortably.'

She continued to rage, sending the saucer and teapot the same way as the cup, and ignoring Rose, who edged towards the door and made her escape. The butler suggested she should slip out through the kitchens to avoid the growing number of tradesman at the front of the house.

Rose followed his advice and collected her horse. She trotted out of the yard and was cantering away down the drive before any of the irate crowd at the front door could accost her. Once out on the road she turned onto one of the many lanes that led up onto the hills, forcing herself to concentrate on pushing the mare on until she was at last on the moor with the icy wind whipping at her cheeks. The occasional drift of snow remained in a ditch or against a north-facing ridge, in stark contrast to the dull winter browns of the moor.

So, Lawrence had been telling the truth all the time. She turned her face up to the heavens. She had willingly given him her body, so why had she been so afraid to trust him, to believe him? Rose looked around, suddenly restless. She needed to see Lawrence, to beg him to forgive her, but that was impossible. He was miles away by now. But he would come back, wouldn't he? He would return and she would throw herself on his mercy. She remembered the stony, implacable look on his face when he had left her.

I shall not trouble you again.

The bleak wind cut through her cloak and she shivered. The moor stretched away on all sides, no sign of life in any direction. Even the stunted trees looked black and decayed. Lifeless. Perhaps it was already too late

She turned her horse and headed for home.

Chapter Eleven

'Well, I am pleased that business is out of the way!' George Craven followed Lawrence out of the lawyer's office and into the waiting carriage. 'Can't tell you how grateful I am to you for sorting out that little matter, Daunton. With the cargo recovered, and the ship's captain making a full confession, we have a strong case against Emsleigh. And I've learned it is not the first time the man has come up against the law—it seems he's been sailing close to the wind for years, with his lawyers successfully defending him against several charges of smuggling. He's always escaped because there's never been enough evidence, but this time we've caught him fair and square. Well done, my friend.'

Lawrence settled himself into his seat.

'How soon will it come to court, do you think?'

'Oh, not 'til the spring,' replied Craven cheerfully. 'Until then Emsleigh is safe enough in Newgate; he seems to have enough funds for a few luxuries while he waits for his trial. Brrr!' He shivered. 'If I'm not mistaken we shall have snow before morning. The sooner we get out of the cold, the better. I'll drop you at your rooms and collect you again in, say, two hours. Will that be time enough for you to change? I am going to buy you the best dinner White's can provide!'

'Really, George, there is no need—'

'Nonsense, man, you have saved me from ruin. And you are in no rush to go to Hampshire?'

'None at all. In fact, I may well remain in town for Christmas.'

'What, you will stay away from Daunton House for another year? My family will be deeply disappointed. They hoped that after the amount of time you have spent there this year you would be making it your home.'

'And I probably shall—but not yet.'

'Ah, I understand.' George nodded and gave him a knowing wink. 'Christmas time. You would have that army of aunts, uncles and cousins descending upon you and they would be colluding with *my* family, doing their best to make you forget your grief over m'sister, but only making it worse with their dismal sighs and sympathetic looks.'

'Exactly.'

'No wonder, then, you would rather remain here! I'd stay with you, but—well—you know how it is. Having come so close to ruin this summer, I am minded to settle down. M'father is getting too old to manage the estate now, so I thought I would live at home and help him.'

'Very commendable,' said Lawrence gravely.

'Aye, I think so,' said George, pleased with himself. 'But I don't travel down until tomorrow, so tonight you and I will have one final spree!'

Lawrence frowned up at the imposing frontage of Samlesbury House as the carriage drew up before the door.

'Really, Craven, I am not sure I am in the mood to be sociable.'

'Nonsense, you are out of practice, having lived like a monk this past year! This isn't one of your starched-up *ton* parties—Nancy Samlesbury will have packed the place with dashing young matrons, every one of 'em eager for a little light-hearted dalliance.' George Craven jumped out of the carriage and held open the door. 'Come along, Daunton, I have already told our hostess I would be bringing you with me and I daren't disappoint her.'

Stifling a sigh, Lawrence followed him into the house and up the curving staircase towards the noisy ballroom. Lady Samlesbury swept across to them as they were announced.

'So you have brought him.' After flashing a smile at Craven, she turned her attention to Sir Lawrence, holding out her hand and fixing him with kohl-rimmed eyes that held more than a hint of an invitation. 'My dear Sir Lawrence, you have become a positive stranger at our little parties.' Her fingers tightened their grip as he bowed over her hand. She waited until George had moved away, then she lowered her voice to murmur in his ear, 'I was afraid you had forgotten me and our... time together.'

The corners of his mouth curved upwards.

'How could I ever forget such a pleasurable experience?'

She moved closer, peeping at him over the top of her fan.

'Perhaps we should try to recreate it...'

'Fie, Nancy, that was two years ago, before you married Samlesbury and became a respectable married woman. Would you make him jealous?'

'No, alas.' She sighed, fingering the exquisite diamonds at her neck. 'Not when he is so generous to me.' With a laugh she tucked her hand into his arm.

'No, Lawrence, you are right, I must behave myself now. But there are many ladies here who are eager to renew their acquaintance with you...'

By midnight Lawrence's cheeks ached from incessant smiling and his head was beginning to throb. It was not from the wine—he had drunk very little, needing to keep his wits about him to avoid the wiles of the numerous ladies who were intent upon flirting with him. He felt like a fox, being hunted at every turn. His first dance partner had twisted her ankle and needed to be helped to a secluded alcove; the next had felt a little faint and insisted he accompany her to a deserted balcony, where the arctic temperatures came to his aid in persuading her that dalliance in such circumstances would undoubtedly result in a severe inflammation of the lungs. Then there was the serious-looking matron who disputed with him over certain lines in 'The Lady of the Lake' and carried him off to the book room, where she threw herself against the door and refused to let him leave until he had kissed her.

A year ago Lawrence would have joined in their games, shrugged his broad shoulders and indulged these rapacious women with a fast, furious flirtation. One of them might even have ended up in his bed. Now there was only one woman he wanted in his arms, only one pair of eyes he wanted to find fixed upon him, and if he could not have Rose, he would have no one. These society ladies with their strong, cloying perfume and knowing smiles left him unmoved. It had taken rapid thinking and a great deal of tact and charm to avoid all the snares set for him, but somehow he had succeeded; so well, in fact, that when he dragged his friend out of the house in the early hours of the morning his hostess assured him that he was welcome at Samlesbury House at any time. And that he had secured his place as a firm favourite with her guests.

Unbelievably weary, Lawrence bundled George into a hired cab and gave the driver his instructions.

'Charming party,' declared George, slurring his words a little. 'Nancy always knows how to entertain her guests. Did you dance with that little redhead?'

'Yes, I danced with her,' said Lawrence, bringing to mind the freckle-faced matron who had pushed herself against him and told him the days he might find her at home alone.

'What a flirt. And with her husband standing by, too! By Gad, she was a tempting little thing.'

Lawrence turned his head to peer across the carriage.

'Tell me truthfully, George—did you really enjoy yourself tonight?'

'Why, yes, of course! Couldn't fail to enjoy myself with such a charming set. Did they not please you?'

'No, not really.'

'Extraordinary.' George sat up. 'Not coming down with something, are you, old boy? Touch of gout, perhaps?'

'I think not. Old age, perhaps.'

'Aye, could be,' came the serious reply. 'You are thirty now, after all. But if you no longer enjoy the society, there's precious little reason to stay in town for Christmas.'

'I know.'

'Dashed if I can understand you,' exclaimed Craven, shaking his head. 'You won't go to your family home, you dislike London—what *do* you want to do?'

Lawrence sighed and turned his head to look out at the night. The streets were still busy; lamps burned outside many of the houses, lighting the way for the non-stop procession of carriages that picked their way between the soil carts and the nightwatch, who cried the hour while keeping a wary eye upon the little groups of revellers making their way home. He had friends enough in town, but if he stayed they would be pressing him to join them—how could he explain that he wanted nothing more than to be alone, to ponder on his future?

As he watched, a few fat flakes of snow drifted past the carriage window.

'I don't know, George. I may go back to Knightscote.'

'Exmoor—in December?' Craven gave a crack of laughter. 'From what you've told me your lodge is in the middle of nowhere—you might not see anyone for weeks!'

Lawrence looked at him, a glimmer of a smile in his eyes.

'Perfect!'

Christmas Eve. A sharp icy wind had been scouring the moors for days and it howled around Knightscote Lodge, whispering under the doors and making the fires burn with an extra-bright glow. Lawrence pulled his chair closer to the hearth and sat down, stretching his long legs before him. He had arrived at the lodge at dusk that day, which had sent Mrs Brendon into a flurry of activity. She hurriedly despatched a man to Exford to buy more provisions and bustled about the house, muttering darkly about the difficulties of working for a man who says one minute he might never come back again and the next turns up without so much as a by your leave. The only one genuinely happy to see him was the pointer bitch, Bandit. Lawrence's keeper had gone off to visit his family for a few days and left the dog in the care of the stable boy. Thus, when Lawrence had arrived and ridden to the stables, Bandit had come running out, fawning around his legs and making it impossible for Lawrence to proceed until he had greeted her.

He had retreated to the drawing room while his

housekeeper bustled about putting the house into what she considered a fit state for its master, but by the time he had complimented her upon a fine dinner and declared himself well satisfied with all her arrangements, harmony had been restored.

That had been some hours ago. Knowing the staff would be up early the following day to walk to church, Lawrence had sent them all to bed. He had fetched Bandit for company and a bottle of brandy for solace and was now settling down to while away the evening in front of the fire. He was in a reflective mood and his brandy glass remained untouched as he lounged in his chair, staring into the flames.

A year ago today it had all started. Rose Westerhill had burst into his life and changed it for ever. She had accused him of wallowing in self-pity and in his attempts to prove her wrong he had reformed his way of life. That had not been difficult, but making Rose believe that he was a changed man had proved impossible. A log shifted, sending a shower of sparks into the air and waking Bandit from her slumbers at her master's feet. Lawrence put out a hand and stroked the smooth head.

'Perhaps it's mere conceit,' he addressed the pointer, who was gazing up at him adoringly, 'but I thought she would know that I was different.'

Bandit merely licked his hand. Lawrence gave her a final pat and sank back in his chair. They remained thus, unmoving, until Lawrence heard the sound of hoofs clinking on the cobbles. In a flash he was at the window, throwing back the heavy curtains to peer out.

A thin covering of snow lightened the darkness, but he could see nothing moving save the bushes at the edges of the drive, bending before the driving wind.

'There's no one there, you fool.' He returned to the chair and picked up his glass.

Wishful thinking. Perhaps it had been a mistake to return to Knightscote. The place held too many memories. He should sell it; there was nothing here for him any longer. As he leaned forwards to throw another log onto the fire a sudden gust of wind moaned through the house, rattling the door. Bandit was immediately on the alert.

'Easy, now. It's an old house, full of creaking boards and rattling windows.' Lawrence sipped at the brandy. 'Perhaps I will build myself a new hunting lodge in Leicestershire. What do you say to that?'

Bandit was not listening. She rose and padded towards the door, ears pricked.

Lawrence was about to order her back when the candlelight glinted on the turning handle. He put down his glass and rose to his feet.

'I am dreaming.'

Rose entered the drawing room and stood with her back pressed against the door, her powder-blue cloak glistening with melting snow. She remained there for a long moment, uncertain of her welcome, until Bandit's effusive greetings could no longer be ignored.

Lawrence watched, transfixed, as she bent down to make a fuss of the dog.

'How did you get in?'

'Through the kitchen. I could see no lights, so I rode round to the stables.' She gently pushed Bandit away and straightened. 'May I come in?'

Lawrence looked at the glass on the table beside him. It was almost full. So this was not a brandy-induced fantasy. His spirits lifted.

'Have you lost your way?'

'No.' A smile trembled on her lips. 'I think I may have found it.'

In two strides he crossed the room, reaching out for her. With a sob she fell into his arms, turning her face up to receive his kiss. He swooped, capturing her mouth, demanding a response that she was eager to give. Her arms crept up around his neck. He registered the damp leather of her gloves, felt the chill of her clothes as she pressed against him.

'You are like ice.' He led her towards the fire. 'Come and warm yourself.'

He unfastened her cloak and tossed it aside before pushing her down into the chair.

'If you are not lost, then what the devil are you doing abroad so late?'

His voice was rough with concern, but she did not appear to notice.

'I could not rest. I wondered—' A rueful smile played about her mouth. 'After my getting stranded last year, it was decided I should not go to Exford this Christmas. Indeed, my family have become so protective I have not been allowed to go anywhere alone. But I needed to know if—if you were here, so I waited until they retired, then slipped out and bribed a sleepy stable boy to saddle my mare.'

'And what would you have done if I had not been here?'

'"Made me a willow cabin at your gate,"' she quoted. '"And called upon my soul within the house."'

Lawrence wanted to be angry at such foolishness, but found he could not stop smiling.

'Ninnyhammer,' he murmured.

She blushed and looked away, suddenly shy. She stripped off her gloves and looked at her fingers. They were red and aching with the cold.

'Here, let me.' Lawrence knelt before her and took her hands between his own.

He pulled her fingers towards him and kissed first one pink tip, then the next, gently warming each one with his lips while his palms cradled her hands, infusing them with his own heat. When her skin had lost the raw redness, he pressed a kiss into one palm. Rose raised the other hand to cradle his cheek, slipping from the chair to kneel before him. He pulled her gently into his arms and began to kiss her face with the same slow care he had given to her fingers.

She gave a little murmur of disappointment when he broke off. He pulled her to her feet and swept her up into his arms.

'We will continue with this in my bed.'

His low whisper sent a delicious shiver running through her. Rose twined her arms around his neck and laid her head on his shoulder.

With a muttered command to Bandit to go and lie

down, Lawrence strode out of the room. Rose lay passive and silent in his arms, marvelling at the way he carried her, as if she weighed no more than a feather. He took the stairs two at a time and continued without pause until they reached his bedchamber, where he carried her over to the bed and laid her gently down upon the covers.

There was no light in the room save the flickering flames in the hearth, but Lawrence did not waste time lighting the candles. He lay down beside Rose and drew her into his arms, his mouth seeking her lips. The faint doubts that had begun to creep into her mind as they traversed the chill dark passages of the old house immediately fled. She sighed, closing her eyes and relishing the close attention he was giving to every inch of her skin. She breathed in the familiar scent of his cologne: the heady mix of lavender, rosemary and bergamot with a hint of bitter oranges. The fragrance awoke the most sensual memories of times shared, both here at Knightscote and the all-too-brief moments they had been together at Mersecombe. The last shreds of consciousness fled and Rose abandoned herself to the pleasures of his lovemaking. She tilted up her chin, allowing him access to the slender column of her throat. His lambent kisses sent waves of pleasure pulsing through her body and seemed to melt her very bones.

He began to unfasten her jacket, all the time anointing her neck and shoulders with tantalising kisses. She moaned as his hand slid over one breast. The chill in her limbs was replaced with burning desire. It was no longer enough to lie passively in his arms. Urgently she pulled his mouth to hers and began to kiss him. It was a deep, demanding kiss and he responded with equal energy. She tore at his clothes, desperate to feel his flesh pressed against hers. Hastily they undressed each other, pausing only to kiss and caress each newly exposed section of skin. Every touch, every kiss awoke a memory; they were joyfully rediscovering each other. As their clothes were discarded so the excitement grew. Blood pounded through their bodies; all sense of time and place was lost, nothing mattered but pleasuring each other until they reached the ultimate delight of their bodies uniting in a heady, exhilarating climax that left them both exhausted, their bodies entwined together, a tangle of limbs bathed in the red-gold glow of the dying fire.

Rose lay very still, eyes closed, arms wrapped tightly about Lawrence. He took her face between his hands and kissed her.

'Mmm.' She snuggled closer. 'I would like to stay like this for ever.'

He chuckled.

'Once the euphoria wears off, you will begin to feel the chill. We should get under the covers.'

They slipped between the sheets, their bodies fitting naturally together.

'What made you come here?' murmured Lawrence, nuzzling her ear. 'How could you risk riding out on such a night?'

She did not answer immediately.

'I had to come,' she said at last. 'I was wrong and I had to tell you. It seems everyone in Mersecombe knew the truth about Althea, except me. I should have been the first to know, not the last, because I should have listened to you.' She held him close, running her hands over his back as if to assure herself he was really there. 'I was afraid I would never see you again. There was no word from you; everyone thought you had left for good. Then Sir Jonas said he had heard from the lawyers that you had left London. He did not know where, but I hoped, prayed—so I came to find you.'

'Then thank heaven I was here.'

The warmth from his body was seeping into her own, driving away the aching cold, and when he raised his eyes to her face the message she read in them melted the icy fear that had numbed her heart.

'Yes.' She blinked back the tears that stung her eyes. 'Thank heaven.' She hugged him, burying her face in his shoulder. 'Oh, my love, I was such a fool not to trust you. Can you ever forgive me?'

'Never,' he muttered, covering her face and neck with hot, fervent kisses. 'You will have to make love to me for at least fifty years before I even begin to forgive you.'

Something between a sob and a chuckle escaped her. The familiar tug of desire was welling up inside and she measured the length of her body against his.

'Very well, then.' Her pulse leapt as she felt him pressing hard and aroused against her. 'Let us begin immediately.'

The fire had burned down to a faint glow, but moonlight shone in through the uncovered windows. Rose lay with her head resting on Lawrence's shoulder. Their lovemaking had continued long into the night. Sheets were tangled, covers had slipped to the floor and remained there, unregarded, until the icy night air began to bite and they gathered them up again, giggling like children. Then they had slept, locked in each other's arms.

Rose moved onto her back. Immediately Lawrence's hand closed on her fingers.

'What is it, my love?'

'Nothing. Only how wonderful this has been.'

He rolled over and gathered her against him.

'And it will continue to be. I do not intend to let you go again.'

'But you must,' she said gently. 'At least for a little while. I must go back to Mersecombe as soon as it is light. No one knows I am here—they will worry.'

'Then I shall come with you.'

'You do not have to do that.'

'I want to. I want to be part of your family from now on, Rose.'

His words made her heart soar.

'I would like that, Lawrence. Very much.'

'We need not wait for dawn.' He raised himself on one elbow, his face a shadowy blur hovering above her. 'There is moon enough. We will send for the gig and be back at Bluebell Cottage before your family has finished breakfast. And I will come to the church with you,' he added, his lips brushing hers. 'We can ask Mr Wilkins how soon we can be married.'

She put her hands against his chest.

'If we are to do all that, then ought we not to get ready?'

His voice deepened and he slid his body closer.

'We should, of course. But not *quite* yet.'

'I have checked all her cupboards, ma'am, and she's not taken any of her clothes, but *her bed has not been slept in*!'

Mrs Molland put her hands to her cheeks as she heard Janet's anguished announcement. She glanced at the clock.

'We have a little time yet before we need to set off for church.' She tapped her foot, her brow furrowed, then shot another question at the maid. 'Does Sam know?'

'Not yet, ma'am, but—'

'Hush!' The hinges of the garden gate squeaked and Mrs Molland ran to the window in time to see Rose and Sir Lawrence walking up the path. 'Thank heavens! She—I quite forgot that she has been out for an early-morning drive with Sir Lawrence.' Her eyes slid away from the maid's sceptical gaze. 'Go and let them in, Janet, if you please!'

If anything was needed to confirm Mrs Molland's suspicions, it was the glow of happiness in her daughter's eyes as she came into the room, followed by Sir Lawrence and a bouncing, liver-and-white pointer.

'Have I given you a fright, Mama? I beg your pardon.' Rose came forwards, happiness bubbling in her voice. 'I hope we are not too late for church?'

'Of course not, but where—?' Mrs Molland broke off as Sam came racing into the room. He pulled up quickly when he saw Sir Lawrence, but it was the sight of the puppy bounding up to him that caused him to cry out in delight.

'Bandit!'

Rose bit her lip to stop herself from laughing. Her mother was quite bursting with questions, none of which could be asked in front of Sam. That, of course, was a relief. She would have to explain everything at some stage, but she was quite happy to put it off for a little while.

'Sir Lawrence has come to spend the day with us,' she said, in answer to the unspoken question in Sam's round eyes. 'And he thought you might like to renew your acquaintance with Bandit.'

Sam was on his knees, happily allowing the dog to lick his face.

'I'm afraid we will have to lock her in the outhouse while we go to church,' added Sir Lawrence, apologetically.

'And will you be coming to the Woolers' later, sir?' asked Sam, getting to his feet.

'I had forgotten,' uttered Rose, dismayed. 'Old Mrs Wooler invited us to join them for dinner this evening. We are the only guests. In light of their loss the family is observing a very quiet Christmas and as we were doing much the same thing—we will see them at the church, and I will ask them if they would object to you joining us.'

'Do say you will, sir,' cried Sam, his eyes shining. 'Jem has said there will not be any dancing, but there will be games, like snapdragon and forfeits, and bobbing for apples! Jem says they have decorated the house with garlands—and mistletoe.' He giggled and cast a mischievous look at Rose.

'Then I do hope they will allow me to come,' said Lawrence gravely.

A few minutes later the little party set off for the church. Rose was conscious of the curious stares as she walked in upon Sir Lawrence's arm, but she held her head high. She was encouraged by the vicar's kindly welcome, and by an approving nod and smile from old Mrs Wooler. That lady's keen eyes accurately assessed the situation and as soon as the service was finished she sent Jem over with an invitation for Sir Lawrence to join them for dinner.

'I think we may conclude that our marriage will generally be welcomed,' murmured Lawrence as he escorted Rose away from the church.

'I believe so.' Rose wondered how it was possible to feel so happy without bursting.

'It is starting to snow.' Lawrence turned up the collar of his greatcoat. 'I should have brought you in the gig.'

'No, it is only a few minutes' walk to get home. Besides, you have promised to use it to take us to the Woolers' later.' Mrs Molland and Sam were walking ahead of them and Rose could tell by her son's eager steps that he was keen to get back to the cottage. 'It was kind of you to bring Bandit; Sam is so excited to see her again.'

'Perhaps we should let him keep her, once we have decided where we are to live. It will be company for the boy.'

Rose hesitated.

'There is something I have not told you. I missed my monthly course.' Lawrence stopped immediately and she said quickly, 'It is early days, I know, but I went to see a doctor this week. A new man, just moved from Bath and said to be very experienced. He thinks there is no reason why I should not be able to have another child.'

Lawrence took her hands, giving her such a long, sober look that she began to panic.

'Of course it is not confirmed, and very likely it is not what I think—after all that has happened this year—'

Lawrence put his fingers to her lips, silencing her.

'If you are carrying my child, that would please me more than I can say, but if our family is never more than you, me and Sam, I shall count myself the luckiest man alive.'

'Oh.' She blinked rapidly. 'Oh, what have I ever done to deserve you?'

His lips twitched.

'I cannot think.' The snow was falling heavily now, like a thick, white curtain, deadening all sound. 'You know,' he said, 'if this continues, I might not be able to get back to Knightscote this evening.'

'You should not even attempt it,' said Rose, trying to sound serious. 'We will put you up at the cottage.'

'What, you would risk sharing your house with one of the country's most notorious rakes?'

'Not at all.' She smiled up at him mistily. 'I would share it with my own, true love.'

* * * * *